Read ALL the CAT WHO mysteries!

THE CAT WHO COULD READ BACKWARDS: The world of modern art is a mystery to many—but for Jim Qwilleran and Koko it turns into a mystery of another sort . . .

THE CAT WHO ATE DANISH MODERN: Qwill isn't thrilled about covering the interior design beat for *The Daily Fluxion*. Little does he know that a murderer has designs on a local woman featured in one of his stories . . .

THE CAT WHO TURNED ON AND OFF: Qwill and Koko are joined by Yum Yum as they try to solve a murder in an antique shop . . .

THE CAT WHO SAW RED: Qwill starts his diet—*and* starts a new gourmet column for the *Fluxion*. It isn't easy—but it's not as hard as solving a shocking murder case!

*TURN THE PAGE FOR MORE
CAT WHODUNITS . . .*

THE CAT WHO PLAYED BRAHMS: While fishing at a secluded cabin, Qwill hooks onto a murder mystery—and Koko develops a strange fondness for classical music . . .

THE CAT WHO PLAYED POST OFFICE: Koko and Yum Yum turn into fat cats when Qwill inherits millions and moves into a mansion. But amid the caviar and champagne, Koko starts sniffing clues to a murder!

THE CAT WHO HAD 14 TALES: A delightful collection of feline mystery fiction from the creator of Koko and Yum Yum!

THE CAT WHO KNEW SHAKESPEARE: The local newspaper publisher has perished in an accident— or is it murder? That is the question . . .

THE CAT WHO SNIFFED GLUE: After a rich banker and his wife are killed, Koko develops an odd appetite for glue. To solve the murder, Qwill has to figure out why . . .

THE CAT WHO WENT UNDERGROUND: Qwill and the cats head for their Moose County log cabin for a relaxing summer—but when a handyman disappears, Koko must dig up the buried motive for a sinister crime . . .

THE CAT WHO TALKED TO GHOSTS: Qwill and Koko try to solve a haunting mystery in a historic farmhouse.

THE CAT WHO LIVED HIGH: A glamorous art dealer was killed in Qwill's new high-rise apartment—and he and the cats are about to reach new heights in detection as they try to find out whodunit . . .

THE CAT WHO KNEW A CARDINAL: The director of the local Shakespeare production dies in Qwill's orchard—and the stage is set for a puzzling mystery!

AND DON'T MISS . . .

THE CAT WHO WASN'T THERE: Qwill's on his way to Scotland—and on his way to solving another purr-plexing mystery!

Available in hardcover
from G. P. Putnam's Sons

The Cat Who Moved A Mountain

Lilian Jackson Braun

JOVE BOOKS, NEW YORK

This Jove Book contains the complete
text of the original hardcover edition.
It has been completely reset in a typeface
designed for easy reading and was printed
from new film.

THE CAT WHO MOVED A MOUNTAIN

A Jove Book / published by arrangement with
the author

PRINTING HISTORY
G.P. Putnam's Sons edition published February 1992
Jove edition / October 1992

ISBN: 0-515-10950-9

Jove Books are published by The Berkley Publishing Group,
200 Madison Avenue, New York, New York 10016.
The name "JOVE" and the "J" logo
are trademarks belonging to Jove Publications, Inc.

PRINTED IN THE UNITED STATES OF AMERICA

10 9 8 7 6 5 4 3 2 1

Dedicated to Earl Bettinger,
the husband who . . .

ONE

A MAN OF middle age, with a large, drooping moustache and brooding eyes, hunched over the steering wheel and gripped the rim anxiously as he maneuvered his car up a mountain road that was narrow, unpaved, and tortuous. Unaccustomed to mountain driving, he found it a blood-curdling ordeal. On one side of the road the mountain rose in a solid wall of craggy rock; on the other side it dropped off sharply without benefit of guardrail, and it was narrowed further by fallen rocks at the base of the cliff. The driver kept to the middle of the road and clenched his teeth at each hairpin turn, pondering his options if another ve-

hicle were to come hurtling downhill around a blind curve.
A head-on collision? A crash into the cliff? A plunge into
the gorge? To aggravate the tension there were two passengers in the backseat who protested as only Siamese cats
can do.

It was late in the day, and the gas gauge registered less
than a quarter full. For almost two hours Jim Qwilleran
had been driving on mountain passes, snaking around tri-
ple S-curves, blowing the horn at every hairpin turn, making the wrong decision at every fork in the road. There
were no directional signs, no habitations where he might
inquire, no motorists to flag down for help, no turn-outs
where he could pull over in an effort to get his bearings
and collect his wits. The situation had all the elements of
a nightmare, although Qwilleran was totally awake. So
were the two in the backseat, bumping about in their carrier as the car swerved and jolted, all the while airing their
protests in ear-splitting howls and nerve-wracking shrieks.

"Shut up," he bellowed at them, a reprimand that only
increased the volume of the clamor. "We're lost! Where
are we? Why did we ever come to this damned mountain?"

It was a good question, and one day soon he would
know the answer. Meanwhile he was frantically pursuing
a nonstop journey to nowhere.

Two weeks before, Qwilleran had experienced a sudden
urge to go to the mountains. He was living in Moose
County, a comfortably flat fragment of terrain in the
northernmost reaches of the lower Forty-eight, more than
a thousand miles away from anything higher than a hill.
The inspiration came to him while celebrating a significant
event in his life. After five years of legal formalities that

had required him to live in Moose County, he had officially inherited the Klingenschoen fortune, and he was now a certified billionaire with holdings reaching from New Jersey to Nevada.

During his five years in Pickax City, the county seat, he had won over the natives with his genial disposition and his streak of generosity that constantly benefited the community. Strangers passing him on the street went home and told their families that Mr. Q had said good morning and raised his hand in a friendly salute. Men enjoyed his company in the coffee houses. Women went into raptures over his flamboyant moustache and shivered at the doleful expression in his hooded eyes, wondering what past experience had saddened them.

To celebrate his inheritance, more than two hundred friends and admirers gathered in the ballroom of the seedy old hostelry that called itself the "New" Pickax Hotel. Qwilleran circulated among them amiably, jingling ice cubes in a glass of ginger ale, accepting congratulations, and making frequent trips to a buffet laden with the hotel's idea of party food. He was an outstanding figure, standing out from the crowd: six-feet-two and well-built, with a good head of hair graying at the temples, and a luxuriant pepper-and-salt moustache that seemed to have a life of its own.

Chief among his well-wishers were Polly Duncan, administrator of the Pickax library; Arch Riker, publisher of the *Moose County Something*; and Osmond Hasselrich of Hasselrich, Bennett & Barter, attorneys for the Klingenschoen empire. The mayor, city council members, chief of police, and superintendent of schools were there, as well as others who had played a role in Qwilleran's recent life: Larry and Carol Lanspeak, Dr. Halifax Goodwinter,

Mildred Hanstable, Eddington Smith, Fran Brodie—a list longer than the guest of honor had imagined. None of them dared to hope that this newly minted billionaire, city-born and city-bred, would continue to live in what urban politicians called a rural wasteland. None could guess what he would do next, or where he would choose to live. He had been a prize-winning journalist in several major cities before fate steered him to Moose County. How could anyone expect him to remain in Pickax City?

Kip MacDiarmid, editor of the newspaper in the adjoining county, was the first to ask the question that was on everyone's mind. "Now that you have all the money in the world, Qwill, and twenty-five good years ahead of you, what are your plans?"

When Qwilleran hesitated, Arch Riker, his lifelong friend, hazarded a guess. "He's going to buy a string of newspapers and a TV network and start a media revolution."

"Or buy a castle in Scotland and go in for bird watching," Larry Lanspeak contributed with tongue in cheek.

"Not likely," said Polly Duncan, who had given Qwilleran a bird book and binoculars in vain. "He'll buy an island in the Caribbean and write that book he's always talking about." She spoke blithely to conceal her feelings; as the chief woman in his life for the last few years Polly would feel the keenest regret if he should leave the north country.

Qwilleran chuckled at their suggestions. "Seriously," he said as he loaded his plate for the third time with canned cocktail sausages and processed cheese slices, "the last few years have been the richest in my entire life, and I mean it! Until coming here I'd always lived in cities with a population of two million or more. Now I'm content to live in a town of three thousand, four hundred miles north of everywhere. And yet . . .''

"You're not living up to your potential," Polly said bravely.

"I don't know about that, but I'll tell you one thing: Taking it easy is not my idea of the good life. I don't play golf. I'd rather go to jail than go fishing. Expensive cars and custom-made suits are not for me. What I do need is a goal—a worthwhile direction."

"Have you thought of getting married?" asked Moira MacDiarmid.

"No!" Qwilleran stated vehemently.

"It wouldn't be too late to start producing heirs."

Patiently he explained, as he had done many times before, "Several years ago I discovered I'm a washout as a husband, and I might as well face the truth. As for heirs, I've established the Klingenschoen Foundation to distribute my money—both while I'm alive and after I've gone. But . . .'' He stroked his moustache thoughtfully, "I'd like to get away from it all for a while and rethink my purpose in life—on top of a mountain somewhere—or on a desert island, if there are any left without tourists."

"What about your cats?" asked Carol Lanspeak. "Larry and I would be glad to board them in the luxury to which they're accustomed."

"I'd take them along. The presence of a cat is conducive to meditation."

"Do you like mountains?" Kip MacDiarmid asked.

"To tell the truth, I haven't had much experience with mountains. The Alps impressed me when my paper sent me to Switzerland on assignment, and my honeymoon was spent in the Scottish Highlands . . . Yes, I like the idea of altitude. Mountains have a sense of mystery, whether you're up there looking down or down here looking up.''

Moira said, "Last summer we had a great vacation in the Potato Mountains—didn't we, Kip? We took the kids and the camper. Beautiful scenery! Wonderful mountain air! And so peaceful! Even with four kids and two dogs it was peaceful.''

"I've never heard of the Potato Mountains," Qwilleran said.

"They're just being developed. You should get there before the influx of tourists," Kip advised. "If you'd like to borrow our camper for a couple of weeks, you're welcome to it.''

Arch Riker said, "I don't picture Qwill in a camper unless it has twenty-four-hour room service. We used to be in scouting together, and he was the only kid who hated campouts and cookouts.''

Qwilleran was quaking inwardly at the thought of condensed living in an RV with a pair of restless indoor cats. "I appreciate the offer," he said, "but it would be better for me to rent a cabin for a couple of months—something Thoreau-esque but with indoor plumbing, you know. I don't need any frills, just the basic comforts.''

"They have cabins for rent in the Potato Mountains," Moira said. "We saw lots of vacancy signs—didn't we, Kip? And there's a nice little town in the valley with restaurants and stores. The kids went down there for movies and the video arcade.''

"Do they have a public library? Do you suppose there's a veterinarian?''

"Sure to be," said Kip. "There's a courthouse, so it's obviously the county seat. Neat little burg! A river runs right along the main street.''

"What's the name of the town?"

"Spudsboro!" the MacDiarmids said in unison with wide grins as they waited for Qwilleran's incredulous reaction.

"We're not kidding," said Moira. "That's what it's called on the map. It's right between two ranges of mountains. We camped in a national forest in the West Potatoes. On the east side there's Big Potato Mountain and Little Potato Mountain."

"And I suppose the Gravy River runs through the valley," Qwilleran quipped.

"The river is the Yellyhoo, I'm sorry to say," said Kip. "It's great for white-water rafting—not the Colorado by a long shot, but the kids got a thrill out of it. There are caves if you're interested in spelunking, but the locals discourage it, and Moira is chicken, anyway."

"Where do the Potato Mountains get their name?"

The MacDiarmids looked at each other questioningly. "Well," Moira ventured, "they're sort of round and knobby. Friendly mountains, you know—not overwhelming like the Rockies."

"Big Potato is in the throes of development," said her husband. "Little Potato is inhabited but still primitive. In the 1920s it was a haven for moonshiners, they say, because the revenuers couldn't find them in the dense woods."

Moira said, "There are lots of artists on Little Potato, selling all kinds of crafts. We brought home some exciting pottery and baskets."

"Yes," Kip said, "and there's a girl who does those tapestries you like, Qwill." When his wife nudged him he repeated, "There's a *young woman* who does those tapestries you like . . . How do you bachelors manage, Qwill, without a wife to set you straight all the time?''

''It's a deprivation I'm willing to suffer,'' Qwilleran replied with a humble bow.

''If you're really interested in mountains, I'll call the editor of the *Spudsboro Gazette*. We were roommates in J school, and he bought the newspaper last summer. That's how we found out about the Potatoes. Colin Carmichael, his name is. If you decide to go down there, you should look him up. Swell guy. I'll tell him to have a rental agent contact you. Spudsboro has a chamber of commerce that's right on the ball.''

''Don't make me sound like a Rockefeller, Kip. They'll hike the rent. I want something simple, and I want to keep a low profile.''

''Sure. I understand.''

''How's the weather in the Potatoes?''

''Terrific! Didn't rain once while we were there.''

For the rest of the evening Qwilleran appeared distracted, and he kept fingering his moustache, a nervous habit triggered by a desire for action. He made quick decisions, and now his instincts were telling him to flee to the Potato Mountains and resolve his quandary. Why that particular range of mountains attracted him was something he could not explain, except that they sounded appetizing, and he enjoyed what he called the pleasures of the table.

Arriving home after the reception, he was greeted at the door by two Siamese cats with expectancy in their perky ears and waving tails. He gave each of them a cocktail sausage spirited away from the hotel buffet, and after they had gobbled their treat rapturously and washed up meticulously, he made his announcement. ''You guys won't like this, but we're going to spend the summer in the mountains.'' He always conversed with them as if they were humans with a passable IQ. In fact, he often wondered how he had lived alone for so many years without two intelligent beings to listen attentively and respond with encouraging yowls and sympathetic blinks.

Their names were Koko and Yum Yum—seal-point Siamese with hypnotically blue eyes in dark brown masks and with brown extremities shading into fawn-colored bodies. The female was an endearing lap sitter who was fascinated by Qwilleran's moustache and who used catly wiles to get the better of him in an argument. The male was nothing short of extraordinary—a genetically superior animal gifted with senses of detection and even prognostication in certain circumstances. His official cognomen was Kao K'o Kung, and he had a dignity worthy of his namesake. Koko's exploits were by no means a figment of Qwilleran's imagination; the hard-headed, cynical journalist had documented them over a period of years and intended eventually to write a book.

Before he broke the news to his two housemates he anticipated a negative reaction. They could read his mind if not his lips, and he knew they disliked a change of address. As he expected, Yum Yum sat in a compact bundle with legs tucked out of sight, a reproachful expression in her violet-tinged blue eyes. Surprisingly, Koko seemed excited about the prospect, prancing back and forth on long, elegant legs.

"Have I made the right decision?" Qwilleran asked.

"Yow!" said Koko spiritedly.

In the next few days Qwilleran proceeded with plans, arranging for a summer-long absence, plotting an itinerary, choosing motels, and making a packing list. For good weather and the quiet life he would need only lightweight summer casuals. It never occurred to him to take rain gear.

Soon the mail began to arrive from Spudsboro. The first prospectus invited him to buy into time-share condominiums, now under construction. A realty agent listed residential lots and acreage for sale. A contractor offered to build the house of Qwilleran's dreams. Several rental agents sent lists of cabins and cottages available, no pets allowed. The Siamese watched anxiously as each letter was opened and tossed into the wastebasket. Yet, the more disappointing the opportunities, the more Qwilleran was determined to go to the Potatoes.

The situation improved with a telephone call from Spudsboro. The person on the line was friendly and enthusiastic. "Mr. Qwilleran, this is Dolly Lessmore of Lessmore Realty. Colin Carmichael tells us you want to rent a mountain retreat for the entire summer."

It was a husky, deep-pitched voice that he identified as that of a woman who smoked too much. He visualized her as rather short and stocky, with a towering hair-do, a taste for bright colors, a three-pack-a-day habit, and a pocketful of breath mints. He prided himself on his ability to personify a voice accurately. Yes, he told her, he was considering the possibility of a mountain vacation.

"I thought I'd call and find out exactly what kind of accommodations you have in mind," she said. "We have a lot of rentals available. First off, do you want the inside of the mountain or the outside?"

The choice stumped him for only a second. "The outside. I'll leave the inside to the trolls."

"Let me explain," Ms. Lessmore said with a laugh. "The inside slope faces the valley, overlooking Spudsboro, and you have spectacular sunsets. The outside faces the eastern foothills, and you can see forever. Also, it gets the morning sun.''

''Do you have anything at the summit?'' he queried.

''Nice thinking! You want the best of both worlds! Now, if you'll tell me your birthday, it will help me match you up with the right place.''

''May twenty-fourth. My blood type is O, and I wear a size twelve shoe.''

''Hmmm, you're a Gemini, close to Taurus. You want something individual but practical.''

''That's right. Something rustic and secluded, but with electricity and indoor plumbing.''

''I think we can do that,'' she said cheerfully.

''I like a firm bed, preferably extra long.''

''I'll make a note of that.''

''And at least two bedrooms.''

''For how many persons, may I ask?''

''I have two roommates, a male and a female, both Siamese cats.''

''Oh-oh! That poses a problem,'' she said.

''They're well-behaved and not in the least destructive. I can vouch for that,'' he said. Then, recalling that Koko had once broken a $10,000 vase, while Yum Yum would steal anything that was not nailed down, he added, ''I'll be willing to post a bond.''

''Well . . . that might work. Let me think . . . There's one possibility, but I'll have to check it out. The place I have in mind is rather large—''

''I was hoping for something small,'' Qwilleran interrupted, ''but under the circumstances I'd compromise on large.'' He was currently living in a converted apple barn, four stories high, with balconies on three levels. ''What do you mean by large?''

"I mean *large*! It was originally a small country inn. It was converted into a home for the Hawkinfield family quite some time ago. There are six bedrooms. The last of the Hawkinfields really wants to sell—not rent—and it has great potential as a bed-and-breakfast operation. If you expressed an interest in eventually operating it as a B-and-B, Ms. Hawkinfield might consent to rent it for the summer. How about that?"

"Are you asking me to perjure myself? I have no interest in a B-and-B . . . now or at any time in the future."

"This is all off the top of my head, of course. I have no authority. Ms. Hawkinfield lives out of state. I'll have to consult with her and get back to you."

"Do that," Qwilleran said encouragingly. "As soon as possible."

"By the way, we haven't talked about the rent. How high are you prepared to go?"

"Tell me how much she wants, and we'll take it from there. I'm not hard to get along with."

Within a week the deal was sealed. The owner, who was asking $1.2 million for the property, graciously consented to rent the premises for the summer, fully furnished, to a gentleman with references and two cats, for $1,000 a week. Utilities would be provided, but he would have to pay his own telephone bills.

"It wasn't easy to convince her, but I did it!" Ms. Lessmore said proudly.

Still unaccustomed to limitless wealth, Qwilleran considered the rent exorbitant, but he was determined to go to the Potatoes, and he agreed to take the inn for three months, half the rent payable in advance. Later he would wonder why he had not asked to see a picture of the place. Instead he had allowed himself to be captivated by the agent's bubbling enthusiasm: "It's right on top of Big Potato! There's a fabulous view from every window, and gorgeous sunsets! Wide verandas, eight bathrooms, large kitchen, your own private lake! The Hawkinfields had it stocked with fish. Do you like to fish? And there are lovely walking trails in the woods . . ."

Koko was sitting near the phone, listening, and when the conversation ended Qwilleran said to him, "You'll have a choice of six bedrooms and eight bathrooms, all with a fabulous view. How does that strike you?"

"Yow," said Koko, and he groomed his paws in anticipation. Yum Yum was nowhere about. She had been sulking for days—pretending not to be hungry, sitting with her back turned, slithering out of reach when Qwilleran tried to stroke her.

"Females!" he said to Koko. "They're a conundrum!"

With the agreement signed and the deposit made, he paid a formal visit to the walnut-paneled, velvet-draped office of Hasselrich, Bennett & Barter for a conference with the venerable senior partner. A meeting with Osmond Hasselrich always began with the obligatory cup of coffee served with the formality of a Japanese tea ceremony. The attorney himself poured from an heirloom silver coffee pot into heirloom Wedgwood cups, his aged hands shaking and the cups rattling in their saucers. Their dainty handles were finger-traps, and Qwilleran was always glad when the ritual ended. When the silver tray had been removed and the attorney at last faced him across the desk with hands folded, Qwilleran began:

"After much cogitation, Mr. Hasselrich, I have decided to go away for the summer." Even after five years of business and social acquaintance, the two men still addressed each other formally. "It's my intention to distance myself totally from Moose County in order to plan my future. This agreeable community exerts a magnetic hold on me, and I need to escape its spell for a while in order to think objectively.''

The attorney nodded wisely.

"I'm going to the Potato Mountains." Qwilleran paused until the legal eyelids stopped fluttering. Fluttering eyelids were the old gentleman's standard reaction to questionable information. "No one but you will have my address. I'm cutting all ties for three months. Mr. O'Dell will look after my residence as usual. Lori Bamba handles my mail and will refer urgent matters to you. All my financial affairs are in your hands, so I anticipate no problems.''

"How do you intend to handle current expenses while there, Mr. Qwilleran?''

"Apart from food there will be very few expenses. I'll open a temporary checking account, and you can transfer funds to the bank down there as needed. The bank is the First Potato National of Spudsboro.'' Qwilleran waited for the eyelids to stop fluttering and the jowls to stop quivering. "As soon as I know my mailing address and telephone number, I'll convey that information to your office. My plan is to leave Tuesday and arrive in the Potatoes by Friday.''

Although often disturbed by Qwilleran's seeming eccentricities, Hasselrich admired his concise, well-organized manner of conducting business, little realizing that his client was merely in a hurry to escape from the suffocating environment.

On Monday there was a bon voyage handshake from Arch Riker after Qwilleran promised to write a thousand words for the *Moose County Something* whenever a good subject presented itself. On Monday evening there was a farewell dinner with Polly Duncan at the Old Stone Mill, followed by a sentimental parting at her apartment.

Then, early on Tuesday morning Qwilleran packed his secondhand, three-year-old, four-cylinder, two-tone green sedan for the journey. Despite his new wealth he still spent money reluctantly on transportation. Included in the baggage were his typewriter and computerized coffeemaker, as well as a box of books and the cats' personal belongings. The Siamese observed the packing process closely, and as soon as their waterdish and pan of kitty gravel disappeared out the back door, they made themselves instantly invisible.

TWO

WHEN THE COMPACT four-door pulled away from the apple barn, both cats were in their carrier on the backseat, reclining on a cushion befitting their royal status, and Qwilleran was at the wheel contemplating a new adventure that might change his life. He planned to keep a diary during the journey, using the small recorder that was always in his pocket. It would capture his thoughts and impressions while driving, along with yowling remarks from the backseat, and he could add commentary when they stopped at motels. The following account was recorded on tape:

* * *

TUESDAY . . . Left Pickax at ten-thirty, a half hour later than planned. The car was packed, and I was ready to take off, when the Siamese vanished. Nothing is more exasperating than delay caused by a last-minute cat hunt. First I found Koko on a bookshelf, doing his ostrich act behind the biographies, with six inches of tail protruding from the hiding place. With him it was a game, and the tail was intended to be a clue, but Yum Yum was in deadly earnest. She was huddled on a beam under the roof, accessible only by a forty-foot ladder. Curses! Rather than call the volunteer fire department, I opened a can of cocktail shrimp with an ostentatious rattling of utensils and remarks such as "This is delicious! Would you like a *treat*, Koko?" In our household the T-word is taboo unless a treat is actually forthcoming, so it always works. After a minute or two a series of soft thumps told me the princess was on her way down from her ivory tower.

Having enjoyed their impromptu feast they hopped into their carrier, ready to hit the road. Did I say impromptu? I daresay the entire episode was plotted by those two incorrigible connivers!

To avoid tiring my passengers, who are confined to 360 square inches of cushioned luxury, I plan to limit each day's driving. At rest stops I release them from the carrier, giving them freedom to hop about the car interior, have a drink of water, and use their commode, which is placed on the floor of the backseat. At least, that's the general idea; they usually ignore their commode until we arrive at a motel. Tonight we'll stop at the Country Life Inn, which not only welcomes pets but supplies a friendly cat to any guest who wants feline company overnight. Extra charge for this, of course.

TUESDAY EVENING . . . Here we are in room 17 of

the Country Life Inn. I paid for a room with two beds, and the cats immediately went to sleep on the one I intended for myself. Meanwhile, I went out and had a decent steak at a so-called family restaurant where the waitresses wear granny dresses. More families are dining out these days. I was surrounded by broods of four or six children who screamed, spilled drinks, raced up and down the aisles, threw food, and otherwise made themselves at home. A spoonful of mashed potato and gravy narrowly missed my left ear, and I determined then and there to boycott wholesome family restaurants and patronize murky dives where the waitresses wear mini-skirts and fishnet tights, where sleazy characters hang around the bar, and where all the potatoes are french fried.

WEDNESDAY . . . I gassed up and pulled away from the inn after a breakfast of buckwheat pancakes, eggs, and country sausages. (We have better sausages in Moose County.) Last night after I turned out the lights, the cats started roaming. I could hear their claws scurrying around the bathtub, and I assumed they were wrestling and having a good time. Later I discovered there was more to that caper than met the ear . . . Anyway, I fell asleep and didn't hear another sound until the car doors started slamming at 7 A.M., at which time I opened one eye and looked over at the other bed. It was empty. Both cats and one dead mouse were in bed with me! Tonight we're going to have separate rooms.

We are now approaching urban areas and driving on freeways, and the furry folks in the backseat seem to be lulled by the steady rate of speed and drone of traffic. Or they may be drugged by the diesel fumes and broken-down oil burners on the highway.

For lunch I stopped at a fast-food restaurant and parked

at the rear near the dumpsters, thinking the garbage aromas would entertain the Siamese during my absence. After releasing them from the carrier, I took care to leave the windows ajar for ventilation and lock all four doors before going in for a quick burger and fries. When I left the restaurant fifteen minutes later I could hear a horn blowing—the continuous, annoying wail of an automobile horn that's stuck—a short in the wiring or whatever. Imagine my embarrassment when I realized it was my own car! That roguish Koko was behind the wheel, standing on his hind legs, with his paws planted firmly on the horn button. As soon as he saw me, the rascal jumped into the backseat. I said, ''That's a clever trick, young man, but we could all be arrested for disturbing the peace.''

It was only when I fastened my seat belt and turned the ignition key that I noticed an unauthorized object on the floor. It was below the window on the passenger side. Until I reached for it I couldn't identify the thing. It was a piece of bent wire from a coat hanger. Car thieves—or worse, cat thieves—had tried to break in! I apologized to Koko . . . Was it a coincidence? Or is he now functioning as a burglar alarm? I can never be sure about that cat!

WEDNESDAY EVENING . . . We checked into our motel at four-thirty. This time I paid for two rooms, both singles. The three of us are spending the evening together in room 37, the cats huddled on the bed watching TV without the audio, while I start a Thomas Mann novel I haven't read since college. At bedtime I'll turn out the lights and slip into room 38.

THURSDAY . . . Now we've left the freeways behind. The scenery is more picturesque, but the forested hills are spoiled by billboards advertising discount stores and warehouse outlets. I went into one such store in a town called

Pauper's Cove and bought a pair of slippers, having left mine in Pickax. They had two thousand pairs but only one in size twelve. The slippers weren't the color I wanted, but they were a rare bargain. Then I stopped for lunch at a local eatery and had some very good vegetable soup and cornbread. While I was eating, a guy rushed in and shouted something, and the entire place emptied—customers, cashier, cook, everyone! I followed, thinking it was an earthquake or a forest fire. But no! They were all standing around my car, peering in at the Siamese, who were leaping gracefully about the interior and striking magnificent poses. Whenever they know they have an audience, those two are shameless exhibitionists.

Before starting to drive again, I went into another discount store, just to browse. They had a good price on driving gloves, so I picked up a pair to use in Moose County next winter—that is, if I'm still in Moose County next winter. Time will tell. I may be in Alaska. Or the Canary Islands.

THURSDAY EVENING . . . Tonight I paid for two rooms at the Mountain Charm Motel, which would be improved by better plumbing and mattresses and fewer ruffles and knickknacks. When I put on my new slippers, I found out that the one I had tried on in the store was size twelve, all right, but the other was size eleven. That led me to inspect the driving gloves. They were both for the right hand! There's one thing I like about Moose County: Everyone's honest . . . Tomorrow we arrive in Potatoland.

FRIDAY . . . Last leg of our journey. Koko and Yum Yum have just had their first experience with a tunnel through a mountain. They raised holy hell until we emerged into the sunlight . . . They're getting excited. They know we're almost there.

Directional signs are beginning to assure me that Spudsboro really exists. The purplish ridges in the distance are
turning into rounded mountains of misty blue, and the
highway is heading toward a gap between them. Now and
then it runs close to the Yellyhoo River . . . Just caught a
strong whiff of pine scent from a truckload of logs coming
out of the mountains . . . It's been raining here; there's a
rainbow . . . We're passing a well-kept golf course, a new
hospital, three fast-food palaces, a large mall. Judging by
the number of car dealers, Spudsboro is booming! . . .
Here we are at the city limits—time to stop talking and
concentrate on my driving.

Upon arriving in the small but thriving metropolis of
Spudsboro, Qwilleran found it to be a strip-city, a few
blocks wide and a few miles long, wedged between two
mountain ranges. Three or four winding but roughly par-
allel streets and a railroad track were built on a series of
elevations—like shelves—following the course of the river.
On one shelf a locomotive and some hopper-bottom cars
were threatening to topple over on the buildings below.
Qwilleran imagined the whole town might wash away
downstream if hit by a hard rain.

At the residential end of Center Street a conglomeration
of Victorian cottages, contemporary split-levels, and
middle-aged bungalows coexisted peaceably—with the
usual hanging flower baskets on porches, tricycles on
lawns, and basketball hoops on garage fronts. Next came
the commercial strip: stores, bars, gas stations, small office buildings, barbers, two banks, and one traffic light.
Naturally Qwilleran's eye was quick to spot the newspaper
office, the animal clinic, and the public library. In the
center of town a miniature park was surrounded by the

city hall, fire hall, police department, county courthouse, and post office. Pickets were parading in front of the courthouse, which had a golden dome too grandiose for a building of its modest size, and a police officer was issuing a parking ticket. Altogether it was a familiar small-town scene to Qwilleran, except for the mountains looming on each side of the valley.

Somewhere up there, he kept telling himself, was the hideaway where he would be living and meditating for three months. It was comforting to know that he could rely on police and fire protection; that he could take his cats to the veterinarian and his car to the garage; that he could have his hair cut and his moustache trimmed. Although he wanted to get away from it all, he was reluctant to get too far away.

At the Lessmore & Lessmore office on Center Street he angle-parked and locked all four doors, having rolled down the windows two inches with confidence that he would find no bent coat hanger on his return.

There were two enterprises sharing the building: a real estate agency and an investment counseling service. In the realty office a woman with a husky voice was talking on two telephones at once. She was on the young side of middle age, short and rather pudgy, dressed in bright green, and coiffed with an abundance of fluffy hair. On her desk was a sign that destroyed Qwilleran's preconceived notion of Dolly Lessmore: THANKS FOR NOT SMOKING.

"Ms. Lessmore?" he inquired when she had finished phoning. "I'm Jim Qwilleran."

She jumped up and trotted around the desk with bubbling energy and outstretched hand. "Welcome to Spudsboro! How was the trip? Have a chair? Where are the cats?''

"The trip was fine. The Siamese are in the car. When did you give up smoking?''

She darted a puzzled glance at her client. "How did you know? Last March a charming young doctor at the hospital gave a class in not-smoking.''

"Spudsboro seems to be a lively town,'' he said approvingly, "and right up to the minute.''

"You'll love it! And you'll love your mountain retreat! I'm sure you're anxious to see it and move in, so as soon as I make one more phone call, I'll take you up there.''

"No need. You're busy. Just tell me where it is.''

"Are you sure?''

"No problem whatsoever. Just steer me in the direction of Big Potato Mountain.''

She pointed across the street. "There it is—straight up. Little Potato is farther downriver. I have a little map here that you can have.'' She unrolled a sheet of paper. "Here's Center Street, and over here is Hawk's Nest Drive. That's where you're going, although you can't get there from here—at least, not directly. When you reach Hawk's Nest Drive, just keep going uphill. It's paved all the way. And when you can't go any farther, you're there! The house is known as Tiptop, which is the name of the original inn.''

The map was a labyrinth of black lines like worm tracks, peppered with numbers in fine type. "Don't any of these mountain roads have names?'' Qwilleran asked.

"They don't need names. We always know where we are, where we're going, and how to get there. It may be mystifying at first, but you'll get used to it in no time. Hawk's Nest Drive is the exception to the rule; it was named by J. J. Hawkinfield when he developed Tiptop Estates.''

''Is there anything I should know about the house?''

''All the utilities are connected. Bed linens and towels are in a closet upstairs. The kitchen is completely equipped, including candles in case of a power outage. There are fire extinguishers in every room, but all the fabrics and carpets are flame retardant.'' Ms. Lessmore handed over three keys on a ring. ''These are for front and back doors and garage. We had to make some minor repairs in preparation for your arrival, and a Mr. Beechum will be around to do the finishing touches. He's one of the mountain people, but he's an excellent worker. If you need anyone to clean, there are mountain women who are glad to earn a little money. We had one of them fluff up the place yesterday. I hope she did a satisfactory job.'' While speaking she was swiveling and rocking her desk chair with a surplus of nervous energy.

''What's my mailing address going to be?'' Qwilleran asked.

''There's no mail delivery up the mountain. You can have a rural mailbox at the foot of Hawk's Nest Drive if you wish, but for your short stay, why don't you rent a post office box?''

''And where do I buy groceries?''

''Do you cook?''

''No, but I'll need food for the cats. Mostly I prefer to eat in restaurants. Perhaps you could recommend some good ones.''

At that moment a roughly handsome man in a business suit rushed into the investment office, threw a briefcase onto a desk, and started out again. ''Gonna play some golf,'' he called out to Ms. Lessmore.

"Wait a minute, honey, I want you to meet the gentleman who's renting Tiptop. Mr. Qwilleran, this is my husband, Robert . . . Honey, he was asking about restaurants."

"Give him the blue book," he said. "That has everything. Don't plan dinner, Doll. I'll eat at the club. Nice to meet you, Mr. . . ."

He was out on the sidewalk before Qwilleran could say "Qwilleran."

"Robert's a golf nut," his wife explained, "and we've had so much rain lately that he's been frustrated." She handed over a blue brochure. "This lists restaurants, stores, and services in Spudsboro. If you like Italian food, try Pasta Perfect. And there's a moderate-priced steakhouse called The Great Big Baked Potato."

"And how about a grocery?"

"You'll find a small but upscale market at Five Points on your way to Hawk's Nest Drive. From here you go down Center Street until it curves to the right, then take a left at the Valley Boys' Club and wind around past the old depot, which is now an antique shop, and go uphill to Lumpton's Pizza, where you jog left—"

"Hold on," Qwilleran said. "It sounds as if you have me going west in order to go east. Run through that once more, and let me take notes."

She laughed. "If you think about east and west in the mountains, you'll go crazy. Just concentrate on left and right, and up and down." She repeated the instructions. "Then ask anyone at Five Points Market how to reach Hawk's Nest Drive. It's very well known."

"Thank you for your assistance," he said. "If I get lost I'll send up a rocket."

She escorted him hospitably to the door. "Enjoy your

stay. Be sure to walk through the woods to your private lake. It's enchanting! In fact, you'll love everything about Tiptop and want to buy it before the season's over.''

"If I do," Qwilleran said, "my first move will be to change its name."

Unlocking the car, he said to his passengers, "Sorry for the holdup, but we're on our way now. It won't be long before you can have a good dinner and a new house to explore."

For answer there was some stoic shuffling and squirming in the carrier.

As he started to drive, Big Potato was on his left; soon it was ahead of him; next it was on his right. Yet, he was not aware of having made any turns. It was quite different from downtown Pickax, where streets were laid out north and south and every turn was ninety degrees. He found the market at Five Points, however, and loaded a shopping cart with food for the Siamese, plus ice cream, doughnuts, and a can of pork and beans for himself.

At the checkout counter the cashier surveyed with undisguised curiosity the ten cans of red salmon, six cans of crabmeat, five frozen lobster tails, eight cans of boned chicken, and two packages of frozen jumbo shrimp. "Find everything you want?" he asked helpfully, glancing at the oversized moustache.

"Yes, you have a fine store," Qwilleran said. "Do you take traveler's checks?"

"You bet!" The young man's badge indicated that he was the manager, filling in at the cash register, and he was briskly managerial—a smiling, rosy-cheeked, well-scrubbed, wholesome type. Qwilleran thought, He runs in marathons, pumps iron, coaches basketball at the boys' club, and eats muesli. There's such a thing as looking too healthy.

"We have a good produce department," the manager said. "Just got some fresh pineapple."

"This is all I need at the moment, but I'll be back. I'm staying in the mountains for three months."

"Where are you staying?" The young man seemed genuinely friendly and not merely interested in selling pineapples.

"At a place called Tiptop. Can I get these things home before they thaw? I'm a stranger here."

"You'll be up there in ten minutes if you take the Snaggy Creek cutoff. Did you buy Tiptop?"

"No. Just renting."

As the manager totaled the array of salmon, crab, lobster, chicken, and shrimp he asked politely, "Are you with a group?"

"No, we're only a small family of three, but we like seafood and poultry."

The man nodded with understanding. "Everybody's worried about cholesterol these days. How about some oat bran cookies?"

"Next time. Tell me about this cutoff."

The manager closed the checkout counter and accompanied Qwilleran to the exit. Pointing up the hill he said, "Okay. This street winds around for half a mile and dead-ends at a pond. That's really Snaggy Creek, swollen by the heavy rain. Turn left there and go to the fork. Okay? Take the right spur. It goes downhill, which may look wrong, but don't try to figure it out. Just remember: the *right spur*. Okay? After you cross a culvert—the water's pretty high there—watch for some wet rocks on the left and immediately turn right across a small bridge. Okay?

About two-tenths of a mile farther on, there's another fork . . .''

Qwilleran was scribbling frantically.

"That's the simplest and fastest way to go," the manager assured him. "You won't have any trouble. By the way, my name's Bill Treacle. I'm the manager."

"I'm Jim Qwilleran. Thanks for the directions."

"Hope we have some good weather for you."

"It's more humid than I expected," Qwilleran said.

"That's very unusual, but the weatherman has promised us a nice weekend." Treacle helped load the groceries into the trunk, exclaimed over the Siamese, and said a cheery "Hurry back!"

Two hours later Qwilleran was cursing the friendly Bill Treacle and his Snaggy Creek cutoff. Either the man had misdirected him, or someone had moved the spurs, forks, culverts, bridges, and wet rocks. There was nothing remotely resembling a paved road that might be Hawk's Nest Drive. There were no road signs of any kind, and for the last hour there had been no signs of life, on foot or on wheel. He could no longer see Spudsboro down in the valley.

"Don't tell me I'm on the *outside* of the mountain!" he shouted in exasperation. "How did I land on the other side without going over the top or through a tunnel? Does anybody know?"

"Yow-ow!" said Koko with the infuriating authority of one who has all the answers.

The dirt road Qwilleran was now following was merely a narrow ledge between a towering cliff and a steep dropoff, with no guardrails even at hazardous hairpin turns. Gouged by tires during the recent wet spell, it had been blow-dried by mountain winds into treacherous ruts, bumps, and potholes. The ice cream was melting in the trunk; the frozen shrimp were thawing, but Qwilleran cared little about that. He simply wanted to arrive some-where—anywhere—before dark and before the gas tank registered empty. Suddenly visibility was zero as he drove into a low-flying cloud. And all the time the Siamese were howling and shrieking in the backseat.

"Shut up, dammit!" he bellowed at them.

At that moment the bouncing, shuddering sedan emerged from the cloud and headed into someone's front yard. Qwilleran jammed on the brakes.

It was only a rough clearing. An old army vehicle and a rusty red pickup with one blue fender were parked in front of a weatherbeaten dwelling that was somewhat more than a shack but considerably less than a house. Two non-descript dogs came out from under the porch with a men-acing swagger like a pair of goons. If they had barked, someone might have come forth to answer Qwilleran's question, but they watched in threatening silence from a distance of ten feet. There were no other signs of life. Even in the backseat there was a palpable silence. After a reasonable wait he opened the car door cautiously and stepped out in slow motion. The watchdogs continued to watch.

"Good dogs! Good dogs!" he said in a friendly tone as he proceeded toward the house with his hands in his pock-ets. Through the open windows and half-opened door he could hear a sound of muffled beating. With a certain amount of suspicion he mounted three sagging wood steps to a rickety porch and rapped on the door. The beating stopped, and a shrill voice shouted some kind of question.

"Hello there!" he replied in the same amiable tone he had used to address the watchdogs.

A moment later the door was flung wide and he was confronted by a hollow-cheeked, hollow-eyed young woman with long, straight hair cascading over her shoulders. She said nothing but gave him a hostile glare.

"Excuse me," he said in a manner intended to be disarming. "I've lost my way. I'm looking for Hawk's Nest Drive."

She regarded him with indecision, as if wondering whether to reach for a shotgun.

"You're on the wrong mountain!" she snapped.

THREE

THE MOUNTAIN WOMAN with hollow cheeks and sunken eyes stood with her hands on her hips and glared at Qwilleran. Assuming—from his astonished expression—that he had not heard the first time, she screamed, "You're on the wrong mountain!" Then, half turning, she shouted something over her shoulder, after which she pushed past him, grumbling, "Follow me." She was wearing grubby jogging shoes and a long, full skirt, and with skirt and long hair flying she leaped off the porch, ignoring the steps. Before Qwilleran had sense enough to return to his own car, she had started the spluttering motor of the pickup.

The ordeal of the last two hours had been stupefying, but now he gathered his wits and followed the other vehicle gratefully as it led the way back down the narrow road to a fork, where it turned onto an upbound trail. The lead vehicle was a modified pickup with the chassis elevated high above the wheels to cope with rough terrain like this, but Qwilleran's sedan bounced in and out of ruts, causing non-stop complaints from the backseat.

"Quiet!" he scolded.

"Yow!" Koko scolded in eloquent rebuttal.

The route meandered left and right and dipped in and out of gullies. There was one hopeful sign, however; Spudsboro was again visible in the valley, meaning they were back on the inside of the mountain. When they finally reached a paved road, the woman stopped her truck and leaned from the driver's seat, shouting something.

Jumping out of his car, Qwilleran hurried in her direction, saying, "How can I thank you, ma'am? May I—"

"Just get out of my way," she growled, revving the motor and making a reckless U-turn.

"Which way is up?" he called to her as she drove away. At least he was now on solid blacktop, and if "up" proved to be "down," he had only to turn around and drive in the opposite direction, assuming there was gas enough in the tank. This was the route he should have discovered two hours ago. There were hairpin turns, but the road's edge was marked by white lines and protected by guardrails, and double yellow lines separated the upbound and downbound lanes. The speed limit was posted, as well as warnings about dense fog, fallen rocks, and icy bridges. A creek, rushing alongside the road, occasionally disappeared and emerged somewhere else. At one point Qwilleran met a sheriff's car coming downhill, and he returned the stare of the officer behind the wheel.

Around the next bend he came upon a handsome house in a carefully landscaped clearing, its many levels ingeniously designed for a hillside. Large glass areas overlooked the valley. The russet stain on the board-and-batten exterior looked appropriately woodsy but failed to conceal that this was an architect-designed residence with a three-car garage and a swimming pool. In slowing down to observe the details, Qwilleran was able to read a rustic signboard: SEVEN LEVELS . . . THE LESSMORES.

Farther up the mountain another impressive house was designed with cedar boards applied diagonally to form a herringbone pattern. A satellite dish faced a wide swath cut in the forest. The rustic signboard read: THE RIGHT SLANT . . . DEL AND ARDIS WILBANK.

Hawk's Nest Drive climbed higher and higher, hugging roadside cliffs crowned with trees that were losing their footing and leaning precariously over the pavement. With every turn Koko yowled vociferously and Yum Yum made threatening intestinal noises as their bodies swerved left, right, left, right . . .

Suddenly Tiptop burst into view, brooding above them on a rocky knoll. The clamor in the backseat stopped abruptly, and Qwilleran stared through the windshield in disbelief. He had expected it to be more cheerful, more hospitable. Instead, Tiptop was a dark, glowering, uninviting building in a gray-green stain, the upper floor sided in gray-green fishscale clapboard. The main floor windows were shaded by a gray-green wrap-around veranda, while second floor windows and attic dormers were darkened by deeply overhanging roofs.

"Great!" Qwilleran muttered as he parked in a blacktopped area large enough for ten cars. "Don't go away," he said to his caged passengers. "I'll be right back." It was his custom to check for hazards and feline escape routes before introducing the Siamese to a new environment. Slowly, noting every dismal detail, he walked toward a gray stone arch inset with a mosaic of darker pebbles spelling out TIPTOP INN—1903. From there a broad flight of stone steps—he counted eighteen—led up to the inn, and seven wooden steps painted battleship gray led up to the veranda.

Unlocking one of the French doors that marked the main entrance, Qwilleran walked into a dark foyer—a wide central hall running the length of the building and ending in more French doors at the rear. Their glass panes did little to lighten the foyer, and he switched on lights—three chandeliers and six wall sconces. He flipped switches in the surrounding rooms also—a cavernous living room, a dining room that seated twelve, a hotel-sized kitchen— thankful that electricity was included in the rent.

Next he opened a window to freshen the deadness of the atmosphere and discovered there were no screens to keep the Siamese from jumping out. This was another mark against the place. They liked to sit on a windowsill sniffing the breeze, yet not a single window was screened. In each room he lowered the sash a few inches at the top for ventilation. This done, he brought the cats and their baggage into the kitchen, fed them a can of salmon hurriedly, and pointed out the location of their waterdish and commode in the pantry.

For himself he brought in the computerized coffeemaker without which he never left home. Although he had been obliged to swear off alcohol and had been convinced by an attractive woman M.D. in Pickax to give up smoking, he still insisted upon his coffee; he liked it strong and he liked it often. Carrying a cupful of the brew and with apologies to the Siamese for leaving them in the kitchen, he now wandered through the house with a critical eye. During his days as a roving news correspondent, checking in and out of hotels, his environment had meant little, but his changing circumstances in recent years had given him an awareness of pleasant living quarters.

The interior of Tiptop, though obviously redecorated not too long ago, was depressingly gray: gray plush carpet, gray damask draperies, wallcoverings predominantly gray. Certain items of massive furniture, circa 1903, were appropriate in sixty-foot rooms with ten-foot ceilings, but they were grotesque in design. More attractive were the sofas, chairs, and tables added by recent owners, and yet the rooms looked bleak, as if deliberately stripped of all small objects. There were sculpture pedestals without sculpture, plant stands without plants, bookcases without books, vitrines without curios, china cabinets without china, and lamp tables without lamps. Pictures had been removed, leaving hooks and discolored rectangles on the walls.

And for this, Qwilleran thought, I'm paying $1,000 a week!

Only one picture remained, a painting of mountains, hung in the foyer over a chest on which were a telephone and a phone directory. He looked up the numbers of the Lessmore office and residence and left the identical message in both places: "Tiptop has been burglarized!" Hurried visits to the six bedrooms upstairs and the recreation room on the lower level confirmed the fact. Even the three fireplaces were stripped.

Meanwhile, impatient cries were coming from the

kitchen. "Sorry! Sorry!" he apologized to the rampant Siamese. "Now it's your turn to explore. I hope you like it better than I do."

They entered the dining room warily, slinking under the table in search of crumbs, although the house had been empty for a year. Then Yum Yum sniffed an invisible spot on the carpet in front of the massive buffet while Koko rose effortlessly and silently to the serving surface. Once upon a time, Qwilleran imagined, it had groaned under platters of roast pheasant, chafing dishes bubbling with lobster thermidor, and eight-gallon bowls of brandy punch. That was almost a century ago, but it was no secret to Koko.

In the foyer Yum Yum discovered the balustered staircase and ran up and down like a pianist practicing scales. Koko was attracted to the painting of mountains and jumped to the top of the chest in order to rub his jaw against a corner of the frame.

"Please! Let's not move any mountains," Qwilleran pleaded as he straightened the picture. He had never decided whether Koko had an appreciation of art or a perpetually itchy jaw.

The staircase was wide and well-proportioned for the spacious foyer, which had a group of inviting chairs around a stone fireplace. On either side of the entrance were two old-fashioned hat-and-umbrella stands with clouded mirrors, a couple of tired umbrellas, and some stout walking sticks for tramping about the woods. The most conspicuous item in the foyer, however, was the bulky and unattractive chest holding the telephone. Alongside it were a pair of Queen Anne side chairs matching the ten in the dining room, and above it hung the painting of a mountain range. A very good painting, Qwilleran thought; it expressed the mystery that he sensed about mountains.

Yum Yum had now ventured into the living room and was stretched on an upholstered chair in what Qwilleran called her Cleopatra pose. Koko followed her but went directly to a tall secretary desk that had empty bookshelves in the upper half. He craned his neck and mumbled to himself as if questioning the absence of books; he was an avid bibliophile.

"Okay, let's go!" said Qwilleran, clapping his hands for attention. "Let's go upstairs and see where you guys are going to bunk."

Neither of them paid the slightest heed. He had to carry them from the room, one under each arm. When they reached the staircase, however, Koko squirmed out of his grasp and headed toward the rear of the foyer. First he examined a Queen Anne chair, passing his nose up and down the legs, and then the frame of a French door, which looked newly painted.

"That's enough. Let's go," Qwilleran insisted. "You've got three months to sniff paint."

On the second floor there were two bedrooms at the rear that would get the morning sun, and the view was a breathtaking panorama of distant hills, a panorama unbroken by billboards, power lines, transmitter towers, or other signs of civilization. One of the rooms had a giant four-poster bed, a good-sized desk, and a pair of lounge chairs that appealed to Qwilleran. The back bedroom across the hall would be good for the Siamese. He put their blue cushion on the bed and left them there to explore their new surroundings while he made up his bed and hung towels in the bathroom.

Then he turned his attention to the upstairs hall, a kind

of lounge where guests of the inn, once upon a time, may
have been served their morning coffee. Here the gray walls
were covered with memorabilia in the form of framed documents and photographs, items of no value to the thieves
who had stripped the house. In old, faded photos (circa
1903) there were stiffly formal men in three-piece suits
and derby hats sitting in rocking chairs on the porch, while
women in ankle-length dresses and enormous hats played
croquet on the lawn. Also exhibited in narrow black frames
were photographs of present-day celebrities with inscrip-
tions to "J.J."

Of chief interest to Qwilleran was a clipping from the
Spudsboro Gazette dating back only a few years. It was a
column called "Potato Peelings" written by one Vonda
Dudley Wix in a cloyingly outdated style. Yet it contained
information of historic importance. The copy read:

The fashionable past of our lush and lovely mountain
is about to be revived, gentle reader, in a way un-
heard of in 1903. In that memorable year the Tiptop
Inn opened its snazzy French doors to a galaxy of
well-heeled guests. Those were days of pomp and
circumstance (ta-da! ta-da!), and the gilt-edged elite
arrived by train from New York, Washington, and
Chicago, some of them in their poshly private railway
cars. (Sorry. No names.) They were transported up
the mountain to the exclusive resort in sumptuous car-
riages driven by Dickensian coachmen in red velvet
coats and top hats.

There they spent a gloriously sybaritic week in sa-
lubrious surroundings (look that up in your Webster,
dears). The emphasis was on dining well (no one had
heard of calories), but they also strolled along moun-

tain paths or played battledore and shuttlecock (fun!)
after which they relaxed on the endless veranda or
repaired to the game room for some naughty gambling. Throughout the week they were pampered by
an attentive staff, including an English majordomo, a
French chef, and a bevy of Irish maids. (Oh, those
Irish maids!) During the ten-course dinners a violinist
played "Barcarolle" and Schubert's "Serenade"
(what else?), after which the evening musicale featured art songs by an oh-so-lyric soprano.

So, you are asking, what happened? . . . Well, the
stock market went *boom,* and the richly rich stopped
coming to Tiptop. A prolonged Depression and World
War II delivered the *coup de grâce* to the poor old
inn. After that it was owned by a Philadelphia bank
for many cruel, cruel years, during which it was
boarded up and sadly forgotten.

Then, in the 1950s, the inn was purchased, along
with most of Big Potato Mountain, by Otis Hawkinfield, the highly respected owner of the *Spudsboro
Gazette*, as a summer retreat. After his death his son
(whom we all know and love as J.J.) refurbished the
inn as a permanent home for his lovely wife and their
four beautiful children. Fortune did not smile on
them, alas, but let us skip swiftly to today's happy
news.

J.J. Hawkinfield has announced his intention to
share Big Potato Mountain with the world! (Bless you,
J.J.!)

"For two generations," he announced in an interview today, "the Hawkinfields have been privileged
to enjoy this sublime mountain environment. I can no
longer be selfish, however, about the spectacular

views, the summer breezes, the good mountain water, the wooded trails, and the breathtaking waterfalls. The time has come to share it with my fellow citizens.'' (Cheers! Cheers!)

Yes! J.J. and a syndicate of investors plan to develop the inside of Big Potato for family living. The approach road has already been paved, and architects are working on plans for year-round homes to be built on lots of no less than three acres, in designs integrated with the mountain terrain.

Boasted J.J. with excusable pride, ''I believe that Frank Lloyd Wright would approve of what we are about to do.'' (Hear! Hear!)

Future plans call for a campground for prestige-type recreation vehicles, offering such facilities as a swimming pool, hot tubs, and tennis courts. (That's class, my friends!) Condominiums and a mountain-top high-rise hotel with helicopter pad are also envisioned by J.J.

''Eventually,'' he revealed, ''the outer slopes of Big Potato will have a ski lodge and several ski runs. What I have in mind is the economic growth and health of the entire valley, as well as an opportunity for all to share in sports, recreation, and the joys of nature.''

''Oh, sure,'' Qwilleran said aloud, huffing cynically into his moustache. ''Frank Lloyd Wright was probably throwing up in his grave!'' He had another look at the framed photographs of celebrities. Many of them were posed with a man having a prominent nose and a high forehead. That, he guessed, was J.J. Hawkinfield ''whom we all know and love'' and who probably died of an overdose of compassion for his fellow citizens.

At that moment he was summoned to the telephone.

"How's everything at Tiptop?" asked Dolly Lessmore's cheery voice.

"Didn't you get my message? The place has been ransacked," Qwilleran said.

"Sorry, I neglected to tell you, but Ms. Hawkinfield was very close to her mother and wanted some family mementos—things that her mother loved so much."

"Like the television? That's gone, too."

"I didn't realize that. Well . . . we have an extra TV you can borrow for the summer."

"Never mind. I don't watch TV. The cats enjoy it, but they can live without the summer reruns."

"But you do understand about the accessories, don't you? Ms. Hawkinfield couldn't bear the thought of her mother's favorite things going to strangers who might purchase the house."

"Okay, I'll accept that. I just wanted you to know that they weren't here when I moved in. Not even any fireplace equipment."

"Is everything else all right?"

"One question," Qwilleran said. "When we discussed this place on the phone, did you say it was *roomy* or *gloomy*? Either you're going to run up an enormous electric bill, or the cats and I are going to turn into moles."

"Today wasn't terribly sunny," the realty agent explained, "and you have to remember that twilight comes earlier in the mountains. Ordinarily the light is so bright on the mountaintop that you'll be glad the windows are shaded by a veranda. Did you find the bed linens and towels all right?"

"I went through the entire linen closet," Qwilleran said irritably, "and there was not a single plain sheet. They're all loaded with lace!"

Ms. Lessmore's voice registered shock. "You don't like it? That's all handmade lace! Those bed linens were Mrs. Hawkinfield's pride and joy!"

"Then why didn't her daughter take them?" he snapped. "Sorry. Forget I said that. You'll have to excuse me. I'm tired tonight. I've been traveling for four days with two temperamental backseat drivers."

"You'll get a good night's rest and feel better tomorrow," she said encouragingly. "Mountain air is great for sleeping."

After hanging up the phone Qwilleran had an overwhelming urge to call someone in Moose County. Whether he knew it or not, the loneliness of a mountaintop and the emptiness of the house were making him homesick. Polly Duncan's number was the one that came promptly to mind. The chief librarian was the major link in the chain that bound him to Moose County, although the link had been weakened since her acquisition of a Siamese kitten named Bootsie. Her obsessive concern and maudlin affection for that cat made Qwilleran feel that he was sharing her with a rival. Furthermore, he considered "Bootsie" a frivolous name for a pedigreed Siamese with the appetite of a Great Dane, and he had told Polly so.

Now, consulting his watch, he was inclined to wait until the maximum discount rates went into effect. Despite his net worth and his extravagance in feeding the Siamese, he was thrifty about long-distance calls, and phone service was not included in the rent. He invited the Siamese into his bedroom for a read.

"Book!" he announced loudly, and they came running.

They always listened raptly as if they comprehended the meaning of his words, although more likely they were mesmerized by his melodious reading voice. Being unable to find an ottoman anywhere in the house (that woman, he was sure, had taken the ottomans, too), he pulled up a second lounge chair and propped his feet on it. Then, with Yum Yum on his lap and Koko on the arm of his chair, he read about a fellow who went to the mountains for a few weeks and stayed seven years.

He read until eleven o'clock, at which time he telephoned Polly Duncan at her apartment in Pickax City. It was a carriage house apartment, and he had spent many contented hours there—contented, that is, until the unfortunate advent of Bootsie.

"Qwill, I'm so glad to hear your voice," she said in the pleasing, well-modulated tones that made his skin tingle. "I wondered when you were going to call, dear. How was the trip?"

"Uneventful, for the most part. We had a little difficulty in finding the top of the mountain, but we're here with our sanity intact."

"What is your house like?"

"It's an architectural style called Musty Rustic. I'll be able to appraise it more objectively when I've had a good night's sleep. How's everything in Pickax?" he asked.

"Dr. Goodwinter's wife finally died. She was buried today."

"How long had she been ill?"

"Fifteen years, ten of them bedridden. Just about everyone in the county attended the funeral—as a tribute to Dr. Hal. He's dearly loved—the last of the old-fashioned country doctors. We're all wondering if he'll retire now."

Qwilleran's mind leaped to Melinda Goodwinter, the

young doctor with green eyes and long lashes, who had cured him of pipe smoking. Had she returned to Pickax for her mother's funeral? He hesitated to inquire. She had been Polly's predecessor in his affections, and Polly was inordinately jealous. Approaching the question obliquely he remarked, "I never knew if the Goodwinters had many children."

"Only Melinda. She came from Boston for the funeral. There's speculation that she might stay and take over her father's practice."

Qwilleran recognized the possibility as a hot potato and changed the subject. "How's Bootsie?"

"You'll be glad to know I've thought of a new name for him. What do you think of Bucephalus?"

"It sounds like a disease."

"Bucephalus," Polly said indignantly, "was the favorite horse of Alexander the Great. He was a noble beast."

"You don't need to tell me that. The name still sounds like a disease, although I agree that Bootsie eats like a horse. Back to the drawing board, Polly."

"Oh, Qwill! You're so hard to please," she protested. "How do the cats like the mountains? Does the altitude affect them?"

"They seem happy. We're reading *The Magic Mountain.*"

"Do you have a good view? Don't forget to send me some snapshots."

"We have a spectacular view. The place is called Tiptop, but if I owned it, I'd name it Hawk's Nest."

"You're not thinking of buying, are you?" she asked with concern.

"I make quick decisions, but not that quick, Polly! I arrived only a couple of hours ago. First I have to get some sleep, and then go into Spudsboro tomorrow to do some errands. Also I've got to learn how to drive in these mountains. One drives south in order to go north, and down in order to go up."

The two of them chattered on with companionable familiarity until Qwilleran started worrying about his phone bill. They ended their visit with the usual murmur: "À bientôt."

"That was Polly," he said to Koko, who was sitting next to the telephone. "Bootsie sends his regards."

"Yow," said Koko, batting an ear with his paw.

Qwilleran went outdoors and paced the veranda that circled the entire house, wondering why he was here alone when he had been so comfortable in Moose County among friends. From the front veranda he could see across the dark treetops to the valley, where pinpoints of light traced the city of Spudsboro. Directly below him the mountainside was dotted with the high-powered yardlights of the houses on Hawk's Nest Drive. One bank of lights flooded a swimming pool like a baseball diamond illuminated for a night game.

Elsewhere, the view was one of total darkness, except for a circle of light toward the south. It appeared to be on a nearby mountain, and the circle appeared to be revolving. Qwilleran went indoors for his binoculars and trained them on the circle. It was definitely moving—a phenomenon that would bear investigation.

A chill wind was stirring, and he retired for his first overnight on Big Potato.

FOUR

QWILLERAN TOOK A few precautions before falling into the arms of Morpheus. It was June, and the sun would be rising early; that meant the Siamese would be awake at dawn, clamoring for their breakfast. Fortunately there were blinds on the bedroom windows—opaque, room-darkening roller blinds. Qwilleran pulled them down in the cats' quarters as well as in his own—four in each room. He also took care to leave their door open so they could go downstairs to the pantry and the turkey roaster that served as their commode. It was a long walk to the pantry, and they really needed a second commode, he thought. He added "turkey roaster" to his shopping list for the next day. There was nothing like a turkey roaster, he had discovered, for a non-tip, rustproof, easy-to-clean, long-lasting litterbox.

He expected to sleep well in the fresh mountain atmosphere. There were many claims made for living at high altitudes, he recalled as he started to doze off: People who live in the mountains are nicer . . . They live longer because the water and air are so pure . . . Heavy drinkers have fewer hangovers in the mountains . . .

He slept fairly well, considering the strange bed and the lace the sheets and pillowcases. Whenever he shifted position he felt an alien substance under his chin. Nevertheless, he managed well enough until about five-thirty. At that early hour he was jolted awake.

Was it a gunshot? It brought him to a sitting position even before his eyes were open. At the sound of the second shot he was wide awake! The realization that it was happening *inside the house* catapulted him from the bed just as the third shot rang out! He dashed for the door, fearing for the cats and unmindful of his own safety. He yanked open the door in time to hear the fourth shot!

At that moment he realized it was not gunfire. Two Siamese were walking triumphantly from their sleeping quarters, tails waving. Early morning light was streaming into their room, turning everything rosy. All four window shades were raised!

"You devils!" Qwilleran muttered, shuffling back to his bed. One of them—no doubt Yum Yum the Paw—had discovered how to raise a roller blind with an explosive report. Simply insert a paw in the pull-ring . . . release it . . . and BANG! Up it goes! He had to admit it was a smart maneuver.

Two hours later it was the noisy motor of an aging truck that disturbed his sleep. Checking the parking lot from a second floor window, he saw a bearded man stepping out of a red pickup with one blue fender. His beard was untamed, and he wore old-fashioned striped railroad overalls and a wide-brimmed felt fedora that was green with age. Collecting paint buckets from the truck bed, he walked slowly toward the stone steps with a hitch in his gait. Hurriedly Qwilleran pulled on some clothes and met the workman on the veranda.

"Good morning," he said to the stranger. "Nice day, isn't it? A bit coolish, but fresh." He had lived in Moose County long enough to know about weather as a form of introduction.

"Gonna rain, come nightfall," said the workman. "Gonna be a gully-washer."

"How do you know?" The air was crisp; there was not a cloud in the sky; the mountains were sharply defined. "What makes you think we'll get rain?"

"Earthworms comin' up. See'd a black snake in a tree." The man's face was a crinkled, weatherbeaten tan, but his eyes were keen. "Gittin' too doggone much rain in these parts."

"Are you Mr. Beechum?"

"Dewey Beechum, come to finish up," he said as he started around the veranda toward the rear.

Qwilleran followed. "What needs to be finished?"

They had reached the rear of the house, and Mr. Beechum nodded toward the railing of the veranda. "That there back rail, and that there glass door." He nodded toward the French door that Koko had sniffed the night before.

"What happened to the door?" Qwilleran asked.

"Busted." He applied a final coat of stain to a section of railing and then painted the framework around the small glass panes of the door—without using a dropcloth and without a spill or a smear.

"You do good work, Mr. Beechum."

"Don't pay to do bad. See that there chair?" He nodded toward the Queen Anne chair in the foyer. "Legs was busted, but I fixed 'em. Never know they was busted."

That explained Koko's interest in the chair and the French door; one of them had recently varnished legs, and the other had new glass and a coat of fresh paint on the frame. Clever cat! He never missed a thing. He even knew that the tall secretary desk in the living room was supposed to have books in its upper deck.

"Do you live around here?" Qwilleran asked.

Beechum jerked his head to the south. "Yonder on L'il Tater. That there's a real mount'n."

"Big Potato looks pretty good to me."

"Ain't what it was, years back."

"What happened?"

"Folks from down there"—he nodded toward the valley—"they come up here and rooned it, cuttin' down trees, buildin' fancy houses, roonin' the waterfalls. No tellin' what they'll be roonin' nextways. But they won't git L'il Tater iffen we hafta hold 'em off with shotguns!"

"Good for you!" Qwilleran always agreed heartily with anyone he was trying to encourage, and already he envisioned Mr. Beechum as a colorful subject for a column in the *Moose County Something*. "I've been thinking, Mr. Beechum, that I'd like to have a gazebo built among the trees."

"A what?"

"A small summer house—just a floor and a roof and

screens on all four sides. I don't think it would ruin anything."

"Don't need no screens up here. No bugs."

How could Qwilleran explain to this mountain man that the gazebo was for the cats, so they could enjoy the outdoors in safety? "Just the same," he said, "I'd feel more comfortable with screens. Could you build it for me?"

"How big you want?"

"Perhaps ten or twelve feet square."

"Twelve's better. No waste."

"May I pay you in advance for the materials?"

"Ain't no need."

"I'd appreciate it if you'd use that treated lumber that doesn't need painting."

"That's what I'm aimin' to do."

"Good! We're on the same wavelength. When can you start, Mr. Beechum?"

"When you be wantin' it?"

"Soon as possible."

The workman raised his green fedora and scratched his head. There was a line of demarcation across his forehead—weatherbeaten tan below, pasty white above. "Mebbe Monday," he said.

"That sounds good."

"Mebbe Wednesday. All depends. Could rain." Beechum started back to the pickup with his paint buckets and brushes.

Accompanying him down the steps Qwilleran took another look at the red pickup with one blue fender and said, "I believe I stopped at your house last night, Mr. Beechum, when I was trying to find my way here. A young woman kindly came to my rescue. I'd like to thank her in some way."

"Don't need no thanks," the man mumbled as he started the reluctant motor.

Qwilleran returned to the house to feed the cats, prepare some coffee for himself, and dress for a shopping trip to Spudsboro. Saying goodbye to the Siamese he inquired, "Will you characters be all right if I go out for a while?" They regarded him with a blank feline stare capable of undermining self-esteem. He knew that look. It meant, Just be sure you come back at dinnertime.

Before descending the twenty-five steps to the parking lot, he stood on the veranda and absorbed the view. Directly below him were treetops and an occasional odd-shaped roof or turquoise swimming pool. In the valley the dome of the courthouse glistened in the sunlight, and a meandering line of trees marked the course of the Yelly-hoo River. Across the river the West Potatoes rose majestically. He snapped a few pictures to send to Polly and then walked down the steps, wondering if his car would start, and if he still had a jigger of gas in the tank, and if one could safely coast down the mountain to a gas station in the valley.

There was no cause for concern; the small car could run on a thimbleful. Maneuvering it around the curves of Hawk's Nest Drive he was thankful for the smooth pavements, the guardrails, and the white and yellow lines. He passed the Wilbank and Lessmore houses and other contemporary dwellings with glass where one would expect walls—and walls where one would expect glass. All had neat, circular drives, blacktopped. In one large area cleared of trees a new house was being built, and a powerful back-hoe was gouging out the hillside. At the bottom of the hill the entrance to Hawk's Nest Drive was marked by two

stone pylons and a sign: TIPTOP ESTATES . . . PRIVATE
ROAD.

Qwilleran filled his gas tank and asked for foolproof
directions to Five Points—without shortcuts—and was
amazed how easily he found the star-shaped intersection.
At the Five Points Café he sat in a booth, ordered ham
and eggs, and perused the *Spudsboro Gazette*, in which
the headline news was Friday's excessive rain, seven inches
in two hours. The river was running high, and the softball
field on the west bank was too wet for play. Otherwise,
Colin Carmichael's newspaper was similar to the *Moose
County Something*, although it surprised Qwilleran to learn
that the "Potato Peelings" column was still being written
by Vonda Dudley Wix. She was gushing about Father's
Day.

The radio at the restaurant was playing country music
and advertising a sale of recliners at a local furniture store,
and in an adjoining booth three men were arguing over
their coffee.

A voice with a nasal twang said, "I see the damned
pickets came crawling out of the woodwork again."

"They're there every Friday afternoon and Saturday,"
said another man with a high-pitched voice. "They're trying to embarrass the city when the weekend tourists arrive."

"There oughta be a law!"

"Ever hear of freedom of speech, Jerry?" This voice
sounded somewhat familiar to Qwilleran. "It's their constitutional right. I'd carry a picket sign myself if I had a
legitimate beef. Okay?"

The second speaker said, "The trouble is—things are
going so good in this town. Why do they have to make
waves?"

"They're a bunch of radicals, that's why!" said Jerry. "That whole crowd on Little Potato is radical to the eyebrows!"

"Oh, come off it, Jerry. Okay?"

"I mean it! Always trying to sabotage progress. Just because they live like bums, they don't want the rest of us to live nice and make a little money."

"Listen, Jerry, there should be a way to live nice without spoiling it for everybody else. Okay? Look what happened to the road up Big Potato! They call it Hawk's Nest Drive and put up a sign to keep people out. That's no private road! That's a secondary county highway, and they can't legally stop anybody from driving up there. When I was a kid, my dad used to drive us to the top of Big Potato where the old inn is, and we'd have picnics at Batata Falls. That was before they dammed it and made it Lake Batata. In those days it was nothing but a dirt road. Then J.J. pulled strings and got it paved at taxpayers' expense, after which they try to call it a private drive. I'm gonna get a picket sign myself one of these days. Okay?"

"Bill's right, Jerry. J.J. started it, and now his cronies are selling timber rights and slashing the forest for a motel or hotel or something. Investors, they call 'em. Not even local people!"

"Whoever they are, it's good for the economy," Jerry insisted. "It creates jobs and brings more people in. You paint more houses, and Bill sells more hot dogs, and I sell more hardware."

"Speaking of hot dogs," Bill said, "I've gotta get back to the store. See you loafers next week—okay?" As he paid for his coffee on the way out, Qwilleran recognized the manager of the Five Points Market and would have relished a few words with him about the Snaggy Creek cutoff, but Bill Treacle slipped out too quickly.

Qwilleran himself left the café soon afterward and drove downtown. He parked and walked along Center Street, noting the new brick sidewalks, ornamental trees, and simulated gaslights. Approaching the Lessmore agency, he thought of stopping to ask a couple of questions: Would there be any objection to a gazebo? What were the revolving lights on the mountain? The office was closed, however. Generally, Center Street had the deserted air of a downtown business district on Saturday when everyone is at the mall. There was no one but Qwilleran to read the picket signs in front of the courthouse: SAVE OUR MOUNTAIN . . . NO MORE SLASHING . . . STOP THE RAPE . . . FREE FOREST.

At the office of the *Spudsboro Gazette* a Saturday calm prevailed, and when he asked for Mr. Carmichael, the lone woman in the front office pointed down a corridor.

The editor was in his office, talking to a law enforcement officer, but he jumped up exclaiming, "You must be Jim Qwilleran! I recognized the moustache. This is our sheriff, Del Wilbank . . . Del, this is the man who's renting Tiptop for the summer. Jim Qwilleran used to cover the police beat for newspapers around the country. He also wrote a book on urban crime."

"Am I intruding?" Qwilleran asked.

"No, I was just leaving," said the sheriff. He turned to the editor. "Don't touch this thing, Colin. Don't even consider it—at this time. Agreed?"

"You have my word, Del. Thanks for coming in."

The sheriff nodded to Qwilleran. "Enjoy your stay, Mr. . . ."

"Qwilleran."

The editor, a fortyish man with thinning hair and a little too much weight, came around the desk and pumped his visitor's hand. "When Kip told me you were coming, I flipped! You were my hero when I was in J school, Qwill. Okay if I call you Qwill? In fact, your book was required reading. I remember the title, *City of Brotherly Crime*. Dolly told me you were renting Tiptop. How do you like it? Have a chair."

"I came to see if I could take you to lunch," Qwilleran said.

"Absolutely not! I'll take *you* to lunch. We'll go to the golf club, and now's a good time to go, before the rush. My car's parked in back."

On the way to the club Carmichael pointed out the new public library, the site of a proposed community college, a modern papermill, a church of unconventional design. "This is a yuppie town, Qwill. Most all the movers and shakers are young, energetic, and ambitious."

"I noticed a lot of expensive cars on Center Street," Qwilleran said, "and a lot of small planes at the airport."

"Absolutely! The town's booming. I bought at the right time. The furniture factory is being automated. An electronics firm is building downriver and will be on-line this year. Any chance you'd like to relocate in Spudsboro? Kip said you took early retirement. There's plenty to do here—fishing, white-water rafting, golf, backpacking, tennis . . . My kids love it."

"To be frank, Colin, I plan to be the solitary, sedentary type this summer. I have some serious thinking to do, and I thought a mountaintop would be ideal. How about you? What brought you and your family to Spudsboro?"

"Well, my wife and I had been hoping to find a smaller, healthier community to bring up our kids, and then this opportunity popped up. I'd always wanted to manage my own newspaper. Don't we all? So when the owner of the *Gazette* died and it went on the block, I grabbed it, although I may be in hock for the next twenty years.''

''Are you talking about J.J. Hawkinfield?''

''He's the one! It's his house you're staying in. My kids wanted me to buy that, too, but they were asking too much money for it, and we don't need all that space. We're better off with a ranch house in the valley. And who knows if the school bus could get up the mountain in bad weather—or if we could get down?''

When they arrived at the golf club, groups were pouring into the clubhouse. Saturday lunch, it appeared, was the accepted way to entertain in Spudsboro. Men wore blazers in pastel colors. Women dressed to outdo each other, one of them actually wearing a hat. Altogether they were far different from the sweaters-and-cords crowd that patronized restaurants in Moose County. There were club-shirted golfers as well, but most of them walked through the dining room to a noisy bar in the rear, called the Off-Links Lounge.

Carmichael ordered a Bloody Mary, and Qwilleran ordered the same without the vodka.

''How do you like Tiptop?'' the editor asked.

''It's roomy, to say the least. Something smaller would have been preferable, but I have two cats, and no one accepts pets in rental units. Dolly Lessmore twisted an arm or two to get me into Tiptop.''

''Yes, she's quite aggressive. As they say at the chamber of commerce meetings, he's *less* and she's *more* . . . Cheers! Welcome to the Potatoes!'' He lifted his glass.

Qwilleran said, ''What do you know about your predecessor?''

"I never met J.J., but people still talk about him. They're thinking of naming a scenic drive after him. He was quite powerful in this town and ran the *Gazette* like a one-man show, writing an editorial every week that knocked the town on its ear. Mine must sound pretty bland by comparison."

"What was his background?"

"J.J. grew up here. His family owned the *Gazette* for a couple of generations, but he wanted to go into law. He was in law school, as a matter of fact, when his father died. He dropped out and came back here to run the paper, but he was a born adversary, from what I hear. He stirred things up and made a lot of enemies, but he also spurred the economic growth of Spudsboro—not to mention the circulation of the *Gazette*."

Qwilleran said, "From a conversation I overheard in a coffee shop this morning, there's divided opinion about economic growth."

"That's true. The conservatives and old-timers want everything to stay the way it was, with population growth at zero. The younger ones and the merchants are all for progress, and let the chips fall where they may."

"Where do you stand?"

"Well, you know, Qwill, I'm exposed to both viewpoints, and I try to be objective. We're entering a new century, and we're already engulfed in a wave of technology that's going to break the dikes. And yet . . . the environment must be understood and respected. Right here in the Potatoes we've got to address such issues as the stripping of forests, damming of waterfalls for private use, population density, pollution, and the destruction of wildlife habitat. How are they handling it where you live?"

Qwilleran said, "In Moose County we're always thirty

years behind the times, so the problems you mention haven't confronted us as yet. We haven't even been discovered by the fast-food chains, but the situation is going to alter very soon. The business community is pushing for tourism. So I'll watch the situation in Spudsboro with a great deal of interest. Who are the pickets in front of the courthouse?''

"That's an ongoing campaign by the environmentalists," Carmichael said. "Different picketers show up each weekend—all hill folks from Little Potato, some of them with a personal ax to grind. There are two kinds of people on that mountain, living quite primitively, you might say. There are the ones called Taters, whose ancestors bought cheap land from the government more than a century ago and who still cling to a pioneer way of life, and then there are the artists and others who deserted the cities for what they call plain living. We call them New Taters. They're the ones who are militant about protecting the environment. Strange to say, some of the conservatives in the valley are afraid of the Taters, even though they're on the same side of the fence politically. It's not a clear-cut situation.''

Two golfers walking through the dining room to the lounge attracted a flurry of interest from women who were lunching. One had a shaggy head of sun-bleached hair and the other was neatly barbered. Qwilleran recognized the latter as Dolly Lessmore's husband.

"That's Bob Lessmore and Hugh Lumpton, top guns in the club," the editor explained. "Champion golfers have a certain look, don't they? Their build, their walk, even their facial set. It comes from concentration, I guess. Do you play golf?''

"No," Qwilleran said. "I never thought that anything

smaller than a baseball was worth hitting. Baseball was my game until I injured a knee. I was too short for basketball, too cowardly to play football, too poor to play polo, and too sane to play soccer."

Carmichael recommended the poached flounder, saying that the new chef was introducing a lighter menu to a membership hooked on corned beef sandwiches and sixteen-ounce steaks. Qwilleran ordered the poached flounder, although he noticed that his host ordered a corned beef sandwich and cheddar cheese soup. It proved to be a small piece of fish, lightly sauced and served on an oversized plate along with three perfect green beans, a sliver of parboiled carrot, and two halves of a cherry tomato broiled and sprinkled with parsley. It was accompanied by the starch of the day, mashed turnip flavored with grated orange rind.

Gingerly Qwilleran forked into this repast, and as he did so, he was aware that a woman at a nearby table was staring at his moustache. She had the embalmed look that comes from too many facelifts, and she was wearing a voluptuous brimmed hat that zoomed up on one side and swooped down on the other.

"Who's the woman in the hat who's giving me the eye?" he asked under his breath.

"That's Vonda Dudley Wix," the editor said without moving his lips. "She writes the 'Potato Peelings' column. She's spotted your moustache, I'm afraid, and she'll be nailing you for an interview."

"She'll have to catch me first. I've read her column. What do you think of her style?"

"Overripe, to say the least. I tried to kill the column when I bought the paper, but the readers rose up in protest. They actually like it! Newspaper subscribers are un-predictable.''

Helping himself to a third mini-muffin, Qwilleran was glad he had eaten a substantial breakfast at the Five Points Café. He maintained an amiable composure, however. ''How long does it take to learn your way around the mountains, Colin? All I've got is three months.'' He related his experience of the previous day: how he wound up on the wrong mountain and how he was rescued by one of the Taters. He said, ''Her manner was definitely hostile, and yet she went miles out of her way to help me find Hawk's Nest Drive. I don't understand it.''

''They're not easy to understand,'' said Carmichael. ''In fact, there are some weird characters in them thar hills.''

''The MacDiarmids told me the artists have a community where they sell their handcrafts. Where's that?''

''Potato Cove. It's on the outside of Little Potato. It was a ghost town that they resurrected.''

''Is it difficult to find?''

''It's on a dirt road, but the route is well marked because it's a tourist attraction. Go to Five Points and then follow the signs.''

Qwilleran said, ''I saw something strange last night. It was around midnight. I went out for a lungful of fresh air before turning in and walked around the veranda. On a mountain toward the south there was a circle of light, and it was revolving.''

''Oh sure, we see that once in a while.''

''Is it some kind of natural phenomenon? I have friends in Moose County who'd insist it was an alien aircraft from outer space.''

The editor chuckled. ''Are you ready for this, Qwill? . . . They say there's a witches' coven up on Little

Potato. Apparently they celebrate certain phases of the moon—or whatever.''

"Have you ever done a story on them?"

"Are you kidding? Even if we could find them in that godforsaken wilderness, no outsider could get close enough to take a picture or spy on them. But if you want to take a whack at it, we'll buy the story," Carmichael added in a jocular vein.

"No, thanks," said Qwilleran, "but I think it was one of the witches who came to my rescue last night."

They ordered coffee, and Qwilleran had a slice of double chocolate fudge cake that restored his interest in the golf club. On the way out, at the editor's urging, he signed up for a social membership that would permit him to use the dining room. They gave him a card with the club logo: SGC in embossed gold, on a brown oval representing a potato.

"And now where do you want to be dropped?" Carmichael asked.

"At a furniture store, if there's one downtown. I left my car on Center Street."

"Didn't you rent the place furnished?"

"Supposedly, but I need an ottoman. I like to put my feet up when I read. I also need a small radio for weather reports."

"The hardware store at Five Points is the best for that. Get one that can operate on batteries in case of a blackout."

"Do you lose power often?" Qwilleran asked.

"Only when a tree blows down across a power line."

As they drove back downtown, the editor pointed out some local attractions: the Lumpton furniture factory, offering guided tours every afternoon; the historical museum in an old house on Center Street; the scenic drive about to be named after J.J. Hawkinfield.

"How old was he when he died?" Qwilleran asked.

"Not old. In his fifties."

"What happened to him?"

Carmichael hesitated. "You haven't heard? He was murdered."

Qwilleran put his hand to his moustache. "Ms. Lessmore didn't tell me that." He had sensed something sinister, though.

"Well, you know, Qwill . . . small towns are sensitive about serious crimes . . . and with the emphasis on tourism here, murder is never mentioned to vacationers."

"I had a hunch that something irregular had happened to the owner of Tiptop. What were the circumstances?"

"He was pushed off his own mountain. You can read about it in our files if you're interested. The murderer is in prison, although there's an element here that thinks they convicted the wrong man, but that's par for the course, isn't it? . . . Well, here's your furniture store, Qwill. It's great to have you here. Don't be too solitary. Keep in touch."

FIVE

ACCORDING TO SIGNS plastered on the windows, the furniture store was having a sale of recliners, a fact corroborated by the lineup of chairs on the sidewalk. Qwilleran walked in and asked to see some ottomans.

"Did you see our recliners on sale?" asked a pleasant elderly woman, eager to be of service.

"Yes, but I'm interested in an ottoman."

"All the recliners in the store are twenty-five percent off," she said encouragingly.

"Do you have any ottomans?" he asked with exaggerated politeness.

"Harry!" she shouted toward the rear of the store. "Do we have any ottomans?"

"No!" Harry yelled. "Show the customer the recliners!"

"Never mind," Qwilleran said. "Show me a telephone book."

Consulting the classified section, he found a likely source of ottomans just two blocks away: Peel & Poole Design Studio. It was a juxtaposition of names that appealed to his fancy for words.

At the Peel & Poole studio he was greeted by a smartly suited young woman who reminded him of Fran Brodie, a designer in Pickax. They had the same suave buoyancy and the same reddish blond hair.

"May I help you?" she asked cordially. Her hair flowed silkily to her shoulders, and long, straight bangs drew attention to the blueness of her eyes.

"I need an ottoman," he said. "I'm renting a furnished place for the summer, and I like to put my feet up when I read. I do not—want—a recliner!" he said with measured emphasis.

"You're quite right," she agreed. "I'm a firm believer in ottomans, and we have a nice one that we can order for you in any cover."

"How long does it take for a special order?"

"Six to eight weeks."

"That won't do. I'll be here only three months. I'm renting Tiptop for the summer."

"Really?" she asked in surprise. "I didn't know they were willing to rent. What condition is it in?"

"The building's in good repair and has all the essentials, but it's rather bleak and full of echoes. Someone has cleaned out all the bric-a-brac."

"The Hawkinfield daughter," the designer said, nodding. "When J.J. died, she took everything in the way of decorative accessories to sell in her shop in Maryland. I helped her appraise the stuff. But now, if you'd like any help in making the interior comfortable for the summer, I'm at your service. I'm Sabrina Peel."

"Qwilleran. Jim Qwilleran, spelled with a QW," he said. "Are you familiar with Tiptop?"

"Definitely! Our studio helped Mrs. Hawkinfield with the interior a few years ago—just before she went into the hospital. The poor woman never returned to enjoy it."

"What happened?"

"She was committed to a mental hospital, and she's still there—doesn't even know that her husband is dead. Would you like a cup of coffee?"

"I never say no to coffee," he said.

"Or a glass of chardonnay?"

"Coffee, if you please."

While she prepared the beverage he wandered about the studio, admiring the Peel & Poole taste. He also found the ottoman she had mentioned: large, cushiony, inviting, and labeled "floor sample." After the first sip of coffee, he regarded her with the beseeching eyes that women could rarely resist and asked, "Would you consider selling me your floor sample?"

She took a moment to react, pushing her hair back from her face with an attractive two-handed gesture. "On one condition—if you'll let me spruce up your summer residence. I can use small rugs and pillows and folding screens to make it more livable and without a large investment on your part. You owe it to yourself to have a pleasant environment when you're vacationing."

"Sounds good to me!" he said. "Would you like to drive up and look it over?"

"How about Monday afternoon at one-thirty? I'll take along some accessories for your approval."

"Tell me something about the Hawkinfields," Qwilleran said. "Why did they want such a large house?"

"They had several children and did a lot of entertaining—originally. Then all of a sudden their life went into a tailspin. Three of the boys were killed within a year."

"How?" Qwilleran was always quick to suspect foul play, and since their father had enemies and was a murder victim himself, the possibilities were rife.

"There were two accidents a few months apart, both related to outdoor sports. It was a crushing blow for the parents. After the second incident Mrs. Hawkinfield couldn't cope and had a nervous breakdown. We all felt terrible about it. She was a nice woman, although she let her husband keep her under his thumb. Everyone wished she'd stand up for herself . . . I don't know why I'm telling you this, except that it's Tiptop history, and it goes with the house, along with the carpet and draperies."

"I appreciate knowing," he said. "I've been getting negative vibrations."

"Is that true? How interesting!" the designer said, leaning forward. "I'm very sensitive to the aura of a house. When I visit a client for the first time, I get a definite feeling about the family's past and present."

"Mrs. Hawkinfield seemed to be hooked on gray, if that signifies anything."

"Hooked is the right word! We tried to warm it up with antique gold and Venetian red, but she loved gray and always wore it. Actually it was becoming. She had lovely gray eyes—and prematurely gray hair, which we all blamed on her husband.''

Qwilleran was about to inquire about the murder, but a chime at the front door announced another customer, and he drained his coffee cup. "I'll look forward to seeing you Monday afternoon, Ms. Peel."

"Sabrina," she corrected him.

"Don't bring anything gray, Sabrina. And please call me Qwill."

Driving away from the design studio with the ottoman in the trunk, he felt a bond of camaraderie with Sabrina Peel. He liked designers, especially those with that particular roseate hair tint, which he thought of as "decorator blond." When he stopped at the Five Points Market to stock his bar for possible guests, he included chardonnay with the usual hard and soft drinks.

The friendly Bill Treacle, who was bustling about the store with managerial urgency, saw Qwilleran loading a shopping cart with scotch, bourbon, vodka, rum, sherry, beer, fruit juices, and mixes. "Having a party?" he asked cheerily. "Looks like you found Tiptop okay."

"No problem," Qwilleran replied. After meeting Sabrina he was feeling too good to quibble about the Snaggy Creek cutoff and the thawed seafood and the melted ice cream.

At the same intersection he went into Lumpton's Hardware and asked for a turkey roaster.

"What size?" asked a man with a nasal twang.

"I thought one size fits all."

"We've got three sizes, top of the line. From Germany. How big a turkey are you talking about?"

"Just a small one," Qwilleran said. He was staggered by the price, but he could afford it, and the cats deserved a second facility. He himself had eight bathrooms at Tiptop; why should they be limited to one commode? He also bought a radio with more features than he really wanted, the control panel having several switches, six knobs, and seventeen buttons. Even so, it cost less than the cats' commode.

Upon leaving the hardware store Qwilleran saw a barnwood sign advertising mountain crafts and handmade gifts at Potato Cove. He followed the arrow, thinking he might find a gift for Polly and a ceramic mug for himself. The coffee cups at Tiptop had finger-trap handles and limited capacity; he could empty one in two gulps.

The road to Potato Cove was the kind that map makers call "unimproved," meaning that it was gravel with teeth-rattling bumps and ruts. It was marked at every turn and every fork, however, and it wound through a dense forest where the pines stood tall and straight, as close together as pickets in a fence.

On the way to the cove Qwilleran saw a few dwellings, poor excuses for housing, and yet there were more signs of life than he had found around Tiptop Estates. He saw children chasing each other and climbing trees, two women laughing as they hung diapers on a clothesline, cats and dogs sunning, a man chopping wood, a white-haired woman sitting on the porch of a log cabin, peeling apples. There was something poetic about this humble scene: her placid demeanor as she sat in a rocking chair with a bowl cradled in her lap, leisurely wielding the paring knife as if she had all afternoon. Qwilleran's camera was on the seat beside him, and he would have snapped a picture if it had not been for the shotgun leaning against a porch post.

Farther along the road there was an enterprise that called

itself "Just Rust." A long, low shed was jammed with rusty artifacts that spilled over into the front yard: bed frames, parts of sewing machines, plows, broken tools, folding metal chairs, wash boilers, scythes, bathtubs, bird cages, bed pans, frying pans, wheelbarrows . . .

Next came a streetscene that might have been the set for a low-budget Hollywood western: crude buildings of weathered wood, spaced haphazardly along the road and connected with wooden sidewalks. Yet, even in this ramshackle environment the hand of an artist was evident in the signs painted on barnwood. The first was a parody of small-town hospitality: WELCOME TO POTATO COVE . . . POPULATION 0. Similar signs nailed to the buildings identified the shops of Otto the Potter, Vance the Village Smith, and specialists in woodcraft, leather goods, hand-dipped candles, baskets, and the like. There was wit in some of the signs. The chair caner called his shop The Bottom Line.

Among the visitors who walked up and down the wooden sidewalks there were townspeople wearing Saturday casuals and doing a little shopping, as well as tourists in shorts and sandals, gawking and snapping pictures. Qwilleran followed a few who were walking briskly toward a shed behind Otto's pottery.

"What's going on?" he asked one of them.

"Kiln opening," was the hurried answer.

In the shed, lighted by sunshine streaming through holes in the rusted metal roof, twenty or more bystanders were watching eagerly as a soft-spoken man in a canvas apron removed pots from a large oven, holding them up one by one. "This is my new decorated platter," he said modestly. "And this is a weed holder with the new glaze I've been working on."

Responses shot out from the onlookers: "I'll take it . . .
Let me see that one up close . . . Do you have three more
like that plate? . . . Oh! That's a pretty one! . . . I'll take
that, Otto."

The potter continued his commentary in a quiet monotone. "The ones closer to the fire may have some variation
in color . . . This bowl's imperfect. It got a little too hot
and started bloating. Like we say, the kiln giveth and the
kiln taketh away. Here's one of my new pitchers with pine
tree decoration."

"I'll take that!" said a man in the back row, and the
pitcher was passed over the heads of the others. In a low
voice he said to his companion, "I can sell it in my shop
for three times the price."

Qwilleran noticed that men in designer shirts and gold
jewelry and women in pastel pants suits and expensive
cologne were grabbing four-dollar mugs and seven-dollar
candleholders, handmade and signed by the potter. He
himself found a mug with a handle that accommodated his
fingers comfortably, and when he learned it was one-tenth
the price of the cats' commode, he bought four. At last
the kiln was emptied, and a groan of disappointment went
up from the audience.

"Sorry I don't have more," the potter apologized. "I
really tried to pack the kiln this time, using miniatures to
fill up the corners."

As the purchasers stood in line to pay, voices filled the
small shed with social hubbub—exulting over their finds,
greeting friends, sharing local gossip. Qwilleran overheard two women saying:

"Did you hear about Tiptop? Some crazy fella with a
big moustache and a lot of cats is renting it for $2,000 a
week!"

"Is he a Canadian or Japanese or what?"

"Nobody knows. The Lessmores made the deal. He's supposed to be a writer."

"That could be a front for something else."

"Anyway, it doesn't sound good."

Qwilleran hustled away with his mugs wrapped in newspaper and stashed them in the trunk of his car before joining the parade up the wooden sidewalk. He stopped to watch a man making sandals and a woman caning chairseats. Then, hearing the ring of hammer on metal, he followed the sound to the smithy. Within a barn with doors flung wide there was a glowing forge, and red hot metal was being hammered on an anvil by a sinewy young man with full beard and pigtail. He wore a leather apron and a soiled tee with the sleeves cut out.

"Howya," he said when he saw Qwilleran watching intently. Picking up a rod with tongs, he thrust it into the glowing coals, checked it for redness, fired it again, and finally hammered it into shape. When the hot iron was plunged into a tub of water to cool, the sizzle added to the show of sights, sounds, and smells.

Qwilleran examined the hand-wrought objects for sale: hooks, tongs, pokers, spikes, and cowbells, but his eye was taken by an item in a shadowy corner of the barn. It was a wrought-iron candelabrum, seven feet tall and branched to hold eight candles. An iron vine twisted around the main stem and sprouted a few tendrils and leaves. "Is that for sale?" he asked.

The smith looked at it dubiously. "Guess so," he said.

"How much are you asking?"

"Jeez, I dunno. It was just somethin' I hadda prove I could do. Mosta the time I'm a mechanic down in the valley."

"It's a spectacular hunk of iron," Qwilleran said, thinking of it for his apple barn in Pickax. "Set a price and let me buy it."

"Uh . . . two hundred?" the blacksmith suggested hesitantly.

"Sold! If I pull my car up, will you help me load it? How much does it weigh?"

"Plenty, man!"

By reclining the passenger seat they were able to pack the candelabrum lengthwise inside the car. Next, Qwilleran amazed the candle dipper by buying three dozen handmade, twelve-inch beeswax candles. Pleased with his purchases and hoping to find a cup of coffee, he trudged up the hill. He had a few words with the quiltmaker and a woman making cornhusk dolls, and then he spotted a building that looked like an old schoolhouse, with a sign saying: THE BEECHUM FAMILY WEAVERS. An old army vehicle was parked alongside.

The open door revealed a veritable cocoon of textiles: shawls, scarfs, placemats, pillows, tote bags, even hammocks hanging from the ceiling. Two customers—tourists, judging by their sunglasses, sun hats, and cameras—were fingering placemats and asking questions about washability and price. They were being answered curtly by a tall young woman with hollow cheeks and long, straight hair hanging to her waist. She turned around, caught sight of Qwilleran's moustache, hesitated, then turned back to the shoppers.

At the same moment he heard soft thumping and beating sounds at the rear of the shop. A woman with gray hair pulled severely into a bun at the back of her head was sitting at a loom, rhythmically operating the heddles, throwing the shuttles and pulling the beater. He watched

her work—watched her with fascination and admiration—
but she never looked up.

Examining the products in the shop, Qwilleran found it
difficult to believe that they had been woven, thread by
thread, on that loom. One was a capelike jacket, incredi-
bly soft, in the new brighter blue that Polly now liked.
The pricetag read $100, and he made a quick decision to
buy jackets for four other friends as well. His chief joy in
having inherited money was the pleasure of giving it away.
During his days as an underpaid journalist, generosity had
been a luxury beyond his means, but now he was enjoying
the opportunity to be munificent. Buying capes for Polly,
Mildred, Fran, Lori, and Hixie in Moose County would
also be a way of expressing his gratitude to the aloof young
woman who had rescued him the night before.

He heard her say to the shoppers, "These are woven by
hand on that loom. If you want two-dollar placemats you'll
find them at Lumpton's Department Store in Spudsboro."
She made no attempt to be tactful, and they walked out.

"Hello again," Qwilleran said amiably.

"Howya," she said in a minor key without smiling.

"Is this all your own handwork? It's beautiful stuff!"

"My mother and I are the weavers," she said, wasting
no thanks for the compliment.

"I'm very grateful to you, Ms. Beechum, for steering
me to the right mountain last night. I don't know what I'd
have done without your help."

"We aim to be good neighbors in the mountains."
There was no trace of neighborly warmth in the statement.

"I'd like to buy this blue—this blue—"

"Batwing cape."

"I'd like to send it to a friend of mine up north. Do

you have any others? I could use four more in different colors.''

''They're a hundred dollars,'' she informed him, as if he might have misread the price tag.

''So I noticed. Very attractively priced, I would say. May I see the others?''

The weaver relaxed her stern expression for the first time. ''They're not here. They didn't sell well, so I took them home. Most of the shoppers are looking for things under five dollars. But I could bring the capes to the shop if you want to come back another day.'' She looked at him dubiously as if questioning his sincerity.

''Are you open tomorrow?''

''Sunday's our biggest day.''

''What hours?''

''Noon till dusk.''

''Very well. I'll be here first thing. My name is Qwilleran. Jim Qwilleran, spelled with a QW. And what's your first name, Ms. Beechum?'' She told him, and he asked her to spell it.

''C-h-r-y-s-a-l-i-s.''

''Pretty name,'' he said. ''I met a Dewey Beechum this morning. He's going to build a gazebo for me.''

''That's my father. He's an expert cabinetmaker,'' she said proudly. ''He was one of the best hands at the furniture factory before they automated. He's looking for work now. If you know anyone who wants custom-made furniture—''

''I'll be glad to recommend him.'' As she wrapped the blue cape in tissue and a Five Points grocery bag, he said, ''Pardon my ignorance, but why is this called Potato Cove? I've just arrived in these parts. What is a cove?''

"A cove is smaller than a valley but larger than a hollow," she said. "Are you going to live here?"

"Only for the summer."

"Alone?"

"No, I have two Siamese cats."

"What brought you here?" she asked suspiciously.

"Some friends from up north camped in the national forest across the river last summer, and they recommended the Potatoes. I was looking for a quiet place where I could do some serious thinking."

"About what?" Her blunt nosiness amused him. He was nosy himself, although usually more artful.

"About my career," he replied cryptically.

"What do you do?"

"I'm a journalist by profession . . . Tell me about you. How long have you lived in the mountains?"

"All my life. I'm a Tater. Do you know about Taters? We've been here for generations, living close to nature. We were environmentalists before the word was invented."

"If you'll forgive me for saying so, Ms. Beechum, you don't talk like a Tater."

"I went away to college. When you go into the outside world, you gain something, but you also lose something."

"Can you make a living by weaving?" he asked. If she had license to pry, so did he.

"We don't need much to live on, but we do fairly well in summer. In the winter I drive the school bus."

"You mean—you maneuver a bus up these mountain roads? You have my admiration . . . I'll see you tomorrow," he said as more tourists entered the shop. "Is there any place in the cove where I can get a cup of coffee?"

"Amy's Lunch Bucket," she said, pointing up the hill.

Although she didn't smile, she had lost the chip on her shoulder.

Qwilleran waved a hand toward the silent woman at the loom. "Good afternoon, Mrs. Beechum, and compliments on your weaving!" She nodded without looking up.

Amy's Lunch Bucket was aptly named, being large enough for four old kitchen tables and some metal folding chairs obviously from the Just Rust collection. But it was clean. The floorboards were painted grass green, and the white walls were decorated with an abstract panorama of green mountains against a blue sky. A plump and pretty woman with the healthy radiance of youth presided over a makeshift kitchen behind a chest-high counter. "Nice day," she said.

"Are you Amy?" Qwilleran asked.

"Sure am!" she replied cheerfully. "What can I dish up for you?"

The menu posted on the wall behind her offered vegetable soup, veggieburgers, oat bran cookies, yogurt, apple juice, and herb tea. "Do you have coffee?" he asked.

"Sure don't. Only coffee sub and herb tea."

There was a sudden squawk behind the counter, as if from some exotic bird.

"Goo goo goo," said Amy, leaning down.

Qwilleran peered over the counter. On a table was an infant in a basket. "Yours?" he asked.

"Yes, this is our Ashley. Two months, one week, and three days. He's going to be an ecologist when he grows up."

Qwilleran accepted coffee substitute and two oat bran cookies, which he carried to a table near the front window. The only other patrons were the candle dipper, who was eating yogurt and reading a paperback, and the blacksmith, who had ordered everything on the menu and was tucking into it with ravenous gulps.

"Howya," he said with his mouth full, and the candle dipper looked up and smiled at the man who had bought almost a hundred dollars' worth of beeswax.

A moment later Chrysalis Beechum burst into the restaurant in a hurry, waving a ceramic mug. "Apple juice for Ma," she told Amy. "How's Ashley? Is Ashley a good boy today?"

"Ashley is an angel today. How's business down the hill?"

"Surprisingly good! Put the juice on our bill, Amy."

As Chrysalis started out the door with the brimming mug, Qwilleran stood up and intercepted her. "We meet again," he said pleasantly. "Won't you join me for a cup of coffee substitute and an oat bran cookie?"

She hesitated. "I've left my mother alone at the shop."

The candle dipper spoke up. "I'm all through eatin', Chrys. I'll stay with her till you git back."

"Aw, thanks, Missy. Take this apple juice and tell her I won't be long." Chrysalis turned back to Qwilleran. "My mother doesn't speak, so I can't leave her in the shop alone."

"She doesn't speak?" Sympathy was masking his curiosity as he held a rusty chair for her.

"It's a psychological disorder. She hasn't said a word for almost a year."

"What may I serve you?"

"Just some yogurt, plain, and thank you very much."

In that small restaurant Amy heard the order and had it ready by the time Qwilleran reached the counter.

"How do you like Potato Cove?" Chrysalis asked him.

"Interesting community," he said. "Very good shops. I like everything except the tourists."

"I know what you mean, but they pay the rent. How do you feel about what's happening to the mountains?"

"Having arrived only yesterday, I'm not ready to make a statement, I'm afraid. Are you referring to the land development?"

"That's what they call it," she said aggressively. "I call it environmental suicide! They're not only cutting down trees to ship to Japan; they're endangering life on this planet! They're creating problems of erosion, drainage, water supply, and waste control! They're robbing the wildlife of their habitat! I'm talking about Big Potato. And the Yellyhoo—one of the few wild rivers left—is in danger of pollution. I'm not going to have children, Mr. . . ."

"Qwilleran."

"I'm not going to have children because the next generation will inherit a ravaged earth."

He had heard all this before but never with such passion and at such close range. He was formulating a reply when she demanded:

"You're a journalist, you say. Why don't you write about this frightening problem? They're ripping the heart out of Big Potato, and they'd like to take our land away from us, too. Little Potato will be next!"

"I'd need to know a lot more about this subject than I do," he said. "Are you connected with the group that pickets in front of the courthouse?"

"I take my turn," she said sullenly. "So does Amy. So does Vance." She nodded toward the blacksmith. "Who knows whether it does any good? I get very depressed."

"Answer one question for me," Qwilleran said. "When I was downtown today, there was a picket sign I didn't understand: Free Forest. Are you campaigning for a national park or something like that?''

Her thin lips twisted in a grim smile. ''My brother is Forest Beechum . . . and he's in the state prison!'' She said it bravely, holding her head high and looking at him defiantly.

''Sorry to hear that. What kind of term—''

''He was sentenced to life! And he's innocent!''

Qwilleran thought, *They always say that.* ''What was the charge?''

''Murder!''

Amy called out from behind the counter, ''The trial was a pack of lies! Forest would never hurt a fly! He's an artist. He's a gentle person.''

They always say that, Qwilleran repeated to himself.

The blacksmith, still speaking with his mouth full, said, ''There's lotsa Spuds that coulda done it, but the cops never come up with a suspect from the valley. They made up their mind it hadda be one of us.''

Qwilleran asked, ''Did you have a good attorney?''

''We couldn't afford an attorney,'' Chrysalis said, ''so the court appointed one for us. We thought he'd work to get my brother off, since he was innocent. We were so naive. That man didn't even try!'' She spoke with bitterness flashing in her eyes. ''He wanted Forest to plead guilty to a lesser charge, but why should he? He was totally innocent! So there was a jury trial, and the jury was rigged. All the jurors were Spuds. Not one Tater! It was all so wrong, so unjust, so unfair!''

''Ain't nothin' fair,'' said the blacksmith.

There was a minute of silence in the little restaurant, a moment heavy with emotion. Then Chrysalis said, ''I've got to get back to the shop. Thank you for the yogurt and for listening, Mr. . . . ''

"Qwilleran."

"Do you really want to see the batwing capes tomorrow?"

"I most certainly do," he said, rising as she left the table. No one spoke until Ashley made his lusty bid for attention.

"Goo goo goo," said Amy.

"The cookies were delicious," Qwilleran told her. "Did you make them?"

"No, they're from the bakery up the hill. They have wonderful things up there."

"Good! That will be my next stop."

"It's after four o'clock. They're closed. But you should come back and try their Danish pastries made with fresh fruit, and their sticky buns made with whole wheat potato dough."

"Amy, you've touched the weakest spot in my character." Qwilleran started out the door and then turned back. "About this murder trial . . . who was the victim?" he asked, although a sensation on his upper lip was telling him the answer.

"Big shot in Spudsboro," said the blacksmith.

"He owned the newspaper," Amy added. "Also an old inn on top of Big Potato."

Qwilleran patted his moustache with satisfaction. All his hunches, large and small, seemed to emanate from its sensitive roots. Right again!

SIX

QWILLERAN STOOD IN front of Amy's Lunch Bucket and gazed at the sky. The heavens refuted Beechum's prediction of rain. With the sun shining and the sky blue and the mountain breezes playing softly, it was one of those rare days that June does so well. There were dragon-like clouds over the valley—sprawling, ferocious shapes quite unlike the puffy clouds over Moose County. They looked more dramatic than threatening, however, and the meteorologist on the car radio had promised fair weather for the next twenty-four hours.

As he stood there he doubted not only Beechum's prediction but also the story he had just heard. How many times had he interviewed the parent, spouse, or neighbor of a convicted felon and listened to the same tale! "My son would never harm anyone! . . . My husband is a gentle, peace-loving man! . . . He was a wonderful neighbor, always ready to help anyone!"

Whatever the facts about the Hawkinfield murder and the conviction of Forest Beechum, Qwilleran was beginning to understand his negative reaction to Tiptop. It was not only the gray color scheme and the barren rooms; it was an undercurrent of villainy. Exactly what kind of villainy had yet to be discovered.

Then he remembered that the Siamese had been left alone all day in unfamiliar surroundings, and he drove back to the inn. Hawk's Nest Drive, so smoothly paved and so expertly dished on the curves, made pleasant driving after the discomforts of the road to Potato Cove.

To unload his purchases it was necessary to make several trips up the long flight of steps—with the ottoman, the supply of liquor, the turkey roaster, his new radio, Polly's batwing cape, three dozen candles, four coffee mugs, and a very heavy iron candelabrum. After transporting them as far as the veranda, he sat down on the top step to catch his breath, but his respite was brief. A feline chorus inside the French doors was making imperative demands, Yum Yum saying, "N-n-NOW!"

"All right, all right, I know it's dinnertime," he called out as he turned the key in the lock. "You don't need to make a federal case out of it!"

It was not food that concerned them, however; it was an envelope that had been pushed under the door. Qwilleran ripped it open and read, "Cocktails Sunday at Seven Levels. Come around five o'clock and meet your neighbors. Very casual. Dolly.'' He pocketed the invitation and carried his acquisitions into the house.

"I've brought you a present,'' he told the Siamese. ''You'll be the only cats in the Potato Mountains with a state-of-the-art commode imported from Germany!''

Koko, who had to inspect everything that came into the house, was chiefly interested in the liquor supply as it was lined up on the bar. The sherry particularly attracted his nose. This was Polly's favorite drink, and it would be astounding, Qwilleran thought, if the cat could make the connection. More likely it was the label. Koko had a passion for glue, and the Spanish wine industry might use a special kind of seductive adhesive in labeling bottles.

After opening a can of crabmeat for the Siamese and a can of spaghetti for himself, he checked the house for catly mischief; they could be remarkably creative in their naughtiness when they felt neglected. Surprisingly everything was in order except for the painting of mountains in the foyer, which had been tilted again.

As he straightened it, Koko came up behind him, yowling indignantly.

"Objection overruled,'' Qwilleran said. ''Why don't you go and massage your teeth on that half-ton buffet in the dining room?''

The painting, which had an indecipherable signature in the lower righthand corner, hung above a primitive cabinet built low to the floor on flat bun feet. It was crudely decorated with hunting symbols and a cartouche on which was inscribed ''Lord Archibald Fitzwallow.'' There were two drawers (empty) and cabinet space beneath (also empty). It was no beauty, but it was a handy place to keep the telephone and throw car keys. As Qwilleran was examining the cabinet, Koko impudently jumped to its surface and moved the mountain for the third time.

"Are you trying to be funny?" Qwilleran shouted at him. "We'll put an end to that little game, you rascal!" With this pronouncement he lifted the picture from its hook and placed it on the floor, leaning it against the wall. Koko stayed where he was, but now he was standing on his hind legs and pawing the wall.

"What's that?" Qwilleran exclaimed. Hanging from the picture hook was an old-fashioned black iron key about three inches long. Koko had sensed its presence! He always knew when anything was unusual or out of place.

"Sorry I yelled, old boy. I should have realized you knew what you were doing," Qwilleran apologized, but now he combed his moustache in perplexity. What was the key intended to unlock? And why had it been hung behind the painting?

It was clear, he told himself, that the Tiptop Inn had catered to a wealthy clientele who traveled with their jewels, making security an important consideration. All the bedroom doors were fitted with old-fashioned, surface-mounted brass locks, the kind requiring a long key. Other doors throughout the house—with the exception of cylinder locks at front and back doors—retained the old style as part of the quaint authenticity of the historic building.

Carrying the key and marveling at its inconvenient size and weight, Qwilleran began a systematic check of the house from the fruit cellar on the lower level to the walk-in linen closet upstairs. He found no lock that would take the key, not even the door to the attic stairway. The attic stairs were steep and dusty, and the atmosphere was stifling, but he went up to explore. It was a lumber room for old steamer trunks and cast-off furniture. There was also a ladder to the rooftop, which he climbed. Upon pushing open a hatch, he emerged on a small railed observation deck.

This was the highest point in the entire mountain range, close to the dragon-like clouds that rampaged across the sky as if in battle, the sun highlighting their golden scales. Below were the same views seen from the veranda, but they were glorified by the extra elevation, and there were unexpected sights. To the north, the top of Big Potato had been sliced off, and an extensive construction project was under way. To the south, there was a glimpse of a silvery blue mountaintop lake, and the beginning of a footpath pointed in that direction.

Forgetting his mission, Qwilleran hurried downstairs, threw the key in the drawer of the Fitzwallow eyesore, and grabbed a sturdy walking stick from the umbrella stand in the foyer.

"I'll be back shortly," he called over his shoulder. "I'm going to find Lake Batata. If I don't return in half an hour, send out the bloodhounds." The Siamese followed him to the door in ominous silence and then scampered into the living room and watched from a window when he headed for the woods, as if they might never see their meal ticket again.

A wooden shingle daubed with the word "trail" was nailed to a tree, and from there a sun-dappled path carpeted with pine needles and last year's oak leaves made soft footing. It wound through a dense growth of trees and underbrush, and the silence was absolute. This was what Qwilleran had hoped to find—a secret place for ambling and thinking. The trail meandered this way and that, sometimes circumventing a particularly large tree trunk or rocky outcrop, sometimes requiring him to climb over a fallen tree. It was descending gradually, and he reminded himself that the return walk would be uphill, but he was not concerned; in Moose County he walked daily and rode a bike, and he was in good condition.

Every few hundred yards there was another chip of wood nailed to a tree to reassure him that this was the trail, but Lake Batata had not appeared. Could it have been a mirage? The decline was becoming steeper, the woods more dense, the footing less secure. There were slippery leaves that had not dried in this deep shade, and there were half-exposed roots that made the trail treacherous. Once he tripped and went down on his bad knee, but he pressed on. The inn was no longer visible on its summit, nor was the valley. This was real wilderness, and he liked it. Now and then a small animal scurried through the underbrush, but the only birds were crows, circling overhead and cawing their raucous complaints. Where, he asked himself, are the cardinals, chickadees, and goldfinches we have in Moose County?

Walking downhill put more of a strain on his knee than walking uphill, and he was glad to stumble upon a small clearing with a rustic pavilion, a circular shelter just large enough for a round picnic table and benches. Qwilleran sat down gratefully and leaned his elbows on the table. The wood was well weathered, and the pavilion itself was rotting. It was a long time since the Hawkinfields had picnicked there. He sat quietly and marveled at the silence of the woods, unaware that this was the silence before a storm. Even the crows had taken cover.

After a while his watch told him it was time to start back up the trail . . . if he could find it. From which direction had he come? All the trees and shrubs looked alike, and there were several trampled areas that might be the beginning of a path. While sitting in the circular pavilion he had become disoriented. The sun would be sinking in the west, and the inn would lie to the north, but where was the sun? It had disappeared behind clouds, and the woods were heavily shaded. Beechum's prediction might be accurate.

Without further delay Qwilleran had to make a decision. One path ascended slightly, and the others descended. Common sense told him to take the former, so he started out, but soon it rose over a knob and sloped abruptly downhill. Returning to the clearing he tried another trail, which soon became no trail at all; it led into a thicket. Still, it was ascending, and Tiptop was up there—somewhere. In the long run how could he go wrong? He struck out through low underbrush, catching his pantlegs on thorns, picking his way among shrubs that snapped back in his face and threatened to jab him in the eye. The walking stick was more of a hindrance than a help, and he tossed it aside. All the while, it was getting darker. He could go back, but which way was back? He had a fear that he was traveling in circles.

He stood still, closed his eyes, and tried to apply reason. That was when he heard something plunging through the underbrush. It sounded like a large animal—not one of those small scurrying things. He listened and strained his eyes in the direction of the rustling leaves and snapping twigs. Soon he saw it through the gathering darkness—a large black beast lumbering in his direction. A bear! he thought, and a chill ran down his spine. What was the advice he had heard from hunters? Don't make a sudden move. Keep perfectly still.

Qwilleran kept perfectly still, and the black animal came closer. It was advancing with grim purpose. Cold sweat broke out on his forehead, and then he realized it was a dog—a large black dog. Was it wild? Was it vicious? It was not starving; in fact, it was grossly rotund, and it seemed to be wearing a collar. Whose dog would be up here on this desolate mountaintop? The trimmed ears and tail suggested that it was a Doberman, out of shape from overeating. With relief he observed that it was wagging its tail.

"Good dog! Good dog!" he said, keeping his hands in his pockets and making no sudden move.

In friendly fashion the Doberman came closer and leaned against his legs. The collar was studded with nailheads, spelling a name: L-U-C-Y.

"Good dog, Lucy," he said. "Are you Lucy?" He patted the black head, and the overfed dog leaned harder, applying considerable pressure. She was pushing him to one side. Qwilleran stepped away, and Lucy pushed again.

My God! Qwilleran thought. She's a rescue dog! Where's her brandy keg?

When he started to move in the direction she indicated, she bounded ahead, looking back to be sure he was following. Lucy could penetrate the thicket better than he could, and when he made too little progress, she returned to investigate the delay.

Eventually they emerged onto a carpet of pine needles. "This is the trail!" Qwilleran exulted. "Good dog! Good Lucy!" She bounded ahead. Now he recognized a certain fallen tree and a certain giant oak circumvented by the path. When finally the great gray-green hulk loomed above the treetops, he let out an involuntary yelp, and Lucy raced for the inn. She arrived first and waited for him on the veranda, close by the kitchen door.

Incredible! Qwilleran thought; she wants food, and she

knows exactly where to go. Two yowling voices could be heard indoors. "Too bad, Lucy," he said. "I can't invite you in, but I'll find you some chow. Stay here." On the porch she appeared much smaller than she had when first lumbering out of the dark woods. Gratefully he gave her four hot dogs he had bought for himself. The Siamese disdained hot dogs with withering contempt, but Lucy gobbled them and took off—on another errand of mercy or in search of another handout.

Indoors the Siamese sniffed Qwilleran's pantlegs and made unflattering grimaces.

"Don't curl your whiskers," he reproached them. "Lucy brought me home just in time." Rain was obviously on the way. The wind was rising, creating a menacing roar around the summit of Big Potato, and the dragon sky was raging.

For no reason at all, except relief at being rescued, Qwilleran felt a need to talk with someone in Moose County. This time he phoned Arch Riker, hoping he would be at home. It was Saturday night, and the middle-aged editor of the *Moose County Something* might be dining out with his cranky, middle-aged friend, Amanda— that is, if they were on speaking terms this week.

When Riker answered, Qwilleran said, "Just checking to see if Moose County is still on the map."

"I thought you were going to boycott us," Riker chided him. "What's the matter? Are you homesick?"

"Why aren't you out romancing the lovely Amanda? I thought this was national date night by act of Congress."

"None of your business."

The two men had been friends since boyhood, and their dialogue never needed to be polite or even sequential.

"How's your little cabin in the Potatoes?" the editor asked. "Does it meet your modest needs?"

"It's adequate. I have six bedrooms, and I can park ten cars and seat twelve for dinner. Right now the wind's roaring as if a locomotive is headed for the side of the building. But it was beautiful earlier in the day. I had lunch with the editor of the *Spudsboro Gazette*, and I'm sending you a copy of the paper. Note the column called 'Potato Peelings.' You might want to apply for syndication rights."

"Are you going to write anything for us?"

"I'm sending you my travel notes, and you can edit them if you think they're worth running. Also, I may write about the local conflict between the environmentalists and the proponents of economic growth. Moose County may get into the same kind of pitched battle before long."

"Good! There's nothing like a bloody controversy to bolster circulation. How do the cats like the mountains? Has Koko found any dead bodies yet?"

"No, but there was a murder here a year ago . . . OUCH!"

"What was that?" Riker asked in alarm.

"I thought I'd been shot! It was a clap of thunder right overhead. We're very close to the action up here on the mountaintop. Better hang up. There's a lot of lightning . . . Wow! There it goes again! Talk to you some other time."

Qwilleran felt better after chatting with his old friend, and he went upstairs to read. It had started to rain with ferocity, and between claps of thunder there was prolonged rumbling, echoing among the mountain peaks. With his feet on the new ottoman and with Yum Yum curled up on his lap, he was well into the second chapter before he realized that Koko was absent.

Any variance in the cats' usual behavior concerned him,

and he rushed downstairs to investigate. As he reached the bottom stair he heard murmuring and mumbling in the living room; Koko was talking to himself as he always did when puzzled or frustrated.

Through the archway Qwilleran spotted the cat at the far end of the room, studying the secretary desk. It was a tall, narrow piece of furniture fully nine feet in height, with a serpentine base and a glass-doored bookcase above. Only a room with a ten-foot ceiling could accommodate such a lofty design. There were no books on the shelves to command the attention of the bibliocat. Instead, he was intent on examining the wall behind the desk, thrusting a paw in the narrow space and mumbling frustrated gutturals.

There was another crack of thunder and bolt of lightning directly overhead. "Come on upstairs, Koko," said Qwilleran. "We're having a read. Book! Book!"

The cat ignored the invitation and went on sniffing, pawing, and muttering.

That's when Qwilleran clapped a hand over his moustache. He was beginning to feel a disturbance on his upper lip. Koko never pursued a mission with such single-minded purpose unless there was good reason. The serpentine base of the desk was built down to the floor, so there could be nothing underneath it. That meant that Koko had found something behind it!

Confident that the furniture was in two sections, Qwilleran threw his arms around the bookcase deck and lifted it off, setting it down carefully on the floor. Immediately he realized the object of Koko's quest. The bookcase had concealed the upper half of a door in the wall.

"Of course!" he said aloud, slapping his forehead with the flat of his palm. "What a blockhead!" On his walks around the veranda he had been vaguely aware of a discrepancy in the fenestration on the south side of the building. There were eight windows. Yet, when one was in the living room, there were only six. With other matters on his mind he had failed to make a connection, but Koko knew there was another room back there!

A cat can't stand a closed door, Qwilleran thought; he always wants to be on the other side of it. There was no need to try the large key; he was sure it would fit the lock. But first he had to slide the desk away from the wall. Even after removing the drawers he found it remarkably heavy. It was solid walnut, built the way they built them a hundred years ago.

Koko was prancing back and forth in excitement, and Yum Yum was a bemused spectator.

"Okay, here goes!" Qwilleran told them as he turned the key and opened the door. Koko rushed into the secret room, and Yum Yum followed at her own queenly pace. It was dark, but the wall switch activated three lights: a desk lamp, a table lamp, and a floor lamp. This was J.J. Hawkinfield's office at home, furnished with a desk, bookshelves, filing cabinets, and other office equipment.

The Siamese had little interest in office equipment. They were both under the long library table, sniffing a mattress that had been stenciled with the letters L-U-C-Y.

"You devil!" Qwilleran said to Koko. "Is that what your performance was all about? Is that why I strained my back moving five hundred pounds of solid walnut?"

Nevertheless, he was standing in the private office of a murdered man. The open shelves were empty except for a single set of law books. An empty safe stood with its door open. There was a computer station with space for a keyboard, monitor, and printer, but its surfaces were bare.

On the walls were framed diplomas, awards, and certificates of merit issued to J.J. Hawkinfield throughout the years, as well as family photos.

Having checked the scent on the mattress, Koko was now on the library table, industriously exercising his paws on a large scrapbook. Qwilleran pushed him aside and opened its cover. At that moment there was a thunderous crash overhead, followed by a flash of lightning, and the lights went out. Qwilleran stood in total blackness, darker than anything he had ever experienced.

SEVEN

"Now what do we do?" Qwilleran asked his companions. He stood in the middle of a dead man's office in total darkness, listening to the rain driving against the house. The darkness made no difference to the Siamese, but Qwilleran was completely blind. Never had he experienced a blackout so absolute.

"We can't stay here and wait for the power lines to be repaired, that's obvious," he said as he started to feel his way out of the room. He stumbled over a leather lounge chair and bumped the computer station, and when he stepped on a tail, the resulting screech unnerved him.

Sliding his feet across the floor cautiously and groping with hands outstretched, he kicked a piece of furniture that proved to be an ottoman. "Dammit, Koko! Why didn't you find this room before I bought one!" he scolded.

Eventually he located the door into the living room, but that large area was even more difficult to navigate. He had not yet learned the floor plan, although he knew it was booby-trapped with clusters of chairs and tables in mid-room. A flash of violet-blue lightning illuminated the scene for half a second, hardly enough time to focus one's eyes, and then it was darker than before. If one could find the wall, Qwilleran thought, it should be possible to follow it around to the archway leading to the foyer. It was a method that Lori Bamba's elderly cat had used after losing his sight. It may have worked well for old Tinkertom, who was only ten inches high and equipped with extrasensory whiskers, but Qwilleran cracked his knee or bruised his thigh against every chair, chest, and table placed against the wall.

Upon reaching the archway, he knew he had to cross the wide foyer, locate the entrance to the dining room, flounder through it to the kitchen, and then find the emergency candles. A flashlight would have solved the problem, but Qwilleran's was in the glove compartment of his car. He would have had a pocketful of wooden matches if Dr. Melinda Goodwinter had not convinced him to give up his pipe.

"This is absurd," he announced to anyone listening. "We might as well go to bed, if we can find it." The Siamese were abnormally quiet. Groping his way along the foyer wall, he reached the stairs, which he ascended on hands and knees. It seemed the safest course since there were two invisible cats prowling underfoot. Eventually he located his bedroom, pulled off his clothes, bumped his forehead on a bedpost, and crawled between the lace-trimmed sheets.

Lying there in the dark he felt as if he had been in the Potato Mountains for a week, rather than twenty-four hours. At this rate, his three months would be a year and a half, mountain time. By comparison, life in Pickax was slow, uncomplicated, and relaxing. Thinking nostalgically about Moose County and fondly about Polly Duncan and wistfully about the converted apple barn that he called home, Qwilleran dropped off to sleep.

It was about three in the morning that he became aware of a weight on his chest. He opened his eyes. The bedroom lights were glaring, and both cats were hunched on his chest, staring at him. He chased them into their own room, then shuffled sleepily through the house, turning off lights that had been on when the power failed. Three of them were in Hawkinfield's office, and once more he entered the secret room, wondering what it contained to make secrecy so necessary. Curious about the scrapbook that Koko had discovered, he found it to contain clippings from the *Spudsboro Gazette*—editorials signed with the initials J.J.H. Qwilleran assumed that Koko had been attracted to the adhesive with which they were mounted, probably rubber cement.

The cat might be addicted to glue, but Qwilleran was addicted to the printed word. At any hour of the day or night he was ready to read. Sitting down under a lamp and propping his feet on the editor's ottoman, he delved into the collection of columns headed "The Editor Draws a Bead."

It was an appropriate choice. Hawkinfield took potshots at Congress, artists, the IRS, the medical profession, drunk drivers, educators, Taters, unions, and the sheriff. The man had an infinite supply of targets. Was he really that sour about everything? Or did he know that inflammatory editorials sold papers? From his editorial throne he railed against Wall Street, welfare programs, Hollywood, insurance companies. He ridiculed environmentalists and advocates of women's rights. Obviously he was a tyrant that many persons would like to assassinate. Even his style was abusive:

"So-called artists and other parasites, holed up in their secret coves on Little Potato and performing God knows what unholy rites, are plotting to sabotage economic growth . . . Mountain squatters, uneducated and unwashed, are dragging their bare feet in mud while presuming to tell the civilized world how to approach the twenty-first century . . ."

The man was a monomaniac, Qwilleran decided. He stayed with the scrapbook, and another one like it, until dawn. By the time he was ready for sleep, however, the Siamese were ready for breakfast, Yum Yum howling her ear-splitting "N-n-NOW!" Only at mealtimes did she assume her matriarchal role as if she were the official breadwinner, and it was incredible that this dainty little female could utter such piercing shrieks.

"This is Father's Day," Qwilleran rebuked her as he opened a can of boned chicken. "I don't expect a present, but I deserve a little consideration."

Father's Day had more significance at Tiptop than he knew, as he discovered when he went to Potato Cove to pick up the four batwing capes.

The rain had stopped, and feeble rays of sun were glistening on trees and shrubs. When he stood on the veranda with his morning mug of coffee, he discovered that mountain air when freshly washed heightens the senses. He was seeing details he had not noticed the day before: wildflowers everywhere, blue jays in the evergreens, blossoming shrubs all over the mountains. On the way to Potato Cove he saw streams of water gushing from crevices in the roadside cliffs—impromptu waterfalls that made their own rainbows. More than once he stopped the car, backed up, and stared incredulously at the arched spectrum of color.

The rain had converted the Potato Cove road into a ribbon of mud, and Qwilleran drove slowly, swerving to avoid puddles like small ponds. As he passed a certain log cabin he saw the apple peeler on the porch again, rocking contentedly in her high-backed mountain rocker. Today she was wearing her Sunday best, evidently waiting for someone to drive her to church. An ancient straw hat, squashed but perky with flowers, perched flatly on her white hair. What caused Qwilleran to step on the brake was the sight of her entourage: a black cat on her lap, a calico curled at her feet, and a tiger stretched on the top step. Today the shotgun was not in evidence.

Slipping his camera into a pocket, he stepped out of his car and approached her with a friendly wave of the hand. She peered in his direction without responding.

"I beg your pardon, ma'am," he called out in his most engaging voice. "Is this the road to Potato Cove?"

She rocked back and forth a few times before replying. "Seems like y'oughta know," she said with a frown. "I see'd you go by yestiddy. Road on'y goes one place."

"Sorry, but I'm new here, and these mountain roads are confusing." He ventured closer in a shambling, nonthreatening way. "You have some nice cats. What are their names?"

"This here one's Blackie. That there's Patches. Over yonder is Tiger." She recited the names in a businesslike way as if he were the census taker.

"I like cats. I have two of them. Would you mind if I take a picture of them?" He held up his small camera for her approval.

She rocked in silence for a while. "Iffen I git one," she finally decided.

"I'll see that you get prints as soon as they're developed." He snapped several pictures of the group in rapid succession. "That does it! . . . Thank you . . . This is a nice cabin. How long have you lived on Little Potato?"

"Born here. Fellers come by all the time pesterin' me to sell. You one o' them fellers? Ain't gonna sell."

"No, I'm just spending my vacation here, enjoying the good mountain air. My name's Jim Qwilleran. What's your name?" Although he was not prone to smile, he had an ingratiating manner composed of genuine interest and a caressing voice that was irresistible.

"Ev'body calls me Grammaw Lumpton, seein' as how I'm a great-grammaw four times."

"Lumpton, you say? It seems there are quite a few Lumptons in the Potatoes," Qwilleran said, enjoying his unintentional pun.

"Oughta be!" the woman said, rocking energetically. "Lumptons been here more'n a hun'erd year—raisin' young-uns, feedin' chickens, sellin' eggs, choppin' wood, growin' taters and nips, runnin' corn whiskey . . ."

A car pulled into the yard, the driver tooted the horn, and the vigorous old lady stood up, scattering cats, and marched to the car without saying goodbye. Now Qwilleran understood—or thought he understood—the reason for the shotgun on the porch the day before; it was intended to ward off land speculators if they became too persistent, and Grammaw Lumpton probably knew how to use it.

Despite the muddy conditions in Potato Cove, the artists

and shopkeepers were opening for business. Chrysalis Beechum met him on the wooden sidewalk in front of her weaving studio. What she was wearing looked handwoven but as drab as before; her attitude had mellowed, however.

"I didn't expect you to drive up here in this mud," she said.

"It was worth it," Qwilleran said, "if only to see the miniature waterfalls making six-inch rainbows. What are the flowers all over the mountain?"

"Mountain laurel," she said. They entered the shop, stepping into the enveloping softness of wall-to-wall, floor-to-ceiling textiles.

"Was this place ever an old schoolhouse?" he asked.

"For many years. My great-grandmother learned the three Rs here. Until twenty years ago the Taters were taught in one-room schools—eight grades in a single room, with one teacher, and sometimes with one textbook. The Spuds got away with murder! . . . Here are your capes. I brought six so you'll have a color choice. What are you going to do with them, Mr. . . ."

"Qwilleran. I'm taking them home to friends. Perhaps you could help me choose. One woman is a golden blond; one is a reddish blond; one is graying; and the other is a different color every month."

"You're not married?" she asked in her forthright way but without any sign of personal interest.

"Not any more . . . and never again! Did you have a power outage last night?"

"Everybody did. There's no discrimination when it comes to power lines. Taters and Spuds, we all black out together."

"Where's your mother today?"

"She doesn't work on Sundays."

With the weaver's help Qwilleran chose violet for Lori, green for Fran, royal blue for Mildred, and taupe for Hixie. He signed traveler's checks while Chrysalis packed the capes in a yarn box.

"I never saw this much money all at once," she said.

When the transaction was concluded, Qwilleran lingered, uncertain whether to broach a painful subject. Abruptly he said, "You didn't tell me that J.J. Hawkinfield was the man your brother was accused of murdering."

"Did you know him?" she asked sharply.

"No, but I'm renting his former home."

She gasped in repugnance. "Tiptop? That's where it happened—a year ago today! They called it the Father's Day murder. Wouldn't you know the press would have to give it a catchy label?"

"Why was your brother accused?"

"It's a long story," she said with an audible sigh.

"I want to hear it, if you don't mind."

"You'd better sit down," she said, kicking a wooden crate across the floor. She climbed onto the bench at the loom, where she sat with back straight and eyes flashing.

Qwilleran thought, She's not unattractive; she has good bones and the lean, strong look of a mountaineer and the lean, strong hands of a weaver; she needs a little makeup to be really good-looking.

"Forest went to college and studied earth sciences," she began boldly, as if she had recited this tale before. "When he came home he was terribly concerned about the environment, and he resented the people who were ruining our mountains. Hawkinfield was the instigator of it all. Look what he did to Big Potato! And he set up projects that will continue to rape the landscape."

"Exactly what did Hawkinfield plan?" Qwilleran asked

in tones of concern. His profession had made him a sympathetic listener.

"After developing Tiptop Estates and making a pile of money, he sold parcels of land and then organized syndicates to promote condos, a motel, a mobile home park, even a ski lodge! Clear-cutting has already begun for the ski runs. Isn't it ironic that they're naming a *scenic drive* after that man?"

"What did your brother do about this situation?"

"Perhaps he was a little hotheaded, but he believed in militant action. He wasn't the only one who wanted to stop the desecration, but Hawkinfield was a very powerful figure in the valley. Owning the newspaper and radio station, you know, and having money and political influence, he had everybody up against the wall. Forest was the only one who dared to speak out."

"Did he have a forum for his opinions?"

"Well, hardly, under the circumstances. All he could do was organize meetings and outdoor rallies. He had to pass out handbills to get an audience. At first nobody would print them, but a friend of ours worked in the job-printing shop at the *Gazette* and volunteered to run off a few flyers between jobs. Unfortunately he got caught and was fired. We felt terrible about it, but he didn't hold it against us."

"What kind of response did you get to your announcements?" Qwilleran asked.

"Pretty good the first time, and there was a reporter in the crowd from the *Gazette*, so we thought we were going to get publicity—good or bad, it didn't matter. It would be exposure. But we were so naive! There was not a word reported in the paper, but he photographed everyone in the audience! Is that dirty or isn't it? Just like secret police! People got the message, and only a few brave ones with nothing to lose showed up for the next rally. This environmental issue has really separated the good guys from the bad guys in this county.''

''In what way?''

''Well, for one thing, the board of education wouldn't let us use the school auditorium or playfield, and the city wouldn't let us use the community house, but one of the pastors stuck his neck out and let us use the church basement. I'll never forget him—the Reverend Perry Lumpton.''

''Is he the one with the contemporary-style building on the way to the golf club?''

''No, he has the oldest church in town, sort of a historic building.''

''And what was Hawkinfield's reaction?''

''He wrote an editorial about 'church interference in secular affairs, in opposition to the economic welfare of the community which it pretends to serve.' Those were the very words! But that wasn't the end of it. The city immediately slapped some code violations on the old church building. Hawkinfield was a real stinker.''

''If your brother is innocent,'' Qwilleran asked, ''do you have any idea who's guilty?''

Chrysalis shook her head. ''It could be anybody. That man had a lot of secret enemies who didn't dare cross him. Even people who played along with him to save their skins really hated his guts, Forest said.''

''Were there no witnesses to the crime?''

''No one actually saw it happen. The police said there was a struggle and then he was pushed over the cliff. All the evidence introduced at the trial was circumstantial, and the state's witnesses committed perjury.''

Qwilleran said, ''I'd like to hear more about this. Would you have dinner with me some evening?'' One of his favorite diversions was to take a woman to dinner. Beauty and glamor were no consideration, so long as he found her interesting, and he was aware that women were equally enthusiastic about his invitations. Chrysalis hesitated, however, avoiding his eyes. "How about tomorrow night?" he suggested. "I'll pick you up here at closing time."

"We're closed Mondays."

"Then I'll pick you up at home."

"You couldn't find the house," she said.

"I found it once," he retorted.

"Yes, but you weren't looking for it, and when you got there, you didn't know where you were. I'd better meet you at Tiptop."

Qwilleran, before returning home with his four batwing capes, decided to drive to the valley to have his Sunday dinner ahead of the Father's Day rush. After he parked he looked up at the mountains. Little Potato, though inhabited, looked lushly verdant, while Big Potato was blemished with construction sites, affluent estates carved out of the forest, and Hawk's Nest Drive zigzagging through the wooded slopes. He found himself being drawn into a controversy he preferred to avoid; he had come to the Potatoes to think about his own future, to make personal decisions.

At the Five Points Café the Father's Day Special was a turkey dinner with cornbread dressing, cranberry sauce, and nips. "Hold the nips," he said when he ordered, but the plate came to the table with a suspicious mound of something gray alongside the scoop of mashed potatoes. He was in Turnip Country, and it was impossible to avoid them. As he wolfed the food without actually tasting it, his mind went over the story Chrysalis had told him. He recalled Koko's initial reaction to the Queen Anne chair and the French door at the scene of the crime. How would Koko react to the

veranda railing that the carpenter had been called in to repair? It overhung a hundred-foot drop, straight down except
for projecting boulders on its craggy facade. Qwilleran could
reconstruct the scene: a chair thrown through the glass door
and a violent struggle on the veranda before Hawkinfield
crashed through the railing and fell to his death.

Upon returning to Tiptop he conducted a test, buckling
Koko into his harness and walking him around the veranda
on a leash. The cat pursued his usual order of business: in-
discriminate tugging, balancing on the railing, examining
infinitesimal specks on the painted floorboards. When they
reached the rear of the house, however, he walked cautiously
to the repaired railing, then froze with tail stiffened, back
arched, and ears flattened. Qwilleran thought, He knows
something happened here and exactly where it happened!

"Who did it, Koko?" Qwilleran asked. "Tater or
Spud?"

The cat merely pranced in circles with distasteful stares
at the edge of the veranda.

The experiment was interrupted by the telephone; an-
swering it, Qwilleran heard a woman's sweet voice saying,
"Good afternoon, Mr. Qwilleran. This is Vonda Dudley
Wix, a columnist for the *Gazette*. Mr. Carmichael was
good enough to give me your phone number. I do hope
I'm not interrupting a blissful Sunday siesta."

"Not at all," he said in a monotone intended to be civil
but not encouraging.

"Mr. Qwilleran, I would dearly love to write a profile
of you and your exploits, which Mr. Carmichael tells me
are positively prodigious, and I'm wondering if I might
drive up your glorious mountain this afternoon for an impromptu interview."

"I'm afraid that would be impossible," he said. "I'm getting dressed to go out to a party."

"Of course! You're going to be tremendously popular! A journalistic lion! And that's why I do so terribly want to write about you before all the best people engulf you with invitations. I promise," she added with a coy giggle, "to spell your name right."

"To be perfectly frank, I don't plan to be social while I'm here. My purpose is to do some necessary work in quiet seclusion, and I'm afraid any mention in your popular column would defeat my purpose."

"Have no fear, Mr. Qwilleran. I would cover that aspect in my profile and even envelop you in a protective air of mystery. Perhaps I might run up to see you tomorrow."

As a columnist himself, Qwilleran knew his reaction when a subject declined to be interviewed; he considered it a personal affront. Yet, he had no intention of being peeled as one of Vonda Dudley Wix's potatoes. He said, "I'm still in the process of getting settled, Ms. Wix, and tomorrow I have another appointment downtown, but I could meet you somewhere for a cup of coffee and talk for a few minutes. Just tell me where to meet you."

"Oh, please come to my house and have tea!" she cried. "I live on Center Street in a little Victorian gingerbread cottage. Tell me when it's convenient for you."

"How about ten-thirty? I have an appointment at eleven-fifteen, but I can give you half an hour."

"Delightful! Beyond my wildest dreams!" she said. "May I have a *Gazette* photographer here?"

"Please—no photos," Qwilleran said.

"Are you sure? You're such a handsome man! I saw you lunching at the club, and I adore your moustache! It's so romantic!"

"No pictures," Qwilleran said firmly. Why, he wondered, did strangers feel free to talk to him about his moustache? He never said, "I like the size of your nose . . . Your ears are remarkably flat . . . You have an unusual collarbone." But his moustache was considered in the public domain, to be discussed without permission or restraint.

When he concluded his conversation with the columnist, he found Koko sitting on Lord Fitzwallow's sideboard with ears askew, waiting for a recap.

"That was Vonda Tiddledy Winks," Qwilleran told him as he unbuckled his harness.

"Yow," said Koko, who never wasted words.

"And you're having an early dinner tonight because I'm going to a cocktail party. Maybe I'll bring you some caviar."

Shortly after five o'clock Qwilleran walked down Hawk's Nest Drive, past the Wilbank house, to Seven Levels. There were half a dozen cars parked there, and Dolly Lessmore greeted him at the door, carrying a double old-fashioned glass and wearing something too short, too tight, and too red, in Qwilleran's opinion.

"We were going to have it around the pool," she said, "but everything is so wet after last night's rain. Come into the family room, Jim, and meet your neighbors from Tiptop Estates. May I call you Jim? Please call me Dolly."

"My friends call me Qwill," he said.

"Oh, I like that! What will you have to drink?"

"What are you having?"

"My downfall—brandy and soda."

"I'll have the same—on ice—without the brandy."

"Qwill, you remember my husband, the golf nut."

"Hi there," said Robert with a handshake that was more athletic than cordial.

"Are you getting comfortably settled at Tiptop?" Dolly asked.

"Gradually. Sabrina Peel is coming tomorrow to throw a few things around and liven it up. Is it okay if I have a carpenter build a gazebo in the woods?"

"Sure! Anything you like . . . as long as you pay for it and don't take it with you when you leave," she added with a throaty laugh. She steered Qwilleran into a cluster of guests. "These are your nearest neighbors, Del and Ardis Wilbank. *Sheriff* Wilbank, you know . . . And this is Dr. John and Dr. Inez Wickes, veterinarians . . . Qwill has two cats," she explained to the Wickes couple. "John and Inez have a perfectly enchanting house over a waterfall, Qwill. It's called Hidden Falls. Perhaps you've seen the sign."

"We thought it was a good idea," said Inez with chagrin, "but honestly, it runs all the time, like faulty plumbing. There are nights when we'd give anything to shut it off, especially after all the rain we've had this spring."

"The water table is dangerously high," said her husband, whose sober mien was emphasized by owl-like eyeglasses. "We have unstable slope conditions here, and we have to worry about mudslides. I've never known the ground to be so saturated."

The hostess introduced several other couples living on Hawk's Nest Drive, and their conversation followed the usual formula: "When did you arrive? . . . How long are you staying? . . . How do you like our mountain? . . . Do you play golf?"

Qwilleran was glad that no one mentioned his moustache, although the women stared at it with a look of appreciation that he had come to recognize. There were two other moustaches there, but neither of them could equal his—in luxuriance or character.

It was a stand-up cocktail party, for which he was grateful. He liked to wander in and out of chatty groups or draw one guest aside for a moment of private conversation. He was curious by nature and an interrogator by profession. Catching Del Wilbank standing alone, nursing a drink and staring out at the pool, he went to him and said, "I've admired your house, Sheriff. It's an ingenious design."

"*We* like it," said Wilbank gruffly, "but it's not everybody's idea of a house. Look at those diagonal boards long enough and you start leaning to one side. Our property is three-point-two acres. Ardis wanted to see the sunsets, so we cleared out about fifty trees. The TV reception's not very good."

"I presume you knew Hawkinfield," Qwilleran said.

"Everyone knew J.J."

"It was an unfortunate end to what I understand was a distinguished career."

"But not totally unexpected," the sheriff said. "We knew something was going to erupt. J.J. was an independent cuss and didn't pull any punches. It was a crime waiting to happen."

"I hear he went over the cliff," Qwilleran ventured.

Wilbank nodded grimly. "That's a long way down! There was a violent altercation first."

"What time of day was it?"

"About two in the afternoon. Ardis and I were at home, waiting for our son to call from Colorado."

"Were there witnesses?"

"No. J.J. was home alone. His daughter was visiting from out of town for Father's Day, and she went down to Five Points for groceries. When she got back, she saw broken glass and a broken railing on the back porch. She screamed for her dad and couldn't find him. Then she heard their Doberman howling at the bottom of the cliff. She came running down the hill to our house, hysterical. That was a year ago today. I was just standing here, thinking about it.''

''Were there many suspects?''

''All you need is one, if you've got the right guy. We traced him through his vehicle. When J.J.'s daughter went down the hill for groceries, she saw this old army vehicle coming up. When she got back, it was gone. Good observation on her part! It led us right to Beechum. He'd been a troublemaker all along.''

''Did he have a record?''

''Nothing on the books, but he'd threatened J.J. He was apprehended, charged with murder, brought to trial, and convicted—open-and-shut case. These Taters, you know . . . some of them have a murderous streak. You've heard of the Hatfields and McCoys? Well, that crew didn't live in the Potatoes, but we have the same breed around here. Hot-tempered . . . prone to hold grudges . . . quick with the shotgun.''

Qwilleran said, ''That's odd. I've been to Potato Cove a couple of times, and I didn't get that impression at all. They come across as amiable people, totally involved with their handcrafts.''

''Oh, sure! But don't look at one of them cross-eyed, or you might get the top of your head blown off.''

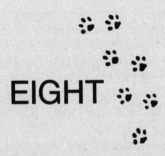

EIGHT

QWILLERAN NURSED HIS glass of soda, sampled the hors d'oeuvres, and listened to the other guests at the Lessmore party as they discussed the problems of mountain living: the inadequacy of fire protection, the high cost of black-topping a circular drive, poor television reception, the threat of mudslides, the possibility of getting street lights and mail delivery on Hawk's Nest Drive.

When he thought it was time to go home, he asked the hostess for a taste of liver pâté for the Siamese—there was no caviar—and started the uphill walk to Tiptop. Hawk's Nest ascending, he discovered, was steeper than Hawk's

Nest descending, and the calves of his legs, accustomed
to the flatlands of Moose County, were already sore from
Saturday's ramble in the woods. He trudged up the slope
slowly and found himself repeatedly smoothing his moustache. It had a peculiar sensitivity to certain stimuli, and
he felt a sensation in its roots whenever he encountered
prevarication, deception, or any degree of improbity. And
now it was sending him signals. Koko, with his twitching
whiskers and inquisitive nose, had the same propensity. In
a way they were brothers under the skin.

Qwilleran spent the rest of the evening reading *The
Magic Mountain* and wishing he had some kind of muscle-
rub. He read aloud to the Siamese, but the day's exercise,
coupled with lack of sleep on the previous night, sent him
to bed early. In spite of the offending lace on the bed
linens, he slept well until seven-thirty, when a noisy en-
gine and broken muffler told him that Dewey Beechum
had arrived to start building the gazebo.

He pulled on some clothes hurriedly and went down to
the parking lot to greet the carpenter. "Better build it over
there," he suggested, pointing to a small clearing.

"T'other side o' them trees is better," said the man.
"That's where I'm fixin' to put it."

"Well, I have to admit you were dead right about the
rain, Mr. Beechum, so I'll take your word for it."

"Rain ain't over yit," the workman mumbled to himself.

Qwilleran watched him unload tools and materials from
his truck and then helped carry them to the building site.
To be sociable he remarked, dropping his subjective pro-
nouns like a Tater, "Had a scare Saturday just before the
rain. Went for a walk in the woods. Got lost."

"Ain't safe 'thout a shotgun," Beechum said. "See any bears?"

"Just a big black dog. Are there bears in these woods?"

"Not more'n two-hun'erd-pounders. Killed five-hun'erd-pounders when we was young-uns. Hard times then. Hadda kill our meat."

Qwilleran listened politely, then excused himself and returned to the house to feed the cats. Feeding the cats, he reflected, was the one constant in his unstructured life—the twice-daily ritual around which his other activities pivoted. A few years ago he would never have believed this to be possible. "Don't be alarmed if you hear hammering and sawing," he told them. "It's being done for your benefit. I'll be back around one o'clock, in case I get any phone calls."

After having breakfast downtown he bought four hot dogs, laid in a supply of flashlights, and opened a checking account at the First Potato National. He was on Center Street when a train rumbled through town on the ledge directly above the bank. The ground shuddered, and the roar of locomotive and freight cars reverberated through the valley.

"Has there ever been a washout here?" he asked the young bank teller. "Did a locomotive ever come crashing down on the central business district?"

"Not that I know of," she said with the detachment of her profession. "Would you like plain checks or the ones with a mountain design? There's an extra charge for designer checks."

"Plain," he said.

At ten-thirty he reported for his appointment with Vonda Dudley Wix. Of all the Victorian houses in the residential section of Center Street, the Wix residence had the fanciest gingerbread trim on gables and porch, as well as the greatest number of hanging flower baskets. Before he could ring the bell, the door opened, and the buxom Ms. Wix greeted him in a blue satin hostess gown and pearls. Her hair, he was sure, was dyed.

"You're so delightfully punctual, Mr. Qwilleran," she cried. "Please come in and make yourself comfortable in the parlor while I brew the tea."

She swept away in ripples of satin that highlighted her rounded contours, while Qwilleran ventured into a room with red walls, rose-patterned carpet, and swagged windows. Reluctant to sit on any of the delicate carved-back chairs, he wandered about and looked at the framed photos on the marble-top tables and shawl-draped piano.

"Do you like Darjeelin'?" she asked when she returned with a silver tea service on a tea cart.

"When it comes to tea, my education has been sadly neglected," Qwilleran said. It was his courteous way of saying he never drank the stuff if he could avoid it. His hostess arranged her folds of blue satin on the black horsehair settee, and he lowered himself carefully to the seat of a dainty chair with a carved back. Then he opened a barrage of questions: "Are these all family heirlooms? . . . How long have you lived in Spudsboro? . . . Does the river ever flood your backyard?"

While giving conscientious answers Ms. Wix poured tea into finger-trap cups that were eggshell thin, using a pearl-handled silver tea strainer.

"An excellent brew," he remarked. "What is your secret?"

"Don't overboil the water!" she said in a confidential whisper. "My late husband adored my tea, but I never revealed my secret."

"How long has Mr. Wix been . . . gone?"

"Almost a year, and I miss him dreadfully. It was a late

marriage. We had only eight years together, eight blissful years."

"My condolences," Qwilleran murmured, waiting a few respectful moments before resuming his interrogation: "Who painted the portrait of you? . . . Do you do your own decorating? . . . When was this house built?" He noticed a small recording device on the tea table, but she had forgotten to turn it on.

"Isn't it a charming house? It was built more than a hundred years ago by a Mr. Lumpton who owned the general store. Spudsboro was a sleepy old-fashioned town for decades until J.J. Hawkinfield took over the newspaper and brought the community to life."

"Was your husband a journalist?"

"Oh, no! Wilson was a highly successful building contractor. He had the contract to build all the houses on Hawk's Nest Drive. He was also on the city council. Wilson was responsible for introducing trash containers and parking meters on Center Street."

"I suppose you studied journalism in college?" he asked slyly.

"Oh, dear, no! I simply had a natural gift for writing, and J.J. elevated me from subscription clerk to columnist overnight! That was twenty-five years ago, and I've been 'peeling potatoes,' so to speak, ever since. I'm afraid I'm telling you my age," she added with coy girlishness.

"Then you knew J.J. very well. How would you describe him?"

"Let me see . . . He had black, black eyes that could bore right through a person . . . and a very *important* nose . . . and a stern expression that made everyone toe the line—employees, city officials, everyone! I believe that's how he achieved such great things for the city. Better schools, new sewers, a good library . . .''

"Did you feel intimidated?"

"Not really," she said with a small, guilty smile. "He was very nice to me. Before I married Wilson, J.J. used to invite me to swimming parties at Lake Batata and wonderful Christmas parties at Tiptop. It was very exciting."

"What happened to their three sons?" Qwilleran asked.

She set down her teacup and turned to him with a doleful face. "They were killed—all three of them! The two younger boys were buried in an avalanche while skiing, and the older boy was lost on the river. Their mother, poor soul, had a nervous breakdown and is still hospitalized somewhere in Pennsylvania . . . May I pour you some tea?"

Qwilleran allowed his cup to be refilled and then asked, "What was the local reaction to J.J.'s murder?"

"We were all simply ravaged with grief! He was the most important personage in the Potatoes! Of course, we all knew it was one of those awful mountain people, and it's a wonder he wasn't lynched before he came to trial."

Qwilleran glanced at his watch and rose abruptly. "I regret I must tear myself away. This has been a most enjoyable visit, but I have another appointment."

"I understand."

"Thank you for the delicious tea."

Vonda Dudley Wix escorted him to the door and said goodbye with effusive expressions of goodwill, and Qwilleran went on his way with smug satisfaction at his handling of the interview.

Returning to Tiptop, he prepared for the visit of Sabrina Peel with somewhat more enthusiasm, chilling wine glasses, re-hanging the mountain painting, placing the iron candelabrum alongside the Fitzwallow chest. He also took care to move the secretary desk back across the door to J.J.'s office; someone had a reason for wanting him to keep out, and he thought it wise to preserve appearances.

Promptly at one-thirty the designer arrived with a vanload of accessories and a young man named Jimmie to carry them up the twenty-five steps. There were wall hangings, toss pillows, a pair of eight-foot folding screens, accent rugs, lamps, and boxes of bric-a-brac.

She said, "You don't have to buy these things, you know. They were on the floor in our studio, and I'm renting them to you. The florist is on the way here with some rental plants. Do you intend to do much entertaining?"

"I might have one or two persons in for drinks, that's all," Qwilleran said.

"Then let's close the French doors to the dining room and bank some large plants in the foyer . . . I never saw *that* before!" She pointed to the seven-foot, eight-branch iron tree.

"I bought it from the blacksmith in Potato Cove."

"You have a good eye, Qwill. It shows some imagination, and it's not overdone. Happily it distracts the eye from that hideous Fitzwallow huntboard, which I hasten to say did not come from our studio."

"You call it a huntboard? That's appropriate. My cat is always hunting for something underneath it."

"You didn't tell me you have a cat."

"I have two Siamese, and they're up there on the stairs, watching your every move."

"I hope they're not destructive," the designer said, and she called up to them, "If you scratch it, kids, you've bought it!"

"Yow!" Koko retorted.

"He's a sassy brat, isn't he?" said Sabrina. "Now let's go to work on the living room. We'll create a more intimate setting by stopping the eye with folding screens as room dividers.''

Qwilleran watched her work with manifest enjoyment as she whirled around the room, her pleated skirt swirling about her knees and her silky mop of hair swirling around her shoulders. With crisp authority she directed Jimmie in placing screens, grouping chairs, skirting tables, setting up lamps, throwing throw rugs, tossing toss pillows, and hanging wall hangings. She herself arranged brass candlesticks, ceramic bowls, carved boxes, and stacks of design magazines. When she had finished, the room looked inhabited by a person of taste, although not necessarily Qwilleran's taste. Nevertheless, he was grateful for the metamorphosis.

Then the florist arrived with indoor trees and large potted plants.

"Do I have to water these things?" Qwilleran inquired.

"No, sir," said the florist. "For rental plants we send a visiting nurse once a week to test the soil for moisture."

As the room was transformed, Koko's curiosity overcame his misgivings, and he watched from the archway. Yum Yum held back, poised for flight.

Qwilleran said to Sabrina, "Would you stay for a glass of chardonnay?"

"I'd love to," she said without hesitation. "Jimmie can go back downtown with the florist . . . Jimmie, tell Mr. Poole where I am, and if my four o'clock client comes in, tell her I'm running late. Give her an old magazine to read." To Qwilleran she explained, "She's my doctor's wife, and revenge is sweet."

Sabrina with her chardonnay and Qwilleran with his apple juice sat in the portion of the living room that was now pleasantly secluded by screens and plants. It was made comfortable with chatty new furniture groupings and made lively with red and gold accents.

"My compliments to the designer," he said, raising his glass. "I hope the screens are sturdy; the cats are sometimes airborne when they're in a good mood."

"You'll find them quite stable," she assured him. "They were custom-made to do heavy duty in the studio. What are you building in the woods?"

"A screened gazebo, so the cats can take an airing if it ever dries up. No one told me it rains so much in the mountains. Also, no one told me that Hawkinfield had been murdered."

"Didn't you know?" Sabrina asked. "What's more, you have a painting done by the murderer." She waved a hand toward the foyer.

"Forest Beechum? Is that his work?" Qwilleran said in surprise. "That fellow really knows how to paint mountains!"

"He did several mountain studies for my clients. Too bad he got himself in such bad trouble."

"Were you satisfied with the verdict?"

"Frankly, I didn't follow the trial, but—from what I hear—there's no doubt that he was guilty." Her wineglass was empty.

"Will you have a touch?" Qwilleran asked, tilting the wine bottle. "How did you get along with Hawkinfield as a client?"

"Fortunately we had very little contact with him," the designer said. "We worked with Mrs. Hawkinfield, but after she was hospitalized we ran into trouble with J.J. He refused to pay a rather sizable bill for what his wife had ordered, saying she was incompetent and we had taken advantage of her disturbed condition. That's the kind of person he was." Sabrina tapped her fingers irritably on the arm of the chair.

"Were you able to collect?"

"Not until we took him to court, and—believe me!—it took a lot of nerve to sue a man as powerful as Hawkinfield. It infuriated him to lose the case, of course, and he relieved his spite by writing a scathing editorial about the moral turpitude (whatever that means) of artists in general and interior designers in particular. I don't think anyone really liked the man—except the woman who writes the 'Potato Peelings' column. He was not only opinionated but ruthless, and he had a completely wrong-headed attitude toward women. A man of his intelligence, living at this moment in history, should have known better." She tossed her head and flung her hair back gracefully, using both well-manicured hands in an appealing gesture. "We all knew he was psychologically abusive to his wife and daughter. He worshipped his sons, and after they were killed, he sent the girl away to boarding school—away from her mother, away from her friends, away from these mountains—everything she loved."

Qwilleran liked designers. They circulated; they knew everyone; they were in touch. He asked, "Why did she leave the mountain painting and take everything else of value?"

"She thought mountains would be too regional to sell in her shop. It's in Maryland, and she gets a sophisticated clientele from Washington and Virginia."

"What kind of shop does she have?"

"It's called *Not New But Nice*. Sort of an upscale, good-taste jumble shop."

"Clever name."

"Thank you," Sabrina said, patting her bangs. "It was my idea."

"Do you keep in touch with her?"

"Only to help her appraise things now and then. All J.J. left her was this house and contents, and she's trying to get all she can out of it. I suppose you can't blame her, but she's really turning out to be a greedy little monster." There was more finger-tapping on the chair arm. "She expects me to do appraisals gratis, and she's asking more than a million for this—this *white elephant*. I imagine she's charging you an arm and a leg for rent."

"I still have one of each left," Qwilleran replied. "What happened to the rest of J.J.'s assets?"

"They went into a trust for the care of his wife. You know, Qwill, you could buy this place for a lot less than she's asking. Why don't you make an offer and open a B-and-B? I could do wonders with it, inside and out." Sabrina construed his scowl. "Then how about a chic nursing home?" she suggested with a mischievous smile. "Or an illegal gambling casino? . . . No? . . . Well, I must get back to the valley. These mountain retreats lull one into a false sense of something or other. Thanks for the wine. I needed it. Where did I leave my shoulder bag?"

"On a chair in the foyer," he said. "May I take you to lunch at the golf club some day?"

"I know a better place. I'll take you to dinner," she countered.

As they left the living room, the designer stopped in the archway to view her handiwork. "We need one more splash of color over there between the windows," she said. "A couple of floor pillows perhaps."

Qwilleran had entered the foyer in time to see two furry bodies leaping from a chair. Sabrina's handbag was slouched on the chair seat, and it was unzipped. He then realized that the Siamese had been too quiet for the last half hour and too suspiciously absent. There was no way of guessing what larceny they might have committed.

"Thank you, Sabrina, for what you've accomplished this afternoon," he said. "And you make it look so easy! You're a real pro."

"You're entirely welcome. My bill will be in the mail," she laughed as she shouldered her handbag and zipped the closure.

He walked with her down the twenty-five steps, and when he returned to the house he said, "Okay, you scoundrels! What have you done? If you've stolen anything, she'll be back here with Sheriff Wilbank."

Koko, sitting on the stairs halfway up, crossed his eyes and scratched his ear. Yum Yum huddled nonchalantly on the flat top of the newel post while Qwilleran searched the foyer. He found nothing that might have come from a woman's handbag. Shrugging, he went out to check Beechum's progress with the gazebo. The carpenter had gone for the day, but the structure was taking shape—not the shape Qwilleran had requested, but it looked good. When he returned to the house he encountered a disturbing scene.

Koko was on the living room floor in a paroxysm of writhing, shaking, doubling in half, falling down, contorting his body.

Qwilleran approached him with alarm. Had he been poisoned by the plants? Was this a convulsion? "Koko! Take it easy, boy! What's wrong?"

Hearing his name, Koko rose to a half-sitting position and bit his paw viciously. Only then did Qwilleran realize that something virtually invisible was wrapped around the pad and caught between the spreading toes. Gently he helped release Koko from the entanglement. It was a long hair, decorator blond.

NINE

QWILLERAN GAVE THE Siamese an early dinner. "Will you excuse me tonight?" he asked them. "I'm taking a guest to the golf club." He had some crackers and cheese himself, having gone hungry at the club on his last visit.

While he was dressing, the telephone rang, and he ran downstairs with lather on his face; there was no extension upstairs.

Sabrina Peel was on the line. She said, "Qwill, I lost a letter while I was at Tiptop. If you find it, just drop it in the mail; it's all stamped and addressed. It may have slipped out of my handbag when I was fishing out my car keys.''

He said he had not seen the letter but promised to look on the veranda and in the parking lot. Hanging up, he gave an accusing scowl at Koko, who was sitting near the phone. Koko stretched his mouth in a yawn like an alligator.

At the appointed time a chugging motor alerted him to the arrival of Chrysalis Beechum in one of the family wrecks. The Beechums were the only two-wreck family he had ever known. He went down the steps to greet her as she climbed out of the army vehicle, looking almost attractive. Her long hair was drawn back and twisted in one long braid hanging down her back, and she wore a stiff-brimmed black hat like a toreador's. The sculptured planes of hollow cheeks and prominent cheekbones gave her face a severe but strikingly handsome aspect. Her clothes were much the same: jogging shoes, long skirt, and a top that was obviously handwoven.

"Good evening," he said. "I like your hat. You wear it well."

"Thank you," she said.

"Have you ever seen the interior of Tiptop?"

"No."

"Would you like to come in for a quick tour? The proportions are quite impressive, and there's some historic furniture."

"No, thanks," she said, her eyes flashing.

"Then let's take off. Your car or mine?" he quipped without getting any amused response. He opened the car door for her. "I've reserved a table at the golf club. I think you'll approve of the food. It's quite wholesome—almost too wholesome for my depraved taste.'' Still, his small talk with a light touch fell flat.

"Do you play golf?'' she asked.

"No, but I have a membership at the club that permits me to use the dining room and bring guests.''

As they started down Hawk's Nest Drive he pointed out the homes of the sheriff, the realty couple, and the veterinarians. His passenger looked at them without interest or comment.

"How was business in Potato Cove today?'' he asked in an effort to involve her.

"We're closed Mondays,'' she said moodily.

"That's right. You told me so . . . Your father came this morning to start building my gazebo. He said it's going to rain some more.''

"How do you like his hat?'' she said.

"It looks as if it might have historic significance.'' That was Qwilleran's tactful way of saying that it was moldy with age and mildew.

With a revival of interest Chrysalis said, "It's a family heirloom. My grandfather chased some revenuers with a shotgun once, and they ran so fast that one of them lost his hat. Grampa kept it as a trophy. He was a hero in the mountains.''

"Was your grandfather a moonshiner?''

"Everyone was running corn liquor in those days, if they wanted to support their families. It was the only way they could make any money to buy shoes, and flour for making bread, and seed for planting. Grampa went to jail once for operating a still, and he was proud of it.''

"How long has your family lived in the mountains?''

"Since way back, when they could buy a piece of land in a hollow for a nickel an acre. They chopped down trees to build cabins and lived without roads—just blazed trails.''

"One has to admire the pioneers, but how did they survive?''

"By hunting and fishing and raising turnips. They carried water from a mountain spring and made everything with their own hands: soap, medicines, tools, furniture, everything. My grandmother told me all this. The affluent ones, she said, had a mule and a cow and a few chickens and an apple tree.''

"When did it change?''

"Actually, not until the 1930s, when road building started and electricity came up the mountain. Some of the Taters didn't want electricity or indoor plumbing. They thought it was unsanitary to have the outhouse indoors. We still resist the idea of paved roads on Little Potato. We don't want joyriders polluting our air and littering our roadsides. There are some older Taters who've never been off the mountain.''

Qwilleran said, "I have a lot to learn about mountain culture. I hope you'll tell me more about it.''

They arrived at the golf club and presented themselves at the door of the dining room—Qwilleran in his blue linen blazer with a tie, Chrysalis in her jogging shoes and toreador hat. The tables were dressed for dinner with white cloths, wineglasses, and small vases of fresh flowers. "Reservation for Qwilleran, table for two, nonsmoking,'' he told the hostess.

"Oh . . . yes . . .'' she said in bewilderment as she glanced at her chart and then the roomful of empty tables.

"We're a little early,'' he said.

"Follow me.'' The hostess conducted them to a table for two at the rear of the dining room, adjoining the en-

trance to the Off-Links Lounge, where golfers were celebrating low scores or describing missed putts with raucous
exuberance.

Chrysalis said, "It sounds like a Tater horse auction."

"May we have a table away from the noise?" Qwilleran
asked the hostess.

She appeared uncertain and consulted her chart again
before ushering them to a table between the kitchen door
and the coffee station.

"We'd prefer one with a view," he said politely but
firmly.

"Those tables are reserved for regular members," she
said.

Chrysalis spoke up. "The other one is all right. I don't
mind the noise."

They were conducted back to the entrance of the lounge.
Dropping two menu cards on the table the hostess said,
"Want something from the bar?"

"We'll make that decision after we're seated," Qwilleran replied as he held a chair for his guest. "Would you
like a cocktail or a glass of wine, Ms. Beechum?"

"I wish you'd call me Chrysalis," she said. "Do you
think I could have a beer?"

"Anything you wish . . . and please call me Qwill."

"I learned to like beer in college. Before that I'd just
had a little taste of corn liquor, and I didn't care for it."

A waiter in his late teens was hovering over the table.
"Something from the bar?"

"A beer for the lady—your best brand," Qwilleran ordered, "and I'll have a club soda with a twist." The drinks
arrived promptly, and he said to his guest, "The service
is always excellent when you're the only customers in the
place."

"Want to order?" the young man asked. His nametag identified him as Vee Jay.

"After we study the menu," Qwilleran replied. "No hurry." To Chrysalis he said, "I see you're wearing something handwoven. There's a lot of artistry in your weaving."

"Thank you," she said with pleasure. "Not everyone really notices it. The women in my family have always been weavers. Originally they raised sheep and spun the wool and made clothes for their whole family. I was weaving placemats to sell when I was seven years old. Then, in college I learned that weaving can be a creative art."

"Do you ever do wall hangings? I like tapestries."

"I've done a few, but they don't sell—too expensive for the tourist trade."

Consulting the menu she decided she would like the breast of chicken in wine sauce with pecans and apple slices, explaining, "At home we only have chicken stewed with dumplings."

Qwilleran ordered the same and suggested corn chowder as the first course. He asked the waiter to hold the food back for a while and to serve the salad following the main course.

The chowder arrived immediately.

"Return it to the kitchen," Qwilleran said to Vee Jay. "We're not ready. We requested that you hold it back." Vee Jay shuffled away with the two bowls.

Chrysalis said, "You know, just because the Taters cling to some of the old ideas like stewed chicken and dirt roads and no telephones, it doesn't mean that they're backward. They maintain old values and old customs because they know something that the lowlanders don't know. Living close to the mountains for generations and struggling to be self-sufficient, they develop their minds in different ways.''

''You're probably right. I'm beginning to believe there's something mystical about mountains,'' Qwilleran said.

When they were finally ready for the soup course, the waiter returned with the two bowls. By this time the chowder was cold.

Qwilleran addressed him stiffly. ''Vee Jay—if that is really your name—we would have ordered vichyssoise or gazpacho if we had wanted cold soup. Take this away and see that it's properly heated.'' To his guest he said, ''I apologize for this.''

In due time the chowder returned, accompanied by two salads. ''We asked to have the salad served *after the entree*,'' Qwilleran complained, losing patience.

The sullen waiter whisked the salads away and, before the diners could raise their soup spoons, served two orders of chicken in wine sauce, maneuvering the table setting to find room for the large dinner plates.

Now angry, Qwilleran called the hostess to the table. ''Please look at this vulgar presentation of food,'' he said. ''Is it your quaint custom to serve the entree with the soup?''

''Sorry,'' she said. ''Vee Jay, remove the soup.''

''Madame! If you please! We have not yet started the soup course! Remove the chicken and *keep it hot* until we're ready.'' He explained to Chrysalis, ''This is the first time I've had dinner here. We should have gone to Amy's Lunch Bucket. It would have been more congenial.''

''Don't worry,'' she said. ''I don't go out enough to know the difference.''

After a few moments of silent sipping of chowder,

Qwilleran asked, "Are the shops in Potato Cove considered successful?"

"I don't know what you mean by 'successful,' " she said, "but we were kind of surprised when some promoters in Spudsboro invited us to move down into the valley. They want to build an addition to the mall and call it Potato Cove."

"How do your people react to that offer?"

"Most of us want to stay where we are, although the promoters tell us there'd be publicity and we'd get more traffic. The rent would be low, because the mall management would consider us an attraction."

"Don't do it!" Qwilleran said. "Potato Cove is unique. It would lose its native charm in a mall. You'd have to stay open seven days a week, eleven hours a day, and the rent would go up as soon as you were installed. They're trying to exploit you."

"I'm glad to hear you say that. I don't trust the Spuds. They do everything for their own benefit with no consideration for us. They drive up our mountain and dump trash and used tires in our ravines instead of going to the Spudsboro landfill where they'd have to pay fifty cents."

"Have you protested?"

"Often! But Taters never get a square deal from the local government. You'd think we didn't pay taxes! And now they're trying to push us off our mountain."

"How can they do that?"

"Well, you know how it is. Old folks have to sell their land because they need money or can't pay their taxes. The Spuds buy the land for next to nothing and then turn around and sell it to developers for a lot of money. That's what Hawkinfield did on Big Potato, and that's what we're afraid will happen to us. The developers will come in;

taxes will go up; and more and more Taters will have to sell out. When you live on land that's been in your family for generations, it's heartbreaking to lose it. Lowlanders who don't have roots like ours don't understand how we feel.''

The meal progressed with a minimum of annoyance after that, although Qwilleran found the chicken unusually salty for a dining room that prided itself on flavoring with herbs. He did his best to maintain a pleasant attitude, however. He said, ''I must ask you about something that baffled me the first night I was here. It was Friday, around midnight. The atmosphere was very clear, and I saw a circle of light on Little Potato. It was revolving.''

Chrysalis rolled her eyes. ''I don't know whether I should tell you about that. It's kind of far-out . . . You have to understand my mother. She's a positive thinker, you know. She believes that sheer willpower can make things happen. Do you buy that?''

''I'll buy anything,'' he said, thinking of Koko's supranormal antics.

''It's not just her own idea. My grandmother and great-grandmother believed the same way. They survived hard times and both lived to a ripe old age. I wish I had their conviction.''

''How about your mother? Has she been able to make things happen?''

''Well . . . my father was in a terrible accident at the factory once, and the doctors said he couldn't possibly pull through. But my mother and grandmother willed him to live. That was twenty-five years ago, and you'd never know anything had happened to him, except for a slight limp.''

''That's a convincing story.''

"Some people call it witchcraft."

"Tell that to Norman Vincent Peale," Qwilleran said. Noticing that she was picking at her food, he inquired how she liked the chicken.

"It's rather salty. I'm not used to much salt."

"I agree the chef has a heavy hand with the saltshaker. Someone should set him straight . . . Are there any other examples of your mother's positive thinking?"

"She always used to arrange good weather for our family reunions," Chrysalis said with a whimsical laugh. "Seriously, though, she made up her mind that Forest and I would go to college, and you know what happened? The state started offering free tuition to mountain students!"

"With all that you've told me, how do you explain your mother's speech affliction?"

She stared at him with the hollow-cheeked sadness he had seen when she spoke of her brother's imprisonment. "She blames herself for the terrible thing that happened to Forest."

"I don't understand," Qwilleran said.

"She used all her mental powers to stop Hawkinfield from ruining the mountains. She didn't want him murdered; she just wanted him to have a change of heart!" Chrysalis stopped and stared into space until Qwilleran urged her to go on. "The horrible irony was that my brother was convicted of the murder—and he was innocent. She made a vow never to speak another word as long as he's in prison."

Qwilleran murmured sympathy and regrets and then said, "What about the circle of light on the mountain?"

She shook her head. "Some of our kinfolk go out on top of Little Potato at midnight, carrying lanterns. They walk in a silent circle and meditate, concentrating on getting Forest released—somehow." She shook her head.

"Do they think the moving circle increases their effectiveness?" he asked gently, although he had his doubts.

"It's supposed to concentrate the force of their collective will. That's what they say."

"You sound as if you're not entirely convinced."

"I don't know . . . I don't know what to think. When we picket the courthouse, we march in a circle, the same way."

"Now that you mention it," he said, "it seems to me that pickets always move in a circle."

"The picketing was Amy's idea," said Chrysalis. "She and Forest were getting ready to marry when he was arrested. They were going to be married at the waterfall at the cove, where the mist rises up like a veil. All the plans were made . . . and then this happened. He was held without bail and railroaded to prison. It's my brother's baby that Amy takes to the Lunch Bucket every day. His name is Ashley . . . I'm sorry. I've been talking too much, but it's good to have a considerate listener who's not a Tater. Lately, I've been getting to be like my mother, not wanting to speak."

"You must not let that happen, Chrysalis. Tell me about the trial. What did you think was wrong about it?"

"Well, first, the court-appointed attorney wasn't even there for the arraignment. He phoned to say he'd be late, but the court didn't want to wait around."

"That sounds like a violation of constitutional rights," Qwilleran said.

"How did we know? We were just Taters. Then Forest was held without bail, and the attorney said it was for his personal safety because the whole town was out to get him. *My brother!* I couldn't believe it!''

''If there was so much animosity, didn't he try for a change of venue?''

She nodded. ''It was denied.''

''What was the attorney's name?''

''Hugh Lumpton.''

Qwilleran huffed into his moustache; another one of those ubiquitous Lumptons!

Chrysalis said, ''He didn't put a single defense witness on the stand, and he let the state's witnesses get away with lies! The jury brought in a guilty verdict so fast, we hardly knew it was over!''

''I'm no lawyer,'' Qwilleran said, ''but it seems to me you should be able to get a new trial. You'd need a different attorney—a good one.''

''What would it cost? We tried to borrow money to hire one when Forest was first accused, but the banks—being mixed up with the land speculators, you know—refused to give us a mortgage. They advised us to sell, but you wouldn't believe what the speculators offered for our choice piece of the mountain. But now it doesn't matter; we'd sell our land for any amount of money if it would get Forest out of prison.''

''There might be another way,'' Qwilleran said, smoothing his moustache. ''Let me think about it. But your brother would still have to convince a jury that he's innocent.''

They finished the meal with sparse conversation. The salad dressing also was salty. Chrysalis moodily declined dessert and simply sipped a cup of tea, silent behind her staring, hollow-cheeked mask.

When they left the dining room, it was still only partially occupied, and there were plenty of empty tables with a view of the golf course. Qwilleran told his guest to wait in the vestibule while he had a few words with the hostess. Eight words were sufficient. Speaking calmly he said, "Give this to the management with my compliments," and he tore up his membership card.

It was still full daylight, and Chrysalis said, "Would you like to drive up to Tiptop the back way? It's only a logging trail, but it goes up the outside of Big Potato, and there's something I want you to see." She directed him through a maze of winding roads in true wilderness. "There!" she said when they reached the top of a knob. "Stop the car! What does that look like?"

Qwilleran saw a vast area of wiped-out forest—a tangle of stumps, fallen trees, and dead branches. "It looks like the aftermath of a tornado or a bombing raid."

"That's slashing!" she said. "Everything is leveled, and then they take the good straight hardwood and leave the rejects. Maybe you've seen the logging trucks leaving the mountains. This is what'll happen to the whole outside of Big Potato if we don't stop them, and this is what speculators would like to do to L'il Tater."

The logging trail narrowed to a mere wagon track twisting upward. She pointed the way, and Qwilleran clutched the wheel as the car lurched through the rough terrain.

"Would you care to come in for a nightcap?" he asked when they finally reached the Tiptop parking lot.

"No, thank you, but I enjoyed the evening, and thank you for listening. It was very kind of you."

He walked her to the decrepit army vehicle. "I'm sincerely sorry about your brother's predicament. I hope something can be done."

She climbed into the driver's seat. "It would be easier to move a mountain," she said with a helpless shrug.

Qwilleran watched her leave before mounting the steps to the veranda. Koko was waiting for him in the foyer, prancing back and forth as if he had something urgent to report, but Qwilleran had other things on his mind. He went directly to the phone and called Moose County without waiting for the discount rates.

"Polly, this is Qwill!" he announced abruptly.

"Dearest! I'm so thankful you called. We have terrible news. Halifax Goodwinter has taken his own life!"

"NO!"

"He buried his wife last Friday, you know, and last night he overdosed."

"This is hard to believe! Did he leave an explanation?"

"Nothing. Nothing at all. But the rumor is circulating that his wife's death was a mercy killing. She'd been hopelessly ill for so long, and the poor man was going on eighty. There'll never be another country doctor like Dr. Hal. The whole county is grieving. Melinda is definitely moving back from Boston to take over his practice, but it won't be the same."

"I agree," said Qwilleran with a gulp. He was worrying less about Moose County's medical prospects than about his own personal relationships. Before Melinda moved to Boston, she had been hell-bent on marriage, and he had been equally determined to stay single, even though he found her disturbingly attractive.

"Now that you've heard the bad news, Qwill," Polly was saying, "how's everything in the mountains?"

"I'm spittin' mad," he said.

"That sounds like mountain vernacular, and you've been there only three days."

"I've just had an infuriating experience at a restaurant."

"What did they do wrong?"

"Everything! They gave me the worst table in the place. The service was abominable. The soup was cold. The food was too salty. It was the salty food that explained the whole conspiracy."

"Are you saying it was done purposely?"

"Damn right it was! I made the mistake of taking the wrong person to dinner. My guest was a mountaineer. They're called Taters around here."

"Really! Are they so undesirable?"

"They're an unpopular minority, although they were here first, and they get a rotten shake at every turn. In Moose County we have cliques but no prejudice like this, and I was unprepared. The whole dinner was an embarrassment."

"What are you going to do?" Polly knew Qwilleran was not one to turn the other cheek.

"I've got to think about it."

"I'm sorry you're so upset."

"Don't worry," he said, his anger subsiding. "I'm going to consult Koko. He'll come up with an idea. How's Bootsie?"

"He's fine. He weighs ten pounds."

"Ten pounds going on thirty! And how are you?"

"I'm fine. The library board is giving a formal dinner Friday, and I'm altering the neck of my long dress so I can wear my pearls. I miss you, dearest."

"I miss you, too." There was a breathy pause. Despite his facility with words, Qwilleran found terms of endearment difficult. "À bientôt," he said with feeling in his voice.

"À bientôt, dearest."

He went outdoors and walked briskly around the veranda a few times. The sun was dropping behind the West Potatoes, and the dragon clouds were waging a riotous battle—violent pink and purple against a turquoise sky. When a damp chill from the northeast chased him indoors, Koko was still prancing.

"What's on your mind?" he asked absently.

"Yow!" said Koko with urgency, running back and forth through the living room arch.

"Where's Yum Yum?" It occurred to Qwilleran that he had not seen her since returning from dinner. Immediately he checked all the comfortable chairs in the living room and all the beds upstairs. Calling her name he rushed from room to room, opening closets, cabinets, and even drawers. Then—back in the living room—he saw Koko dive under the floor-length skirt that Sabrina had draped on a round table.

"You devils!" he muttered as he fell on his hands and knees and peered under the skirt. There they were, both of them, wearing beatific expressions, and on the floor between them was a stamped, addressed letter with perforations in two corners. "Who stole this?" he demanded, although he knew Koko was the culprit, attracted by the adhesive on the stamp and the envelope. Although Yum Yum's famous paw pilfered Scrabble tiles and cigarette lighters, Koko specialized in documents, leaving fang marks as evidence. Qwilleran dropped the Peel & Poole letter in a drawer of the Fitzwallow huntboard for safekeeping until he could mail it, noting as he did so that it was addressed to Sherry Hawkinfield in Maryland—probably a bill for Sabrina Peel's appraisal services.

Before going upstairs to finish the evening with a book,

he gave the Siamese their bedtime snack, a dry food concocted by a gourmet cook in Moose County. Qwilleran watched them gobble and crunch, but his mind was elsewhere. He had no desire to take sides in local politics and no intention of becoming a gullible confederate in a Tater obsession. Yet, the shabby treatment at the golf club and the emotional outpourings from his dinner guest were stirring his blood.

The matter of a good attorney could be handled easily; he had only to call Hasselrich, Bennett & Barter in Moose County, but old Mr. Hasselrich—he of the fluttering eyelids and quivering jowls—would expect a well-organized brief. Some kind of preliminary investigation of the Father's Day murder would be necessary, something that could be done quietly without causing alarm in the valley.

As Qwilleran absentmindedly watched the Siamese washing up after their snack, he started patting his moustache; an idea was formulating. For cover he would use a ploy that had worked on a previous occasion. It would explain his presence in the Potatoes and his need to see a transcript of the Beechum trial, and it would enable him to question a number of local residents, especially those victimized by Hawkinfield's damaging editorials. To spread the word and establish his credentials he would first break the news to Carmichael at the *Gazette*.

"Colin," he would say, "I want you to be the first to know. I plan to write a biography of J.J. Hawkinfield."

TEN

BEECHUM HAD BEEN right again. It rained all night, charging in like a herd of elephants, battering the trees, beating on the roof, soaking the earth. By Tuesday morning the downpour had abated leaving the trees dripping, the atmosphere soggy, and the ground muddy. Qwilleran doubted that the carpenter would show up to work on the gazebo.

While he was preparing his breakfast coffee and thawing a four-day-old doughnut, the telephone rang, and a man's voice said genially, "How are you, Qwill? Getting settled? I hear you had dinner at the club last night. This is Colin Carmichael."

"Let's say that I participated in a farce that masqueraded as dinner," Qwilleran retorted in a bad humor. "How did you hear about it?"

"They called me because I sponsored you."

"If they want to apologize, it's too late. I've torn up my card."

"It's not exactly an apology. It's an explanation," the editor said. "They thought I should explain the situation to you. To put it bluntly, you brought a Tater to the club as your guest, and the members don't care for that."

"That's what I suspected," Qwilleran said belligerently. "Tell the members they know what they can do. Editors excluded, of course."

"Honestly, I hated to call you, Qwill. Sorry it happened."

"So am I. It tells me something about Spudsboro that I didn't want to know."

"Don't hold it against me. How about lunch?"

"I think it would be better if I dropped into your office. There's something I want to discuss with you, and I'd like to see some back copies while I'm there."

"Sure. Any time after two will be okay. We're putting a special to bed at two, and it's quite important. I want to be on top of it."

"What kind of special?"

"Sixteen pages of June brides, heavy on advertising, of course."

"Of course," said Qwilleran. "See you after two."

To his surprise, the red pickup with one blue fender pulled into the lot, and he went to the building site to greet the carpenter.

"Morning, Mr. Beechum. That was quite some rain we had last night."

"Gonna git worse."

"Hmmm . . . well . . . but the job is shaping up nicely. I didn't know it was going to be hexagonal, though."

"Hex what?"

"It has six sides instead of four."

"Figgered to git you sumpin' special."

"I appreciate that." Qwilleran sauntered around with his hands in his pockets. "Nice view from here. You were right about that, too."

"Lotsa purty sights in the mount'ns." The carpenter straightened up and pointed with his handsaw. "They's a purty trail down thataway."

"Thanks, but I'm not taking any more chances on getting lost in the woods."

"Iffen you git lost, jes' keep on goin'. You bound to come out somewheres."

"I admire your philosophy, Mr. Beechum. What about the caves? I hear there are some interesting caves in the mountains. Do you know anything about the caves?"

"Fulla bats. You like bats? Know a feller was bit by a bat. Kicked the bucket."

"I gather you don't recommend the caves. How about the spectacular waterfall at the cove?"

"Purty sight! Lotsa pizen snakes back there, but it's a mighty purty sight!" The carpenter's eyes were twinkling roguishly.

Qwilleran thought, This is mountain humor—scaring lowlanders with tales of snakes, bears, and bats. Let him have his fun. "When do you think this job will be finished?" he asked.

"Like 'bout when I git it done. Gonna rain some more."

"The man on the radio said the rain is over for a while," Qwilleran assured him.

"Them fellers don't know nothin' on radio," said the weather expert.

Qwilleran returned indoors to dress for downtown, and while he was shaving he heard another vehicle pull into the parking lot. A peek out the front window of the upstairs hall revealed Dolly Lessmore in brilliant yellow stepping out of her white convertible. He toweled the lather off his face and rushed downstairs to admit her.

"Hope I'm not interrupting anything," she said gaily. "I just wanted to see what Sabrina did for you. The plants do a lot for the foyer, don't they? Where'd you get that gorgeous candleholder?"

"From Potato Cove," Qwilleran said. "Go into the living room and sit down. I'll bring some coffee."

"I was hoping you'd say that."

"Shall I add a surreptitious soupçon of brandy?"

"What I don't know won't hurt me," she said, "but not too much, please; I'm on my way to the office . . . Are these the cats?" The Siamese were walking regally into the room as if they expected to be the main attraction.

"Some persons call them that," he said. "I think of them as domestic software."

Dolly turned away. "I don't know anything about cats. We've always had dogs."

At that pronouncement Koko and Yum Yum turned around and walked out, their long, lithe bodies making U-turns in unison. Foreparts seemed to be leaving the room while hindparts were still coming in.

Qwilleran served coffee in the new mugs, explaining that they were handmade by Otto the Potter and remarking, "The cove's an interesting little business community. I hope no one convinces them to move into a mall."

"Don't worry! Those Taters don't have enough sense to

grab a good offer when they get one. They'd rather play store all summer and go on welfare all winter. Don't get friendly with Taters, Qwill.''

He huffed into his moustache. Now he knew the reason for her impromptu visit; the club had notified her of his *faux pas*. ''Didn't you hire a Tater to make repairs to this house?'' he challenged her.

''Well, you know, Mr. Beechum does very good work for not much money.'' Dolly surveyed the living room with approval. ''Sabrina did a super job here. She's a Virgo. That's a good sign for a designer.''

''What's your sign?'' he asked. ''Or is that a trade secret?''

''I'm a Leo.''

''I assume that's a good sign for selling real estate.''

''It's a good sign for selling anything,'' she said with a throaty laugh.

''How about Hawkinfield's sign? Does anyone know?''

''Oh, sure. He was a Capricorn, meaning he was tough and power-hungry and always seemed to win, but he had a sensitive side that not many people knew. When he lost his three sons, his life was wrecked. Did you know about that?''

''I knew there were a couple of fatal accidents.''

''The thing that drove him half-mad,'' said Dolly, turning suddenly serious, ''was the suspicion that the mountain people were responsible.''

''How did he figure that?''

''You don't know the story. I'll tell you . . . There was an avalanche on a ski trail. A group from the Valley Boys' Club went cross-country skiing with an adult counselor. They always hired a Tater guide, of course, who knew the mountains. Well, the skiers were strung out along the trail, with the guide leading and the counselor bringing up the rear, and most of them had squeezed through this one narrow pass when the snow started to slide off the cliff above. The counselor yelled a warning, but the two young Hawkinfield boys panicked and got tangled up in their skis. Snow and ice came thundering down on top of them.''

"How do you know all these details?" Qwilleran asked.

"The counselor told us; he plays golf at the club. He yelled for help, but the rest of them were too far ahead. The pass was blocked. He dug frantically with his hands at the mountain of snow, but it was hopeless. There were tons of it! It was two days before they found the bodies. J.J. wrote an editorial on the loss of his sons that would break your heart! Privately, though, he was furious. He imagined a Tater plot. The guide, he thought, had spaced the skiers out along the trail, and an accomplice on top of the cliff started the snowslide."

"That's a far-fetched scenario, Dolly. Having someone to blame may have been a safety valve for his emotions, but . . . do you believe Taters would be so malicious?"

"You haven't heard the whole story. The following summer his one remaining son went rafting on the river with a couple of high school buddies. It was after a heavy rain—a real mountain downpour—and the river was turbulent. That's what the kids like, of course—risks! Their raft turned over, and the other two saved themselves, but the body of the Hawkinfield boy was never found. J.J. hired private detectives, thinking his son had been kidnapped by Taters; that's how crazed he was! Those were rough years for him. His wife ended up in a private mental hospital, and he lived alone in this big house."

"What about his daughter?"

"He thought it would be better for her if she went away to school."

Qwilleran said accusingly, "You didn't tell me he'd been

murdered on the premises. As it happened, I found out from other sources.''

"Oh, come on, Qwill. You're not spooked by anything like that, are you?'' she asked teasingly.

"I myself don't object to a homicide or two,'' he retorted, ''but a purchaser of the inn could sue you if you don't reveal the skeletons in the closet.''

"Well, now you know,'' Dolly said with a shrug. "J.J. had made enemies, but we never dreamed it would end the way it did, and now that his murderer turned out to be a Tater, we can't help wondering about the other incidents involving his sons.''

"Did you attend the trial?''

"Yes, I was there with Sherry Hawkinfield. The poor girl had no one, you know.''

"What convicted Forest Beechum?''

"The crucial testimony came from her. She was here for Father's Day, and on Saturday she went to Potato Cove to buy a gift for her dad. She bought a painting and asked the artist to deliver it on Sunday as a surprise. Robert and I were supposed to come up here for a drink on Sunday afternoon and then take J.J. and Sherry to dinner at the club. While we were dressing, we heard police cars and an ambulance going up the mountain. We phoned the Wilbank house, and Ardis told us there'd been a murder at Tiptop. We couldn't believe it!''

"What time was that?''

"We were due there at three. I think it was about two-thirty when we found out.''

"Del Wilbank told me there were no witnesses to the actual incident. Where was Sherry?''

"She'd gone down to Five Points to buy cocktail snacks. The artist was coming up the mountain as she drove down, and he was gone when she returned . . . You seem quite interested in this, Qwill.''

''I should be! I'm living at the scene of the crime, and I might hear chains rattling in the middle of the night,'' he said lightly. ''Seriously, though, I've been searching for a writing project, and I've come to the conclusion that J.J. would be a good subject for a biography.''

''That would be super! Absolutely super!'' Dolly said. ''It would put Spudsboro on the map, for sure. If there's anything Robert and I can do to help . . . Well, look, I've got to hie myself down to the office. Thanks for the coffee. The brandy didn't hurt it a bit!''

Qwilleran walked with her down the long flights of steps, and she said, ''Are you sure you don't want to buy Tiptop and open a country inn? You'd make a charming host.''

''Positively not!''

''It'll be a year-round operation when the ski runs are completed. This could be another Aspen!''

''If it doesn't stop raining, Tiptop could be another Ark,'' Qwilleran said.

Returning to the foyer he found Koko prowling aimlessly. ''Any comment?'' he asked the cat. Koko merely stretched out on the floor of the foyer, making himself a yard long, and he rolled over a few times in front of the Fitzwallow huntboard.

''Treat!'' Qwilleran announced, striding toward the kitchen. Koko scrambled to his feet and raced him to the feeding station, but Yum Yum failed to report. For either of them to ignore the T-word was cause for alarm. Qwilleran went looking for her, starting with the new hiding place under the table skirt in the living room. There she was!

''Yum Yum! *What are you doing?*'' he said in shock.

She was completely absorbed in an aggressive ritual,

biting small clumps of fur from her flanks. Feathery tufts
were scattered on the gray carpet. Briefly she stopped and
gave him a deranged look with slightly crossed eyes, then
went on biting.

"What's the matter, sweetheart?" Qwilleran asked ten-
derly as he drew her out from her retreat. She made no
protest but cuddled in his arms as he walked back and
forth in the foyer. She made no protest, but neither did
she squeeze her eyes in bliss or extend a paw to touch his
moustache. "Are you homesick?" he asked. "Is it
stress?" She had been yanked away from familiar surroundings and subjected to four days on the road, after
which she found herself in a strange house with an unhappy history. Furthermore, he had neglected her for three
days while pursuing his own interests. Koko might be
tough and self-reliant, but Yum Yum was sensitive and
emotionally vulnerable, having been an abused kitten before Qwilleran rescued her.

With one hand he punched the phone number of Lori
Bamba in Moose County, still cradling Yum Yum in his arm.
Lori, his part-time secretary, was knowledgeable about cats.

"Qwill!" she cried. "I didn't expect to hear from you
for three months! Is everything all right?"

"Yes and no," he said. "I'm concerned about Yum
Yum. Suddenly she's started tearing her fur out."

"Where?"

"On her flanks."

"Mmmm . . . yes . . . that sometimes happens. It could
be an allergy. Has it just started?"

"I noticed it for the first time today. She was hiding
and doing this secret thing to herself, and it seemed, well,
obscene! I know she's been under stress lately."

"The vet can give her a shot for that," Lori said, "but

wait a day or two and see what develops. Give her some extra attention. It could be a hormonal thing, too. If it continues, take her to the doctor.''

''Thanks, Lori. That relieves my mind. I thought I had a feline masochist on my hands. How's everything in Moose County? I heard about Dr. Halifax.''

''Wasn't that a shame? I don't know what we'll do without that dear man. The whole county is upset. Otherwise, everything's okay. I've been able to handle your correspondence without bothering Mr. Hasselrich.''

''And how's the family?''

''The family's fine. Nick is still looking for a different kind of work. We were thinking of starting a bed-and-breakfast.''

''Don't move too quickly,'' Qwilleran cautioned. ''Give it plenty of thought. Get some advice.''

After talking with Lori, he willingly changed his plans for the morning. He had intended to spend time at the public library, have lunch somewhere, and call on Colin Carmichael after two o'clock. Instead, he spent the next few hours sweet-talking Yum Yum, scratching her chin, fondling her ears, stroking her fur, and doing lap service. Only when she fell into a deep, contented sleep did he steal out of the house and drive down the mountain.

Upon reaching Five Points he was undecided. He had seen a certain bowl at the woodcrafter's shop in Potato Cove, and it kept haunting him. About fifteen inches in diameter, it was cut from the burl of a cherry tree and turned on a lathe until the interior was satin-smooth. In contrast, the top edges and entire exterior were rough and gnarled. He liked it. There had been a time in his life when art objects held little appeal for him, but that had changed along with his circumstances and increased leisure. On a previous visit to the cove he had lingered over the bowl, and now he decided to go back and buy it. He could have lunch at Amy's, walk around for a while, and reach the *Gazette* office in Spudsboro around two o'clock.

"Sumpin' told me you'd be back to git it," said Wesley, the wood crafter, gleefully. Word had spread around the cove that a stranger with an oversized moustache, who claimed to be a journalist, was hanging around the shops and buying high-ticket items.

Qwilleran loaded the bowl in the trunk of his car—it was even heavier than it looked—and drove to the Village Smithy to tell Vance that his candelabrum was a great success. While there he also bought a hand-forged cowbell with a tone that reminded him of Switzerland.

The blacksmith said, "Somethin's screwy with your car. It don't sound right. You git it from bouncin' 'round these mount'n roads."

"Glad you mentioned it," Qwilleran said. "Where's a good repair shop?"

"I kin fix it. Are you gonna be around? Gimme your keys."

"That's very good of you, Vance. I'll have lunch at Amy's and see you later."

At the Lunch Bucket the plump and pretty proprietor was behind the high counter, smiling as usual, and the baby was burbling in his basket.

Qwilleran said, "I have to confess I've forgotten the baby's name."

"Ashley," she said proudly. "Two months, one week, and six days."

"I like your mountain names: Ashley, Wesley, Vance, Forest, Dewey. Names like that have dignity."

"It's always been that way in the mountains; I don't know why. Women have first names like Carson and Tully and Taylor and Greer. I think it's neat. With a name like Amy, wouldn't you know I'm from the prairie?'' She made a comic grimace.

"What brought you to Little Potato?"

"I dated Forest in college and loved the way he painted mountains—so real and yet out of this world. He painted all the signs for Potato Cove, too. They wanted him to paint the signs for Tiptop Estates, but he refused because he didn't believe in what Hawkinfield was doing to Big Potato. Anyway . . . we were going to be married at the waterfall last June when all the wildflowers were out. Here's his picture.'' Amy opened the locket that she wore and showed Qwilleran the face of a lean, unsmiling young man with long, black hair. "Suddenly our whole life caved in. I'll never be able to think of Father's Day without getting sick . . . What can I get you to eat?''

Qwilleran ordered soup and a veggieburger, and while she was preparing it, he said, "There are conflicting reports on what happened at Tiptop on that day.''

"I can tell you God's honest truth. Wait till I finish this burger.'' She ladled up a bowl of vegetable soup. "Here, you can start with this. It's especially good today. I hit it just right, but be careful—it's very hot.''

"That's the way I like it,'' he said, thinking of the corn chowder at the golf club. It was thick with vegetables, including turnips, which he swallowed without complaint. "Excellent soup, Amy! A person could live on this stuff!''

"Sometimes we have to,'' she said as she carried the burger to his table and sat down.

Qwilleran was the only customer, and he wondered how this tiny, unpopular restaurant could survive. "Where do you buy your groceries?'' he asked.

"We belong to a co-op where we can buy in bulk. Other

things come from the Yellyhoo Market on the river. We buy right out of the crates and off the back of trucks. There's a big saving.''

''You were going to tell me Forest's story, Amy.''

''Hope it doesn't spoil your lunch, Mr. . . .''

''Qwilleran.''

''Well, here goes. It started the Saturday before Father's Day, when Sherry Hawkinfield came into the weaving studio. Forest was minding the store while Chrys did a few errands. He used to show his mountain paintings there—all sizes. The tourists bought the small ones, but Sherry wanted a large one as a Father's Day gift and tried to haggle over the price. Imagine! It was only $300. Forest told her the painting would be worth $3,000 in a big-city gallery, and if she wanted something cheap, she should go to Lumpton's Department Store. He was never very tactful.''

''I can see that,'' Qwilleran said.

''So, anyway, she wrote a check for $300 and asked him to deliver the painting the next day as a surprise for her father. She wanted it exactly at one o'clock . . . Would you like coffee sub with your burger, Mr. . . .''

''Qwilleran. No, thanks. I'll skip the beverage today.''

''Well, he drove to Tiptop on Sunday, and Sherry told him where to hang the painting in the hallway. Just as he was pounding the nail in the wall, the Old Buzzard rushed in—that's what Forest called him. The Old Buzzard rushed in from somewhere and said to his daughter, 'By God! What's that damned rabble-rouser doing in my house? Get him out of here!' She didn't say anything, but Forest said, 'I'm delivering a painting of a mountain, sir, so you'll know what mountains used to look like before you started mutilating them, *sir*!' And the man said, 'Get out of my house and take that piece of junk with you, or I'll have you arrested for trespassing and littering!' And he grabbed a stick out of the umbrella stand and was threatening him. Forest won't stand for abuse, verbal or otherwise, so he said, 'Go ahead! Hit me, sir, and I'll have the publisher of the *Gazette* charged with assault and battery!' The Old Buzzard was getting as red as a beet, and Sherry told Forest he'd better leave.''

"He left the painting there, I gather."

Amy nodded. "She'd paid for it, you know. Anyway, he stomped out of the house and drove back to the cove, madder than I've ever seen him."

"What time was that?"

"About one-thirty, I think. At three o'clock the police came, and Forest was charged with murder! We couldn't understand it! We didn't know what it was all about! We were all so confused. And then—when Sherry told such horrible lies at the trial—it was like a nightmare! . . . Excuse me."

Two tourists had walked into the restaurant, and Amy went behind the counter, greeting them with her usual smile, her eyes glistening unnaturally. There was a happy squawk from Ashley.

"Goo goo goo," she said. "His name is Ashley," she told the customers. "He's two months, one week, and six days."

Qwilleran smoothed his sensitive moustache. He thought, If Amy's story is true, and if Forest didn't kill J.J., who did? And why is Sherry Hawkinfield protecting the murderer?

ELEVEN

As QWILLERAN WAS leaving Amy's Lunch Bucket she said meekly, "If you want real coffee, you can get it at the bakery up the hill."

"Thanks, Amy. You're a real friend," he said.

"Have you ever seen the waterfall? It's very exciting. The trail starts behind the bakery."

"Are there poison snakes back there?"

"Of course not! There are no poison snakes in the Potatoes, Mr. . . . ."

"Qwilleran."

He ambled up the gradual incline on the wooden sidewalk until he scented a yeasty aroma and came upon an isolated building with the remains of a steeple. The weaving studio occupied an abandoned schoolhouse; the bakery occupied an abandoned church. Hanging alongside the door was a barnwood sign shaped like a plump loaf of bread, but he read the lettering twice before he could believe what he saw: THE HALF-BAKED BAKERY. A screened door flapped loosely as he entered.

"Why the screened door?" he asked by way of introduction. "I thought you didn't have flying insects in the Potatoes."

"It's the damned health code," said a man in crumpled whites with a baker's hat sagging over one ear like a deflated balloon. "They make us wear these stupid hats, too."

The same uniform was worn by a woman taking a tray of crusty Italian bread from an oven. Like all the equipment—grinders, mixers, dough tables, scales and whatnot—the oven looked secondhand if not actually antique. At the front of the shop were four wooden student chairs with writing arms, as well as a coffeemaker with instructions: "Help Yourself . . . Pay at Counter . . . Cream in Fridge." Separating the bakery from the snack area was a scarred glass case displaying cookies, muffins, Danish pastries, and pecan rolls, although very little of each. What elevated this humble establishment to the sublime was the heady fragrance of baking bread.

Qwilleran helped himself to coffee and bought an apple Danish from the baker. "If you don't mind my saying so," he said as he pulled out his bill clip, "you picked a helluva name for your bakery."

"Tell you why we did it," the man said. "Everybody told us we were half-baked to open a whole-grain bakery in Potato Cove, but we're doing all right. Overhead's low, and we wholesale to a food market and a couple of restaurants in the valley, so we have a little cash flow we can count on.''

"Do you supply the golf club?" Qwilleran asked slyly.

"Hell no! But you see that tray of bread? It's going to an Italian restaurant. They pick it up every day at four o'clock." He looked at Qwilleran's moustache. "Are you the fella that bought Vance's big candlestick?"

"Yes, I'm the proud possessor of fifty pounds of iron." Qwilleran looked around the shop. The unifying note in the bakery was paint; everything paintable had been painted orchid: walls, ceiling, shelving, tables, student chairs, even the floorboards. "Unusual paint job you have here," was Qwilleran's comment.

"Thrift, man! Thrift! Lumpton Hardware advertised a sale of paint, and all those fakes had was pink and blue. It was my wife's idea to mix 'em."

Qwilleran carried his purchase to an orchid student chair and bit into a six-inch square of puffy, chewy pastry heaped with large apple slices in thick and spicy juices. It was still warm.

"I'm forced to tell you," he said, "that this is absolutely the best Danish I've ever eaten in half a century of pastry connoisseurship."

The baker turned to the woman. "Hear that, sugar? Take a bow." To Qwilleran he said, "My wife does the gooey stuff. Wait till you taste the sticky buns! Everything we use is whole grain and fresh. Apples come from Tater orchards—no sprays, no chemicals. We stone-grind our flour right from the wheat berries. Bread's kneaded and shaped by hand. Crackers are rolled the same way."

"That's my job," said his wife. "I like handling dough."

"Bread untouched by human hands may be cheaper, but nobody says it's as good," the baker said. "You're new around here."

"I'm here for the summer. My name's Jim Qwilleran. What's your name?"

"Yates. Yates Penney. That's my wife, Kate. How do you like the Potatoes, Mr. . . . ?"

"Qwilleran. I'm not sure I like what's happening to Big Potato."

"You said it! The inside of Big Potato looks like a mangy cat, and the outside looks like a war zone. City people come up here because they like country living, and then they drag the city along with 'em. The Taters have the right idea; they build themselves a rustic shack and let everything grow wild, the way Nature intended. We're from Akron, but we know how to fit in. Right, sugar?"

Qwilleran said, "What is this waterfall I've heard about?"

"You mean Purgatory?"

"Is that what it's called? I'd like to see it."

The baker turned to his wife. "He wants to go to Purgatory." They communicated silently for a few moments until she nodded, and then he explained, "We don't encourage sightseers because they throw beer cans and food wrappers in the falls, but you don't look like the average tourist."

"I take that as a compliment. Is the trail well-marked? I'd like a quiet, leisurely walk without getting lost."

"It's quiet, all right," said Kate. "Nobody goes back there on a Tuesday afternoon. Only on weekends."

"You can't get lost either," Yates assured him. "Just

follow the creek upstream. It's about half a mile, but all uphill.''

''That's okay. I've been practicing. Where did Purgatory get its name?''

''Some old-time Taters named it, I think. It's not an Indian name, I know that. Anyway, the water drops off a high cliff and down into a bottomless pit, and the mist rises like steam. Quite a sight!''

''Good! I'll take a little ramble. I have some time to kill while Vance works on my car.''

''What's wrong with it?''

''Nothing serious. Mountain-itis, I guess you'd call it. While I'm standing here I'd like to pay for some Danish and sticky buns. I can pick them up when I finish with the falls.''

''We close at four,'' Kate warned him.

''If it's only half a mile, I'll be back well before that,'' Qwilleran said.

''Take care!''

''Don't fall in,'' the baker said with a grin.

Behind the bakery Qwilleran could hear the creek before he could see it. Swollen by heavy rain, the waters were rushing tumultuously over boulders in the creek bed. An irregular path on the edge of the stream had been worn down by generations of Taters and perhaps by Indians before them, who made the pilgrimage without benefit of handrails, curbs, steps, or warning signs. This was raw nature, and the footing was muddy and treacherous. Sharp rocks and wayward roots protruded from the walkway, camouflaged by pine needles and oak leaves that were wet and slippery. Tufts of coarse wet grasses grew over the edge, dripping and ready to chute an unwary wanderer into the stream.

After a few stumbles Qwilleran realized the impossibility of ogling the rushing stream and walking at the same time. Only by alternating a few careful steps with a few motionless moments could he appreciate the wild beauty. Brilliant green ferns abounded, thriving in the damp shadows. Every cleft rock had its trickle of water trying to find the creek and soaking the ground en route. Then there were the wild flowers—clumps of them in yellow, white, pink, blue, and red, growing among the wild grasses or in the crevices of rotting logs or across the face of rock outcroppings. Hundred-foot pine trees rising like the vaulted ceiling of a cathedral filtered the sun's rays through their sparse upper branches. Moose County could never produce a show like this!

The course of the creek angled sharply and sometimes plunged out of sight, only to reappear with added force. Qwilleran was following it upstream, of course, and its exuberance increased—in noise and in turbulence. When the waters were not splashing wildly over boulders, they were cascading smoothly over rock ledges in a series of naturally terraced waterfalls. And Qwilleran, when not picking his way along the precarious path, was clicking his camera. Take it easy, he told himself, or you'll run out of film.

The higher he climbed, the more dramatic the views and the louder the thunder of water, until he groped his way around the last projecting cliff and found himself in a rock-walled atrium. There it was! Purgatory! An immense column of water, four times higher than its width, poured over a lofty cliff with unimaginable force and deafening roar—tons of water dropping straight down into a black hole in the rock from which rose clouds of vapor.

Qwilleran caught his breath. To be alone in the woods

with this mighty dynamo gave him an eerie sensation, as if he were a supplicant consulting an oracle in a rock-walled temple, somewhere in the distant past. Perhaps Native Americans had worshipped their spirits here. Perhaps, he thought for one giddy moment, this was where he would find the answers. Overwhelmed by the experience, he had forgotten the questions.

Then the hypnotic moment passed, and he was a summer vacationer with a camera. Climbing carefully over the surrounding boulders he found numerous photogenic angles and clicked the shutter recklessly until he realized he had only one picture left. For the final shot he wanted to try a profile of the cascade entering the cauldron of billowing steam.

The path had ended, but he edged around the perimeter of the atrium until he found the right angle. Studying the view-finder critically for his final shot, he made one impulsive move—a step backward.

Immediately his feet shot out from under him and—sprawled on his back—he started to slide slowly but inexorably toward the abyss. Twisting his body in panic, he clutched at wet rocks and grabbed handfuls of shallow-rooted weeds. Nothing stopped his slide down the muddy slope. His bellowing shouts were drowned by the pounding waters . . . and now he was enveloped in fog . . . and now he was slipping into the black hole. He grabbed for the rim, but it crumbled. Grasping wildly at the nearly vertical walls of the chasm, he managed to slow his descent and find a ledge for his toe. It bore his weight. It was a wisp of hope.

He clung to his perch and tried to think. Spread-eagled against the face of the rock he ran bleeding hands over its surface in search of a projection. Behind him the shaft of water was thundering, and he was drenched like a drowning man. Something flashed into his mind then: mountain climbers in Switzerland . . . scaling the flat face of a peak . . . with infinite patience. Patience! he told himself. The mist stung his face and blinded him, but he fought his panic. Running his hands painstakingly over the flat surface in search of crevices, testing craggy ledges for strength, he inched upward. Time lost its meaning. He spent an eternity clinging and creeping, never knowing how much farther he had to climb. Patience! When the darkness lessened he knew he was approaching the rim, although he was still enveloped in mist.

Eventually one exploring hand felt level ground. It was the rim of the pit, but the trial by mud was not over. He had to hoist himself out of the hole, and one misstep or one miscalculation could send him plunging back into the depths. The terrain above him was slimy, but it was blessedly horizontal. After several tries he found something growing from a crevice, something tough and fibrous that he could grab as he clambered out. Facedown in the mud he crawled and squirmed out of the mist and away from the pit until he felt safe enough to collapse and hug the earth. No matter that he was muddied from head to foot, his clothing in shreds, his hands and knees bloodied, his watch smashed, his camera lost; he was on terra firma.

Only then did he pay attention to a shooting pain in his ankle. It had been torturing him throughout the ordeal, but the life-or-death struggle had superseded all else. When he turned over and tried to sit up, he yelped with pain and shock; his ankle was swollen as big as a grapefruit. Rashly he tried to stand up and fell back with a cry of anguish. For a moment he lay flat on the ground and considered the problem. A little rest, he thought, would reduce the swelling.

He was wrong. His ankle continued to throb relentlessly, responding to every move with agonizing spasms. How do I get out of here? he asked himself. At the bakery they had said no one went to the waterfall on a Tuesday afternoon. Having great lung power, he tried a shout for help, but it was drowned out by the roar of the falls. Suppose he had to stay in the woods all night! Beechum had predicted more rain. The nights turned cold in the mountains, and his lightweight clothing was wet and tattered.

With a burst of determination he proposed to drag himself along the trail, an inch at a time if necessary. Fortunately it was all downhill; unfortunately the path was studded with sharp rocks, and his hands, elbows, and knees were already lacerated. Even so, he squirmed downhill a few yards, trying to save his ankle, but the pain was non-stop and the swelling had reached the size of a melon. Defeated, he dragged himself to a boulder and leaned against it in a sitting position.

For a while he sat there thinking, or trying to think. Vance would wonder why he hadn't called for his car; Yates would wonder why he hadn't picked up his baked goods.

Now that he had inched his way out of the atrium, the crashing noise of Purgatory was somewhat muffled. "HELP!" he shouted, his voice echoing in the rocky ravine. There was no answering cry. The sky, glimpsed between the lofty treetops, was now overcast. The rain was coming. If he had to spend the night in the woods, wearing cold, wet clothing and lying on the drenched ground, covering himself with wet leaves like a woodland animal, he would be ready for an oxygen tent in the morning . . . that is, if anyone found him in the morning. They might not find him until the weekend.

"HELP!"

Then a chilling thought occurred to him. The Taters may have intended him to disappear in the Purgatory abyss. If so, they could have only one motive; they suspected his purpose in visiting their precious mountain. They may have mistaken him for a federal agent. What were they growing in the hidden coves and hollows? What was stockpiled in those caves? Beechum's banter about bears and bats and poisonous snakes may have been something more than mountain humor.

"HELP!"

Did he hear a reply, or was it an echo?

He tried again. "HELP!"

"Hallo," came a distant cry.

"HELP!"

"Coming! Coming!" The voices were getting closer. "Hold on!" Soon he could see movement in the woods, screened by the underbrush, then heads bobbing along the trail. Two men were coming up the slope, and they broke into a run when he waved an arm in a wide arc.

"For God's sake! What happened?" the baker shouted, seeing the tattered, mud-caked figure leaning against a boulder. "What happened to your ankle?"

"You look like you been through a *ce*-ment mixer!" the blacksmith said.

"I sprained my ankle, and I was trying to drag myself back to the cove," Qwilleran said shortly. He was in no mood to describe his ordeal or confess to the careless misstep that sent him sliding ignominiously into the pit.

They hoisted him to a standing position, with his weight

on his right foot, and made a human crutch, unmindful of the mud being smeared on their own clothes. Then slowly they started down the precarious slope to Potato Cove. Qwilleran was in too much pain to talk, and his rescuers were aware of it.

At the end of the trail a group of concerned Taters waited with comments and advice:

"Never see'd nobody in such a mess!" said one.

"Better hose him down, Yates." That was the baker's wife.

"Give 'im a slug o' corn, Vance. Looks like he needs it."

"Somebody send for Maw Beechum! She's got healin' hands."

Qwilleran's rescuers stripped off his rags behind the bakery and turned the hose on the caked blood and dirt, the icy water from a local well acting like a local anesthetic. Then, draped in a couple of bakery towels, he was assisted into a backroom and placed on a cot among cartons of wheatberries and yeast. Kate, serving hot coffee and another Danish, explained that Mrs. Beechum had gone home to get some of her homemade medicines.

When the silent woman arrived, she went to work with downcast eyes, making an icepack for the ankle and tearing up an old sheet for bandages. Then she poured antiseptic from a jelly jar onto the wounds and larded them with ointment.

Yates said, "With that stuff you'll never get an infection, that's for sure. When you feel up to it, we'll fix you up with pants and a coat and drive you home. You can say goodbye to those shoes, too. What size do you take? . . . Hey, Vance, get some sandals from the leather shop, size twelve." He appraised the bandaging. "Man, you look like a mummy!"

The wrappings on Qwilleran's hands, elbows, and knees restricted his movement considerably, but the ankle torture was somewhat relieved after the ice pack and tight bandaging. He wanted to thank Mrs. Beechum, but she had slipped away from the bakery without so much as a nod in his direction, leaving him a jar of liniment.

Kate said, "You should use ice again tonight and keep your foot up, Mr. . . . ."

"Qwilleran."

Yates buckled on the sandals, and Wesley brought him a carved walking stick, which looked more like a cudgel. "I don't know how to thank you people," he said.

"We aim to be good neighbors," said Kate.

The three men drove away, Yates driving Qwilleran in his newly repaired car, and Vance following in his pickup. Qwilleran was abnormally quiet, still dazed by his experience. He felt that his precipitous slide into the black hole had never happened. Yet, if it were true and if he had not survived, would anyone ever know his fate? What would have happened to Koko and Yum Yum, penned up in a house that no one had reason to visit?

The baker respected his silence for a while but threw curious glances at him repeatedly. Finally he said, "What really happened at Purgatory, man?"

Qwilleran was jolted out of his reverie. "What do you mean?"

"You don't wind up in that condition just by twisting your ankle."

"I told you I was trying to drag myself back to the cove. The path was muddy and full of sharp rocks."

"You were soaking wet from head to foot."

"There's a lot of mist at the falls. You should know that."

Yates grunted, and no more was said for a few minutes. When they reached Hawk's Nest Drive, he tried again. "See anybody in the woods?"

"No. It was just as your wife said: no one around on Tuesday. This is Tuesday, isn't it? I feel as if I've been on that trail a week!"

"Did you hear anything unusual?"

"Not with the water roaring! I couldn't hear myself think!"

"See anything strange?"

"What are you getting at?" Qwilleran said with slight annoyance. "I saw the creek, boulders, fallen trees, mud, large and small waterfalls, flowers, more mud . . ."

"Okay, okay, I'll shut up. You had a rough time."

"Sorry if I barked at you. I'm feeling edgy."

"You should be! You've been through hell!"

At Tiptop his rescuers helped him up the twenty-five steps, and the sight of Qwilleran dressed in baker's whites and supported by two strangers sent the Siamese flying upstairs, where they watched from a safe elevation. He offered the men a beer and was glad when they declined; he needed a period of rest in which to find himself again. There were moments when he was still in the abyss, clinging to a slippery wall of rock.

"I'll bring up your baked goods," Yates said. "Anything more we can do? Be glad to do it."

"There's a burl bowl in the trunk of my car that you could bring up. And again, I don't know how to thank you fellas."

When they had gone and Qwilleran had dropped on the

gray velvet sofa with his ankle elevated on one of Sabrina's pillows, the Siamese walked questioningly into the room.

"You'll have to bear with me awhile," he told them. "You almost lost your chief cook."

They huddled close to his body, playing the nursing role instinctive with cats, and made no demands, although it was past their normal dinnertime. At intervals Koko ran his nose over the white uniform and grimaced as if he smelled something rotten.

When the telephone rang, Qwilleran was undecided whether to answer, but it persisted until he grabbed his walking staff and moved to the foyer with halting steps.

"I thought you were going to drop in this afternoon," said Colin Carmichael.

"I dropped into a waterfall instead," Qwilleran said, recovering some of his spirit.

"Where?"

"At Potato Cove. I'm lucky I got out alive."

"Are you all right?"

"Except for a sprained ankle. Do you happen to have an elastic bandage?"

"I could pick one up at the drug store easily enough and run it up the mountain in no time. Anything else you need?"

"Perhaps one of those cold compresses that can be chilled in the freezer."

"No problem. Be right there."

"The front door's unlocked, Colin. Just walk in."

Having maneuvered successfully to the foyer, Qwilleran hobbled to the kitchen to feed the cats. They were used to dodging his long strides and found his new slow-motion toddle with a stick perplexing. He was back on the sofa when the editor arrived.

Carmichael frowned at the ankle. "That's quite a balloon you've got there. Is it painful?"

"Not as bad as it was. Excuse my attire; the baker at the cove had to lend me some clean clothes. Go out to the kitchen, Colin. There's a bar in the pantry. Help yourself, and you can bring me a ginger ale from the fridge. You might also throw the compress in the freezer."

The editor lingered. "I hated to call you about the Tater thing, Qwill. Don't hold it against me."

"Forget it. I'm not here to get involved in local politics or prejudices."

"What happened to your hands?"

"I tried to save myself and grabbed some unfriendly rocks. The bandages make them look worse than they are."

When they settled down with their drinks, Carmichael glanced around the living room. "This is a lot of house for one guy."

"It was the only place that would rent to cats. I have two Siamese," Qwilleran said.

"Where are they?"

"In hiding. They avoid veterinarians and editors."

"Our star columnist is going around with a red face since her interview with you. It seems you asked all the questions, and she did all the talking. She's too embarrassed to call you again."

"Let's leave it that way, Colin. Tell her I'm on a secret mission and don't want her to blow my cover. Tell her anything. Tell her I'm opening a health spa for men only, with retired burlesque strippers as masseuses."

"There's some speculation anyway—as to your identity, and your reason for being here, and why you're willing to pay such high rent."

"I'm beginning to wonder about the rent myself."

"Well, tell me how you sprained your ankle, Qwill."

Qwilleran related the episode in cool, journalistic style without histrionics, underplaying his descent into the pit and his heroic struggle to climb to safety. In concluding he said, "Let me tell you one thing: I wouldn't be sitting here tonight if it weren't for some of those Taters . . . Your glass is empty, Colin. Go and help yourself."

"Not this time, thanks. My family's expecting me home for dinner. We're having a backyard barbecue for my little girl's birthday . . . But tell me what you wanted to discuss in my office."

"It's only a wild notion. How would you react to a biography of Hawkinfield? I've thought of writing one, but it would require a lot of research."

"That's a great idea!" said the editor. "You can count on our complete cooperation. We can line up interviews for you. Everyone will be glad to talk."

"It's only in the thinking stage," Qwilleran said. "I might open with the murder trial, then flashback to J.J.'s regime at the *Gazette*, his civic leadership, the loss of his family, and his violent end."

Carmichael was pounding the arm of his chair. "That would make a damn good movie, too, Qwill! You've got me all fired up! After this news a backyard barbecue is going to seem like small potatoes."

"I'll need to get a transcript of the trial, of course, and there are considerations I'll want to discuss with an attorney. Would you recommend Hugh Lumpton?"

"Well," said the editor, "he's a great golfer. Drives a $40,000 car. Always has a lot of women around him. But—"

"That doesn't tell me what I need to know, does it?"

"Just between you and me, Qwill, I wouldn't even hire

him to write my will—not that I have any firsthand experience, you understand. It's just what I pick up at the club and at the chamber. You'd be better off going to one of the lawyers next door to the post office . . . Well, see here, is there anything I can do for you before I leave? Anything I can send you from the valley?''

''Not a thing, thanks. I appreciate the items from the drugstore. And tell your daughter that Koko and Yum Yum said happy birthday.''

''Great! She'll flip! She loves cats, especially ones that talk.''

After Carmichael had left, Qwilleran undertook a slow trek to the kitchen in search of food for himself, but he was intercepted by Koko, who was rolling and squirming on the floor in front of the Fitzwallow huntboard. Whatever his motive, the performance was a subtle reminder to Qwilleran that he had forgotten to mail Sabrina's letter to Sherry Hawkinfield. It was still in the drawer of the cabinet, fang marks and all. He looked at the address and then called directory assistance for a telephone number in Maryland: a shop called *Not New But Nice*. He had to repeat it twice to make himself understood.

When he punched the number, a recording device answered, but he was prepared; it was early evening, and he presumed the shop would be closed. In his most ingratiating voice he left a message that was purposely ambiguous:

''Ms. Hawkinfield, please call this number in Spudsboro regarding a valuable painting by Forest Beechum that belongs to you . . .''

Qwilleran turned to Koko. ''Do you think that will get results? The key word is *valuable*.''

''Yow!'' said Koko, hopping on and off the huntboard in excitement.

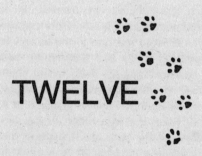

TWELVE

QWILLERAN WAS SURE that Sherry Hawkinfield would not return his call until morning. It was her place of business that he had phoned. He sat on a kitchen chair trying to eat soup with a bandaged hand that could hardly hold a spoon, while his left leg was propped on another chair with a cold compress wrapped around the ankle. Watching him from a respectful distance were two Siamese with anxious eyes, and their solicitude did nothing but make him jittery.

"I appreciate your concern," he said, "but there are times when I wish you would go away." They edged closer, looking doubly worried. Then suddenly they became agitated, running to and from the back door, Koko with his ears swept back and Yum Yum with her tail bushed. A moment later there was snuffling on the veranda and the click of claws.

"It's Lucy," Qwilleran said morosely. "Keep quiet and she'll go away." But the cats only increased their frenzy, and Lucy started to whine.

In no mood for domestic drama and muttering under his breath, Qwilleran kicked off the compress and limped to the refrigerator, where he found the four hot dogs he had bought for himself. He threw them to the overfed Doberman, and soon the commotion subsided, indoors and out.

His irritability was a delayed reaction to the unnerving experience at the waterfall. *Why did I come to these damned mountains?* he asked himself. Polly would blame it on his impulsiveness; she often questioned his precipitate actions, doing so with a polite sideways glance of mild reproach. So did Arch Riker but with blunt disapproval. How could they understand the messages telegraphed to Qwilleran through his sensitive moustache? How could he understand them himself?

He would have paced the floor if he had two good ankles. He would have enjoyed a pipeful of Scottish tobacco if he had not given it up. His books and radio were upstairs; so was his ottoman; so was his bed. Sooner or later he would have to tackle the ascent.

To reach the top he sat down on the second stair and went up backward, dragging his hand-carved walking staff and accompanied by the Siamese, who were always entertained by the eccentric behavior of humans and who had determined not to leave him alone in his travail.

As soon as he had sunk into his lounge chair and cushioned his left foot on the ottoman, the telephone rang.

"Yow!" Koko yowled in his ear.

"I'm not deaf!" he yelled back.

There was a slim chance that it might be the call from Maryland, so he hoisted himself out of the chair and— groaning and muttering—bumped down the stairs on his posterior. He reached the foyer and grabbed the handset after the ninth ring.

Qwilleran was taking a moment to adjust his attitude when a woman said impatiently, "Hello? Hello?"

"Good evening," he said with the silky charm and mellifluous voice that had thrilled women for three decades.

Then, rather pleasantly she said, "Are you the one who called me and left a message? I'm Sherry Hawkinfield." She had a young voice, a cultivated voice. She had gone to a good school.

"Yes, I'm the one," he replied. "My name is Jim Qwilleran."

"You sound . . . nice," she said archly. "Who are you? I don't recognize the name."

"I'm renting Tiptop for the summer. Dolly Lessmore made the arrangements."

"Oh . . . yes . . . of course. I just happened to come back to my shop after dinner, and I found your message."

"All work and no play makes . . . money," Qwilleran said.

"You're so right! What did you want to know about the painting?"

"It's a fantastic interpretation of mountains, and I understand it's quite valuable. Is it possibly for sale? If so, what are you asking for it? Also there's an antique English huntboard in the foyer that has a great deal of primitive appeal. Ms. Lessmore tells me you're disposing of some of the furnishings. Is that correct?" In the astonished pause that ensued he could visualize dollar signs dancing in her eyes.

"The whole house is for sale," she said eagerly, "completely furnished. It would make a neat country inn. Dolly says you're a prospect."

"I'm giving it some thought. There are certain details that should be discussed."

"Well, I might fly out there for the weekend to see some friends in the valley. We could talk about it then," she said with growing enthusiasm.

"I'd appreciate that. When would you arrive?"

"If I got a Friday morning flight, I'd rent a car at the airport and drive up to see you in the afternoon."

"Perhaps we could have lunch while you're here," he suggested cordially. "Or dinner."

"I'd love to."

"It would be my pleasure, I assure you, Ms. Hawkin-field."

"Then I'll see you Friday afternoon. What's your name again?"

"Jim Qwilleran, spelled with a QW."

"I'm glad you called, Mr. Qwilleran."

"Please call me Qwill."

"Oh, that's neat!"

"May I call you Sherry?"

"I wish you would. Where are you from?" She was beginning to sound chummy.

"Another planet, but a friendly one. The Beverly Hills of outer space."

This brought a giddy laugh. "I'll look forward to meeting you. Want me to call you from the airport and set a time?"

"Why don't you simply drive up to Tiptop? I'll be here

. . . waiting," he said meaningfully. (With my ankle in a sling, he told himself.)

"All right. I'll do that."

"I don't need to tell you how to find Tiptop," he said, in what he knew was a weak jest.

"No," she giggled. "I think I remember where it is."

There were pauses, as if neither of them wanted to terminate the conversation.

"Bon voyage," he said.

"Thank you. *Au revoir.*"

"Au revoir." Qwilleran waited for the gentle replacing of the handset before he hung up. Turning to Koko, who was waiting for a report, he said, "I haven't had a phone conversation like that since I was nineteen."

Koko replied with a wink, or so it seemed; there was a cat hair in his eye.

Once more Qwilleran went upstairs the hard way. He shooed the Siamese into their room, and as he pulled down the window shades in his own bedroom, he saw the revolving circle of light on Little Potato. Forest's kinfolk were trudging with their lanterns in grim silence.

His sleep that night was reasonably comfortable except when he shifted position rashly, and in the morning the ankle showed noticeable improvement despite the heavy atmosphere that usually aggravates aches and pains. Rain had started to fall—not torrentially but with steady determination, and according to the meteorologist on the radio it would rain all day. There was a danger of flooding in some areas.

Qwilleran slid downstairs to feed the Siamese and make a breakfast of coffee and sticky buns. Also, in spite of his unwillingness to pay for extra telephone services, he called the company to request an extension. By exaggerating his predicament dramatically he wangled a promise of immediate installation.

Next he had a strong urge to confide in someone, and he called Arch Riker at the office of the *Moose County Something* even though the full rates were in effect.

"Don't tell Polly," he cautioned Riker when the editor answered, "but I'm sitting here with a sprained ankle, and I had a narrow escape yesterday."

"What fool thing have you been doing?" his old friend asked.

"Taking some pictures of a waterfall that cascades down for about forty feet and disappears into a black hole. I almost disappeared myself. I'm lucky to get out alive. I lost the camera that Polly gave me, and it was full of exposed film."

Riker said, "I knew you were making a mistake by going into those mountains. You should never stray from solid concrete. How bad is the ankle? Did you have it X-rayed?"

"You know I always avoid X rays if possible. I'm using ice packs and some homemade liniment from one of the mountain women."

"How's the weather?"

"Rotten. If it doesn't rain all day, it rains all night. They never told me I was moving to a rain forest."

"Glad to hear it! Now maybe you'll stay indoors and write a piece for us. We need something for Friday. Could you rip something off and get it faxed?"

"The most interesting possibility," Qwilleran said, "is a topic I'm not prepared to cover as yet—the murder that took place here a year ago."

"I hope you're not going to get sidetracked into some kind of unauthorized investigation, Qwill."

"That remains to be seen. The case involves power politics and possibly perjury on a grand scale. I have a hunch that the wrong man was convicted."

Riker groaned. He knew all about Qwilleran's hunches and found it futile to discourage him from following them up. Reluctant to take him seriously, however, he asked, "What does the Inspector General think about the case?"

"Koko is busy doing what cats do. Right now he's rolling on the floor in front of the telephone chest; somehow it turns him on. I'm worried about Yum Yum, though. I may have to take her to the doctor."

"I suppose you heard about Dr. Goodwinter. I saw Dr. Melinda yesterday, and she asked about you. She wanted to know how you are, and she batted her eyelashes a lot."

"What did you tell her?"

"Blood pressure normal; appetite good; weight down a few pounds—"

"How does she look?" Qwilleran interrupted. "Has she changed in three years?"

"No, except for that big-city veneer that's inescapable."

"Does she know about Polly?"

"The entire county knows about Polly," Riker said, "but all's fair in love and war, and I could tell by Melinda's expression that her interest isn't entirely clinical."

"Gotta hang up," Qwilleran said abruptly. "Doorbell's ringing. It's the telephone man. Okay, Arch, I'll send you some copy, but I don't know how good it'll be."

He limped to the door, leaning heavily on his cane and assuming an expression of grueling physical pain.

"Hey, this is some place!" said the installer when he was admitted. He was a wide-eyed, beardless young man not yet bored with his job. "I never saw the inside of

Tiptop before. The boss said you live here alone and hurt your foot. What happened?''

"I sprained an ankle."

"You'd better get off of it."

Wincing appropriately, Qwilleran shuffled into the living room and sprawled on the sofa.

The installer followed him. "You buy this place?"

"No, I'm renting for the summer."

"This is where a guy was killed last year."

"So I've been told," Qwilleran said.

"Used to be a summer hotel for rich people. My grandmother was a cook here, and my grandfather drove a carriage and brought people up from the railroad station. The road wasn't paved then. He used to talk about drivin' people like Henry Ford, Thomas Edison, and Madame Schumann-Heink, whoever she was."

"Famous Austrian opera singer," Qwilleran said. "What did your grandparents do after the inn closed?"

"Moonshinin'!" the installer said with a grin. "Then they opened a diner in the valley and did all right. They served split-brandy in teacups—that's half brandy and half whiskey. The diner's torn down now, but lots of old people remember Lumpton's famous tea."

"Are you a Lumpton?" Qwilleran asked. He had counted forty-seven Goodwinters in the Moose County phone book but twice that many Lumptons in the Spudsboro directory.

"On my mother's side. My cousins own Lumpton's Pizza. Sheriff Lumpton is my godfather. You know him? He was sheriff twenty-four years. Everybody called him Uncle Josh. He always played Santa for the kids at Christmas, and he sure had the belly for it! Still does. But now they have some skinny guy playin' Santa . . . Well, I better get to work. Where d'you want the extension?"

"Upstairs on the desk in the back bedroom," Qwilleran said from his bed of pain. "Can you find it all right?"

"Sure. If you hear it ring, it's just me checkin' it out."

The phone rang a couple of times, and eventually the young man came downstairs. "Okay, you're all set. I left a phone book on the desk. Your big cat's sure a nosey one! Watched everythin' I did. The little one is bitin' herself like she has fleas."

"Thanks for the prompt service," Qwilleran said.

"Take it easy now."

As soon as Qwilleran heard the van drive away, he went upstairs to find Yum Yum. He could now climb one step at a time if he led with his right foot and leaned heavily on his staff. The telephone, he discovered, had been installed on the desk as requested, but in the wrong room. It was in the cats' bedroom, and Koko was being aggressively possessive about it. Yum Yum was on the bed, gnawing at her left flank, and there were small tufts of fur on the bedcover.

Qwilleran brushed Koko unceremoniously aside and called the Wickes Animal Clinic. Dr. John, according to the receptionist, was in surgery, but Dr. Inez had just finished a C-section and could come to the phone in a jiffy.

When Inez answered, he said, "This is Jim Qwilleran, your neighbor at Tiptop. Do you make house calls? Something's very wrong with my cat, and I'm grounded with a sprained ankle."

"What's wrong?" she asked, and when he described Yum Yum's behavior, she said, "I know it looks kinky, but it's not unusual for spayed females. We can give her a shot and dispense some pills. No need to worry. One of us will run up the hill with the little black bag around five o'clock. What happened to your ankle?''

"I slipped on some wet leaves," he explained.

"Will this rain ever stop?" she complained. "The waterfall under our house is running so high, it may wash out our sundeck. See you at five."

Qwilleran babied Yum Yum until she fell asleep and then went to work on copy for the *Moose County Something*: a thousand words on the feud between the environmentalists and the Spudsboro developers.

"What has happened," he asked his Moose County readers, "to give a negative connotation to a constructive word like 'develop'? It means, according to the dictionary, to perfect, to expand, to change from a lesser to a higher state, to mature, to ripen. Yet, a large segment of the population now uses it as a pejorative." He concluded the column by saying, "The civic leaders of Moose County who are campaigning for 'development' should take a hard look at the semantics of a word that sounds so commendable and can be so destructive."

"And now, old boy," he said to Koko, who had been sitting on the desk enjoying the vibrations of the typewriter, "I've got to figure out how to get this stuff faxed. May I use your phone?" He tottered into the cats' room and called the manager of the Five Points Market, saying, "This is Jim Qwilleran at Tiptop. Do you remember me?"

"Sure do!" said the energetic Bill Treacle. "Did you run out of lobster tails?"

"No, but I have a food-related problem. I sprained my ankle yesterday. Do you make deliveries?"

"Not as a rule. What do you need?"

"Some frozen dinners and half a pound of sliced turkey breast from the deli counter and four hot dogs."

"I'm off at six o'clock. I'll deliver them myself if you can wait that long," said Treacle. "I've never seen the inside of Tiptop."

"I can survive until then. If you wish, I'll show you around the premises and even offer you a drink."

"I'll take that! Make it a cold beer."

At that point some twinges in the left ankle reminded Qwilleran that he had been sitting at a desk too long. He sank into his lounge chair, propping both feet on the ottoman, and thought about Moose County . . . about the sunny June days up there . . . about the old doctor's suicide . . . and about Melinda Goodwinter's wicked green eyes and long lashes. Her return to Pickax after three years in Boston had crossed his mind oftener than he cared to admit. Her presence would definitely disturb his comfortable relationship with Polly, who was a loving woman of his own age. Melinda, for her part, had a youthful appeal that he had once found irresistible, and she had a way of asking for what she wanted. To be friends with both of them, to some degree or other, would be ideal, he reflected wistfully, but Pickax was a small town, and Polly was overpossessive. The whole problem would be tidily solved if he decided not to return to Moose County, and that was a distinct possibility, although he had not given it a moment's thought since arriving in the Potatoes.

Reaching for a pad of paper he jotted down some options, commenting on each to faithful Koko, who was loitering sociably. Yum Yum was on the bed, wretchedly nipping at her flanks and tearing out tufts of fur.

Move back to a large city. "Which one? And why? I'm beginning to prefer small towns. Must be getting old."

Buy a newspaper. "Now that I can afford one, I no longer want one. Too bad."

Travel. "Sounds good, but what would I do about you and Yum Yum?" he asked Koko, who blinked and scratched his ear.

Teach journalism. "That's what everyone says I should do, but I'd rather do it than teach it."

Try to get into acting. "I was pretty good when I was in college, and television has increased the opportunities since then."

Build a hotel in Pickax. "God knows it needs a new one! We could go six stories high and call it the Pickax Towers."

He had been so intent on planning the rest of his life that he failed to hear a car pulling into the parking lot, but Koko heard it and raced downstairs. Qwilleran followed, descending the stairs lamely. Through the glass of the French doors he could see the top of an umbrella, ploddingly ascending the twenty-five steps. It reached the veranda, and Qwilleran—sloppily attired, unshaven, and leaning on a cane—recognized the last person in the world he wanted to see.

THIRTEEN

QWILLERAN RECOGNIZED THE hat waiting outside the front door—a large one with a brim like a banking plane—and wished he could slink back upstairs, but it was too late. She had caught sight of him through the glass panes.

"A thousand pardons!" she cried when he opened the door in his grubby condition. "I'm Vonda Dudley Wix. I'm calling at an inopportune time. I should have telephoned first. Do you remember me?"

"Of course." He remembered not only the hat but also the young-old face beneath it and the scarf tied in a perky bow under her chin. "Come in," he said, exaggerating his limp and his facial expressions of agony.

"I won't stay," she said. "Colin told me about your misfortune, and I brought you some of my Chocolate Whoppers to boost your morale." She was holding a paper plate covered with foil.

"Thank you. I need a boost," he said, brightening at the mention of something chocolate. "Will you come in for a cup of coffee?"

"I don't drink coffee," she said as she parked her umbrella on the veranda. "It goes to my head and makes me quite tipsy."

"I don't have tea. How about a glass of apple juice?"

"Oh, feathers! I'll throw discretion to the winds and have coffee," she said airily, "if it isn't too much trouble."

"No trouble—that is, if you don't mind drinking it in the kitchen. My computerized coffeemaker does all the work."

Leaning on his carved walking staff he conducted her slowly to the rear of the house, while she chattered about her last visit to Tiptop, and how it had changed, and what delightful parties the Hawkinfields used to give in the old days.

Qwilleran pressed the button on the coffeemaker (the dial was set permanently at Extra Strong) and unwrapped the cookies: three inches in diameter, an inch thick, and loaded with morsels of chocolate and chunks of walnuts.

"They're a trifle excessive," said his guest, "but that's how my boss liked them. I used to bake them for J.J. once a week." Qwilleran thought, That's why he let her keep on writing that drivel. "This is the first time I've made them since he died," she added.

"I feel flattered." He poured mugs of the black brew.

"Are the rumors true, Mr. Qwilleran?"

"What rumors?"

"That you're going to buy Tiptop and open a bed-and-breakfast?"

"I'm a writer, Ms. Wix. Not an innkeeper. By the way, the cookies are delicious."

"Thank you . . . Oooooh!" Taking her first sip of coffee, she reacted as if it were turpentine. Then, composing herself, she said, "This is the kind of coffee I used to prepare for my late husband. Wilson never drank alcohol or smoked tobacco, but he *adored* strong coffee. The doctor warned him about drinking so much of it, but he wouldn't listen." She sighed deeply. "It was almost a year ago that he had his massive heart attack."

Qwilleran set down his mug and touched his moustache with misgivings. "Was your husband overweight?" he asked hopefully.

"Not at all! I have his picture right here." She rummaged in her handbag and produced a snapshot of a broad-shouldered, muscular man with close-cropped gray hair. "He worked out at the gym faithfully and was never sick a day in his life!" Mrs. Wix found a tissue in her handbag and touched her eyes carefully. "He died not long after J.J. They were business associates, you know."

Qwilleran thought, It would be interesting to know what kind of stress triggered the attack. Shock at the murder of his colleague? Fear for his own life? Anxiety about his financial future? Guilt of some kind? . . . Stalling for time while he formulated a pertinent question, Qwilleran changed the subject. "You spell your name W-i-x, but there's a street downtown spelled W-i-c-k-s and an animal clinic spelled W-i-c-k-e-s. Any connection there?"

"Are you interested in genealogy?" she asked with

sudden animation. "All three names go back to my husband's great-great-grandfather, Hannibal W-i-x-o-m, who settled here in 1812 and operated a grist mill. He had several daughters but only one son, George, who married Abigail Lumpton and earned his living by making furniture. He shortened the name to W-i-x, and some of his descendents became W-i-c-k-s or W-i-c-k-e-s, because they weren't careful about the spelling on county records in those days."

Qwilleran nodded, although his mind was elsewhere.

"Interestingly," she went on, "I've been able to trace families by the name of W-i-x in Vermont, Indiana, and recently Utah. Actually the name originated in England, the family being founded by Gregory W-i-c-k-s-h-a-m, who fought in the War of the Roses. Subsequent branches of the family altered it to W-i-c-k-s-u-m or W-i-x-x-o-m, one of the latter being quite high up in the English court. Don't you find this intriguing?" she asked.

Qwilleran blinked and said, "Yes, indeed. May I fill your cup?"

"Only halfway. It's very strong. But so good!" She adjusted her hat primly.

"That's a handsome hat, Ms. Wix, and you wear it very well. Not every woman could carry it off."

"Thank you. It's supposed to enhance my best profile." She tilted her head coquettishly.

"How long was your husband associated with Hawkinfield?"

"Ever since the beginning of Tiptop Estates. J.J. thought highly of Wilson as a builder and was instrumental in getting him elected to the city council. Of course, my husband knew how to handle him," she said with a sly, conspiratorial smile. "Wilson simply let him have his own way!"

An ideal pair, Qwilleran thought. The quintessential yes man and the quintessential apple polisher.

"May I remove my scarf?" she was asking. "It's a trifle warm."

"By all means. Make yourself comfortable. Are you sure you won't have a cookie?"

She whipped off her scarf with evident relief. "No, I made them expressly for you."

Qwilleran asked casually, "I imagine you and your husband were shocked by Hawkinfield's murder. Where were you when you heard the news?"

"Let me see . . . It was Father's Day. I gave Wilson a present and took him to dinner at the golf club. As soon as we walked into the dining room, the hostess broke the news, and we were so distressed we turned around and went home. J.J. had been my employer and friend for twenty-five years, and he was *so good* to Wilson after we were married!" Ms. Wix removed her hat and mopped her brow with a tissue. "Wilson was one of the pallbearers, and he was supposed to be a state's witness at the trial, but before he could testify, he collapsed—right there in the courtroom—and died on the way to the hospital."

"Were you there?"

"No. It was all over by the time they notified me. A terrible shock! I was under a doctor's care for three days." She was now fanning herself with a brochure from her handbag.

"You say Wilson was supposed to testify for the prosecution. Do you know the nature of his testimony?"

"I think it was about death threats," she said, gasping

a little. "I'm not sure. He didn't want to talk about it. It was all very upsetting to both of us."

"You mean threats that Forest Beechum had made?"

"I think so . . . yes . . . I didn't want to know about it."

"You don't know if they were verbal or written?"

"May I have a glass of water . . . cold?"

While Qwilleran was adding ice cubes to the glass, the Siamese, who had finished napping upstairs, sauntered into the kitchen in search of crumbs. Moving in a ballet of undulating bodies and inter-twining tails, they performed their complex choreography around chair legs and table legs.

"You have . . . three of them?" she asked between sips of water.

"Only two, Koko and Yum Yum."

"I believe . . . I'm seeing double," she said.

"Does the cold water help?" he asked anxiously.

"This coffee . . . I'd better go home." She stood up and quickly sat down again, her face alarmingly flushed. There were droplets of moisture on her brow and chin.

"Are you sure you're all right? Do you want to lie down? Try eating a cookie."

"Just let me . . . get a breath of fresh air," she said. "Where's my hat?" She clapped it on her head at a careless angle, and he assisted her from the kitchen to the veranda as well as he could, considering his own unstable condition. What could he do? To drive her home would be an impossibility. She might have to stay. He might have to call a doctor.

Slowly they moved around the long veranda, Qwilleran limping and leaning on his staff, Vonda walking unsteadily and leaning on Qwilleran. In the past he had served liquor to guests who had shown an adverse reaction, but this was the first time it had happened with coffee. He should have served her fruit juice.

By the time they arrived at the front of the house and at the top of the twenty-five steps, Ms. Wix was breathing normally. Her flush had faded, and she seemed to be in control, even to the extent of straightening her hat.

"I'm all right now," she said, inhaling deeply. "Forgive me for my little spell of nerves."

"No need to apologize," he said. "It was my fault for serving such strong coffee. Are you sure you can drive?" She was searching for car keys in her handbag.

"Oh, yes, I'm perfectly all right now, and I know this road very well."

He watched her drive away. It had stopped raining, and she had forgotten her umbrella—her scarf, too, he later discovered. Returning them would be a good opportunity to ask a few more questions, he thought as he massaged his moustache.

Qwilleran sequestered the cats in the kitchen in preparation for the doctor's visit. Otherwise they would sense the hospital connection and go flying to the farthest corner of the house. As he climbed upstairs awkwardly to shave and dress, he wondered which of the two doctors would respond. He rather hoped for Inez; a woman might have a more comforting way with the sensitive and high-strung Yum Yum. He also wondered if he should consider reducing his consumption of coffee. Polly had urged him to temper its potency, but the sudden demise of Wilson Wix brought the message home.

It was John Wickes who arrived at five-fifteen, a serious-looking man with large eyeglasses and a thoughtful way of speaking. "Having a little trouble?" he asked soothingly.

Qwilleran described Yum Yum's latest aberration.

"Where is she?"

"They're both locked up in the kitchen. Follow me."

They found the Siamese on the kitchen table, guarding the remains of the Chocolate Whoppers—a mound of nuts and chocolate bits. Everything else had been devoured. When the little black bag appeared, however, Yum Yum rose vertically in space and landed on top of a kitchen cabinet. Koko, knowing instinctively that the thermometer and needle were not for him, moved not a whisker.

"Leave her alone," Wickes said quietly. "She'll come down when she's ready."

"Then pull up a chair and let's have some five o'clock refreshment," Qwilleran suggested. "Whiskey? Wine?"

"A little scotch, I think. It's been a busy day: vacationers walking in with sick cats and dogs, the usual patients for vaccinations, ear crops, spaying, etc. . . . plus surgical emergencies. Inez did a caesarean on a pregnant cat today, and I had to do a sex change on a male because of blockage. So . . . yes, I'll have a little scotch—against the weather."

"Do you always have this much rain in the Potatoes?"

"No, it's very unusual and a little frightening," the doctor said, maintaining his unruffled tone of voice. "The river is running so high we've had to sandbag the clinic property, and here on the mountain I'm worried about Lake Batata. It was man-made by damming the Batata Falls, and if the heavy downpour continues, it could burst its bounds and flood the mountainside. Inez and I are ready to evacuate if necessary."

His matter-of-fact comment led Qwilleran to ask, "Are you serious about this, John?"

"Dead serious."

"Who converted the waterfall into a lake?"

"Hawkinfield, about ten or fifteen years ago."

"Did he get permission?"

"I doubt whether he thought it necessary."

"How well did you know him?"

"I bought my lot from him and took care of his dogs. Beyond that I didn't care to go."

Qwilleran said, "I suppose Lucy was one of them."

"The Doberman? She was the last of his dogs. Has she been hanging around?"

"Once she brought me home when I was lost in the woods, for which I was grateful, and another time she came begging for food, although she's as big as a barrel."

"Lucy was always obese. I tried to convince Hawkinfield that he was hurting his dog by overfeeding, but it was useless to try to tell him anything, and it was never wise to oppose him too strongly. He had ways of retaliating."

"Where were you and Inez when you heard about the murder?"

"Where were we?" he mused. "We were spending Father's Day in the valley with our sons and their families. Someone phoned us the news, and it wasn't greeted with much sorrow. John Jr. is the gadfly on the board of education, and my younger son runs the county animal shelter. Hawkinfield persecuted both of them in editorials because they wouldn't dance to his tune. The man was unhinged, but he had power. That's the worst kind."

"I assume you're a native Spud," Qwilleran said.

"I was born in the valley, but we were all Taters originally. My forebears drifted down out of the mountains and adapted to valley environment—and valley mentality." He drained his glass.

Since Yum Yum showed no intention of deserting her perch, Qwilleran poured again. "Vonda Wix gave me a brief rundown on the genealogy of your family."

"Yes, no matter how you spell it, we all stem from a prolific old stud in the fifteenth century. One of his descendents settled here in the early nineteenth and operated a grist mill, chiefly to grind corn for the moonshiners. Making homemade whiskey was traditional among the pioneers as part of family medicine, you know. There's still a little 'midnight farming' being done on Little Potato."

At that moment there were two soft thumps to be heard, and Yum Yum descended from her lofty perch. She walked slowly and sinuously past the kitchen table, each velvet paw touching the floor like a caress. The doctor picked her up gently and began a leisurely examination while crooning to her in some unknown tongue. She was completely under his spell and reacted not at all when her temperature was taken or when the injection went into her flank. "Here are some tablets," he said. "Follow the dosage on the label."

Qwilleran said, "Your bedside manner is admirable, John."

The doctor shrugged off the compliment with his eyebrows and a flicker of a smile. "How's your ankle, Qwill?"

"On the mend somewhat. I appreciate your coming up here, though."

"Glad to do it. Come down the hill and have a drink with us Sunday afternoon, if our house hasn't washed away."

The Siamese followed the doctor to the door as if reluctant to see him go.

"Our next visitor," Qwilleran told them, "comes bearing turkey, so treat him with diplomacy. But don't expect any dinner from me after stuffing yourselves with my Chocolate Whoppers!"

While they waited for Bill Treacle, Sabrina Peel called to say she had some floor pillows for the living room.

Might she drop them off the next afternoon? She would like to arrive late and then take Qwilleran to dinner at the restaurant called Pasta Perfect.

"You'll have to drive," he said. "I've sprained my ankle."

"Hope you don't object to sharing a town wagon with drapery samples and wallpaper books."

Shortly after six o'clock a car pulled into the parking lot and a smiling Bill Treacle—still exuding pep after an eight-hour shift at the market—appeared at the door with two sacks of groceries. "Hey, you weren't lying!" he said when he saw Qwilleran hobbling with the aid of a stick. "Want me to put this stuff in the refrigerator? Some of it should go in the freezer right away. Okay?"

"First door on the left," Qwilleran instructed him, pointing down the foyer, "and while you're there, help yourself to a beer. You can bring me a ginger ale. We'll sit in the living room."

"This is some barn of a place," the young grocer observed as he started down the hall. When he returned with the drinks he was accompanied by the Siamese, walking beside him like an honor guard, their tails rigidly at attention.

"Friendly brutes, aren't they?" he said.

"Cats are instinctively attracted to a source of energy," Qwilleran explained. "Have a chair, and excuse me if I keep my foot elevated."

"What happened to it?"

"I slipped on some wet leaves."

"There's plenty of those around. I never saw so much rain in June. Let me know if there's anything I can do for you while you're laid up. Okay?"

Qwilleran seized his cue. "There's one thing you could do, Bill. I noticed that Lumpton's Hardware has fax service, and if you'll take some copy and shoot it through tomorrow, I'll be grateful. It's a column I write for my hometown newspaper, and they want to run it Friday."

"Is that your job? Everybody's been wondering who you are and why you're here."

That was another cue. "One reason I'm here is to write a biography of J.J. Hawkinfield."

"No kidding! I didn't know he was that important. I can tell you a few things about the Old Buzzard if you want to know. I used to work for him at the *Gazette*."

"How was he as a boss?"

"Unbelievable! If there was a mistake made, he'd come storming into the production department or newsroom and yell, 'Who's responsible for this stupid error?' And he'd fire somebody on the spot, or else rage around the department and sweep everything off the desks and dump files out on the floor. He was really nuts!"

"Do you know the Beechums?"

"Sure do! Do you know about Forest and the trial? Have you met Chrys? I used to date her before all this happened. Now Forest is locked up without being guilty; their mother has stopped talking; and Chrys has turned off about everything. Bad news all the way around."

"Are you the one who printed handbills for Forest?"

"Maybe it wasn't the smartest thing to do—okay?—but nobody was cooperating, and I had to help somehow. He was a hundred percent right about what was happening to Big Potato. So, being in charge of job printing at the *Gazette*, I ran off a few flyers between orders. The Old Buzzard caught up with me and not only canned me but blackballed me wherever I applied for another job. But I got back at him!" Treacle said with a grin. "I knew the hospital spent a lot of money to print forms and booklets. They were giving the *Gazette* jobbing shop $20,000 of business a year. Okay? So I showed the hospital auxiliary how they could set up their own print shop and do the work with volunteers.''

Qwilleran asked, ''How did Hawkinfield react?''

''They say he nearly busted a blood vessel. It turned out to be a break for me, too. A guy on the hospital board of commissioners owns Five Points Market, and he was so impressed he gave me this job. So that was another kick in the head for the Old Buzzard . . . Hey, the cats kinda like me, don't they?''

Koko and Yum Yum were being sociable as cats do when they have an ulterior motive—sniffing shoelaces, rubbing ankles, purring throatily. They knew he was a grocer and not a printer. He also happened to be sitting in Yum Yum's favorite chair.

Qwilleran said, ''If Forest is innocent, it means the real criminal is free and possibly walking around Spudsboro. Have you thought of that?''

''Yeah, but nobody's ever gonna do anything about it. The public wanted a quick conviction—okay? And they wanted to hang a Tater—okay? The judge and the prosecutor were both coming up for reelection, so what have you got? A beautiful frame-up.''

''How do you explain this prejudice against Taters?''

''Don't ask me! When the first settlers came to the Potatoes, there were Indians here, and it was whites against redskins. Now it's valley whites against mountain whites.''

''Did you attend the trial?''

''Sure did. I took time off from my job. I sat with the Beechums.''

''Were you in the courtroom when Wilson Wix collapsed?''

''He dropped dead right in front of me! He was a Hawksman, you know. That's what they called the Old Buzzard's cronies on the council, zoning board, school board, and all that. Wix was a nice guy, but he was a Hawksman.''

"Do you remember the day Hawkinfield was murdered?" Qwilleran asked.

"Sure do. My sister and I were taking our parents out to dinner for Father's Day—okay? First I drove them up to the top of Big Potato, like my dad used to do when we were kids, before the waterfall was dammed. When we got to the top there were a couple of cars in the Tiptop parking lot, and we heard a dog howling, so we turned around and drove down again.''

"What time was it?"

"Two o'clock, I'm pretty sure, because we had a reservation at The Great Big Baked Potato for two-thirty. Later on, after we found out what happened, I remembered the dog was howling like the Old Buzzard was already dead. So what were those two cars doing in the parking lot? . . . Anyway, after Forest was arrested and charged, I went to his attorney with this information. I didn't have a description of the cars or license numbers. All I knew was that neither of them was the Beechum jalopy, and maybe I could testify to that. He told me I was a known accomplice of Forest and had been fired for dishonesty, so any testimony from me would do more harm than good. That's what he told me.''

"You're referring to Hugh Lumpton?" Qwilleran asked. "Did he do a conscientious job of defending Forest in your opinion?"

"That guy? He did a lousy job! I could've done better myself. In the first place, the county doesn't pay much when they assign a lawyer. In the second place, he's a Spud and he plays golf with the prosecutor. The whole thing was a joke, only it wasn't funny. At the end, all

Lumpton said to the jury was that the prosecution hadn't proved their case. The jury wasn't out long enough to get a cup of coffee, and when they came back with a guilty verdict, I was ready to commit murder myself!''

"I'm curious about the Lumptons. I see the name everywhere."

"Yeah, you can't spit without hitting a Lumpton. They're in pizza, furniture, hardware, everything. They've been here for generations. Some moved to the valley and made good, and some are still Taters. For a long time we had a popular sheriff who was a Lumpton. He was jolly and sort of easygoing. Who says cops have to go around looking fierce and rattling handcuffs? Josh Lumpton was too independent for the Old Buzzard, and he finally got him defeated. Now the sheriff is a guy named Wilbank.''

"Did Wilbank take the stand at the trial?'' Qwilleran asked.

"Yeah, he told how Sherry Hawkinfield came running down the hill to his house and said her dad was missing, and how they found the body at the foot of the cliff, and how the front hall was wrecked. The worst was Sherry's testimony— a bare-faced lie! How can they get away with that? It was her word against a Tater's, so you know who they believed. And then there were other trumped-up lies.''

"I heard something about a death threat.''

"Are you kidding? Forest wouldn't be stupid enough to send an anonymous threat through the mail!''

"Was it produced as evidence?''

"No, that was another fishy thing. It had disappeared, although Robert Lessmore testified he'd seen it.''

"This is all very interesting,'' Qwilleran said. "How about another beer?''

"Thanks, but I'm bowling tonight. Just give me the

papers you want faxed, and I hope your ankle gets better soon—okay?''

Bill Treacle left, and Qwilleran relented and gave the Siamese some turkey for their good behavior. For his own dinner he thawed some beef pepper steak. As he ate his meal at the kitchen table, Koko sat on a chair opposite with his chin barely clearing the edge of the table, his bright eyes watching every move intently.

"Don't just sit there looking omniscient," Qwilleran said to him. "Come up with an idea. What do we do next?"

With a grunt Koko jumped from the chair and ran from the kitchen. His exodus was so abrupt, so urgent, that Qwilleran limped after him, first taking care to cover his plate of beef. He found the cat rolling on the carpet at the foot of the telephone chest, stretching to his full length and muttering to himself.

Qwilleran placed his hand on the telephone. "Do you want me to make a call?" he asked. "Are you on the phone company's payroll?"

Koko scrambled to his feet and raced wildly about the foyer while Qwilleran called Osmond Hasselrich at his home in Pickax. It was his first contact with the attorney since leaving Moose County, and they had a long conversation.

As later events indicated, that was probably not what Koko wanted at all.

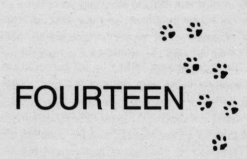

FOURTEEN

ON THURSDAY MORNING the trees were still dripping, but the sun shone intermittently and Qwilleran's ankle was gradually responding to treatment. Drinking his breakfast coffee in the kitchen he recalled how his conversations with the friendly telephone installer, the saturnine veterinarian, the flaky *Gazette* columnist, and the overly energetic grocer had left him with no answers, only conjectures. He guessed that the "death threat" was not received by Hawkinfield in his lifetime but was forged following his murder and shown to Robert Lessmore (a golf buddy of the prosecutor), who thereby testified to seeing such a document, overlooking the discrepancy in timing. Meanwhile, it had been conveniently destroyed by the same hand or hands that forged it. If the instruments of law and order in Spudsboro were as corrupt as Treacle intimated, a veritable network of collaborators could be involved in the frame-up of a Tater, including Sherry Hawkinfield, and all of this was done to protect the actual perpetrators of the crime, there being more than one, Qwilleran surmised.

It occurred to him that Wilson Wix may have been enlisted against his better judgment, and the stress of committing what he knew to be perjury triggered his heart attack. One could not lay the whole blame on caffeine. Qwilleran poured a third cup.

He had a strong urge to visit the Old Buzzard's office once more in search of clues if not answers. The obstacle was the heavy desk concealing the door. Then Dewey Beechum arrived to work on the gazebo, and the problem was solved. The dampness of the season had caused his historic hat to grow moss, and his beard was curling and looking wilder than ever.

Qwilleran called to him from the veranda and beckoned him up the steps. "It's hard for me to leave the house," he explained to the carpenter. "I've hurt my ankle. How's the job progressing? It's impossible to see from here."

"Finish up today, like as not. Built the screens in my barn. Aimin' to save time."

"Good idea! I'll be around here all day. Just add up your bill, and I'll write you a check. Do you think we're going to have any flood damage?"

"Iffen it don't stop rainin'."

"We could use a few hours of sunshine and a little

breeze to dry things up," said Qwilleran, who had learned the banal art of weatherspeak in Moose County.

Beechum gave a sour look upward, perhaps searching for a black snake in a tree. "Won't git it," he pronounced.

Having disposed of the amenities, Qwilleran explained his problem. The workman nodded and followed him into the house, trudged through the living room without looking to right or left, lifted the bookcase off the base with ease, pulled the desk away from the wall without asking any questions, and returned to his work on the gazebo.

Taters were strong, silent types, Qwilleran reflected. They worked hard, lived long lives, never worried about being overweight, and did a little midnight farming as a hobby.

Koko was delighted to see the office open again. He immediately went in to sniff Lucy's mattress. Yum Yum, on the other hand, was sleeping off her medication on a down-cushioned chair in the living room. It was the one chair that was more comfortable than all the rest, and with true feline instinct she had commandeered it.

There was something in Hawkinfield's office that Qwilleran expressly wished to examine: a family photograph hanging on the wall. Seated in the center of the group was J.J. with his lofty brow and "important" nose, obviously the master of the house. Standing behind him were three bright-looking boys of graduated heights, and on either side were seated a pretty woman with a shy smile and a teenage girl with a sullen pout. She had the Hawkinfield nose and an exaggerated overbite. Was this the Sherry Hawkinfield, Qwilleran wondered, that he had invited to dinner? He could only hope she had improved with age.

Sprawling in J.J.'s lounge chair and propping his ankle on J.J.'s ottoman, he delved into another of the editor's scrapbooks and read attacks on the county animal shelter, Mother's Day, and the high school football coach. It was prose written by a madman with a passion for exclamation points. In one tirade he aimed his barbs at a sheriff who was running for reelection. This candidate, Hawkinfield pointed out, was three months in arrears on his water bill, regularly had his wife's parking tickets voided, and at one time succeeded in hushing up his own felonious bad-check charge. No name was mentioned, but even a stranger in the Potatoes like Qwilleran could guess that it was Uncle Josh Lumpton, who forthwith lost his post to Del Wilbank.

Koko, tired of sniffing Lucy's mattress and the law books on the shelf, suddenly landed on the desktop with whiskers twitching and paws digging. He wanted desperately to get into the center drawer, the shallow one that is usually a catchall. Qwilleran obliged him, having an avid curiosity of his own. In the compartments at the front of the drawer there were pencils, pens, paper clips, rubber bands, a few pennies, three cigarettes in a squashed pack, two large screws, and one stray postage stamp. Koko pounced on the stamp and carried it away to sniff and lick in some dark corner. Now how did that cat know it was there? Qwilleran asked himself.

At the rear of the drawer the miscellaneous papers and file folders included a large yellow legal pad on which Hawkinfield apparently drafted his editorials in longhand, using a soft lead pencil. The one on the pad was datelined two days after Father's Day of the previous year. It had never been published and had never journeyed beyond the center drawer of Hawkinfield's desk, but before Qwilleran could read it, the doorbell rang.

Beechum had finished the gazebo and was coming to

collect payment. Qwilleran knew it was rash to pay for the work without inspecting it, but he trusted the man and even added a bonus for prompt service. He then asked the carpenter to move the desk back against the office door—but not before he had retrieved the yellow legal pad. After that it was time to shave and dress for dinner with Sabrina Peel, and Qwilleran transferred the pad to his own desk upstairs.

When Sabrina arrived she brought two pillows in bright red and gold, each a yard square, to stack on the living room floor between two windows. "I think they make the statement we want," she said. "They balance the color accents and add some desirable weight at that end of the room . . . How's the ankle, Qwill?"

"The Pain-and-Anguish Scale went down sixteen points when you walked in," he said, admiring the misty green silk dress that complemented her decorator-blond hair. "Shall we have a drink before we leave?"

"Mmmm . . . no," she said. "I've requested a choice booth, and they won't hold a reservation more than fifteen minutes. I hope you don't object to the no-smoking section . . . Where did you find that fabulous burl bowl? At Potato Cove? . . . I see you need candles. I could have brought you some."

"I have plenty," he said. "The candle dipper sold me a lifetime supply, but I haven't found time to stick them in the candleholder . . . Let me check out the Siamese before we leave."

The two cats were exactly where he thought they would be—perched on top of the new floor pillows, looking haughty and possessive, their cold blue eyes challenging anyone to dethrone them.

With Qwilleran taking one experimental step at a time, he and Sabrina walked slowly down the long flight to the parking lot.

"Do you mind living alone?" she asked.

"I've tried it both ways," he replied, "and I know it can be a letdown to come home to an empty apartment, but now I have the Siamese to greet me at the door. They're good companions; they need me; they're always happy to see me come home. On the other hand, they're always glad to see me go out—one of the things that cats do to keep a person from feeling too important."

On the way down Hawk's Nest Drive she pointed out clients' houses. She had helped the Wilbanks select their wallpapers . . . Peel & Poole was redesigning the entire interior for the Lessmores . . . Her partner had done the windows and floors for the Wickes house.

"Are you the only design studio in town?" Qwilleran asked her slyly.

"The only good one," she retorted, flashing an arch smile at her passenger. "I'd give anything to get my hands on Tiptop and do it over, inside and out."

"Would you kill for it?"

He expected a flip reply, but Sabrina was concentrating on traffic at the foot of the drive and she ignored the remark.

They turned onto a road that roughly paralleled the overflowing banks of the Yellyhoo River and then led into the foothills where the restaurant called Pasta Perfect occupied a dimple in the landscape. It was a rustic roadhouse that appeared ready to collapse.

Qwilleran said, "In the flat country where I live, this place would look like a dump, but in the mountains even the dumps look picturesque."

"It was a challenge to blend its dumpishness with an appetizing interior," Sabrina admitted. "The owners wanted a shirt-sleeve ambiance that looked and felt *clean*, so I had the old wood floors refinished to look like old wood floors, left the posts and beams in their original dark stain, and painted the wall spaces white to emphasize all the cracks and knots and wormholes."

The restaurant was a rambling layout of small rooms that had been added throughout the years, and Sabrina and her guest were seated in the Chief Batata Room, where high-backed booths provided privacy as well as a mountain view through panels of plate glass. The focal point of the room was a painted portrait of an Indian chief smoking a peace pipe.

Sabrina said, "I want you to look at this staggering menu, Qwill. The fifteen kinds of pasta and all the sauces are house-made, fresh daily." For an appetizer he ordered smoked salmon and avocado rolled in lasagna noodles, with a sauce of watercress, dill, and horseradish. Sabrina chose trout quenelles on a bed of black beans with Cajun hollandaise—and a bottle of Orvieto wine.

"How are you enjoying your vacation?" she asked.

"So far, it's been nothing but rain and minor calamities, but let's not talk about that. What do you know about the Fitzwallow huntboard?"

"J.J. bought it at an auction, claiming there was a Fitzwallow in his ancestry. It's a monstrous thing, and his wife hated it."

"My cat has taken a fancy to it," Qwilleran said. "If he isn't jumping on top of it, he's rolling on the floor at the base. I think he has some Fitzwallow blood himself. One thing I wouldn't mind owning, though, is Forest Beechum's painting. What is it worth?"

"It's definitely worth $3,000, Qwill. As an artist he's an unknown, but it's good, and it's big! He did this painting of Chief Batata, too. I thought it would be amusing in the no-smoking room, but I'm afraid no one gets the joke. I suppose you're an ex-smoker like the rest of us."

"I used to smoke a pipe, thinking I looked thoughtful and wise while puffing. Also, re-lighting it filled in lengthy pauses when I didn't know what to say. Now I have to sit and twiddle my thumbs and look empty-headed."

"Qwill, I can't imagine you ever looking empty-headed. What do you do, anyway? There's been a lot of speculation in the valley."

"I'm a wandering writer, searching for a subject, and I think I've found it. I want to write a biography of J.J. Hawkinfield. He was a large, power-mad frog in a small puddle, with a bombastic style of writing, a penchant for making enemies, and a succession of family sorrows ending in his own murder. It's the Greek tragedy of the Potato Mountains! It calls for a Greek chorus of Taters and Spuds!"

"Will it be a whitewash?" she asked. "Or are you going to paint him warts and all?"

"Being a journalist by profession, I'm especially interested in the warts."

"Do you think you can get people to talk?"

"The public," Qwilleran said, "is immensely fond of talking to authors—especially about someone who's dead and can't lash back. I may start with ex-sheriff Lumpton."

Sabrina laughed. "That freeloader! Don't believe a word you get from Uncle Josh."

"What do you know about him?"

"Well, he and J.J. were feuding for years. He's in the trucking business now, and he's building an enormously expensive house. We're doing the interior with a no-limit budget."

"Trucking logs out of the mountains must be lucrative," Qwilleran commented.

"According to conventional wisdom, Uncle Josh was stashing the money away in a coffee can buried in his backyard all the time he was sheriff."

The waiter brought the antipasto on very cold plates, followed by the entrees on very hot plates. Having ordered tagliatelle in a sauce of ricotta, leeks, and ham, Qwilleran twirled his fork in rapt appreciation for a while. Eventually he asked, "Who is this partner you're always mentioning?"

"Spencer Poole. He's an older man and a wonderful person. When I was in high school he gave me a summer job, folding samples and keeping the studio dusted. After I graduated from design school, he took me into the firm because he liked the sound of Peel & Poole."

Uh-huh, Qwilleran thought, grooming his moustache. It was more likely because she's a stunning young woman.

Sabrina said, "I told him it should be Poole & Peel, since he's the senior partner, but he pointed out the importance of vowel sounds in the name of a design studio. He said 'ee-oo' has more class than 'oo-ee,' which is associated with hog calling. Spencer is fussy about details, but that's what makes him a terrific designer. He's taught me a lot," she said, her eyes sparkling. They were green tonight; a few days ago they were blue.

"With a name like Peel, you must be Scottish," he remarked. "My mother was a Mackintosh."

"Say something in Scots," she said teasingly.

"Mony a mickle mak' a muckle," he recited.

"Many small things make a large thing," she guessed.

"That's its popular meaning, although the dictionary defines mickle and muckle as synonyms. George Washington used the expression in the popular sense, however, and if it's good enough for the Father of our Country, it's good enough for me."

"My partner would love the sound of it," she said.

Speaking seriously in a lower voice, Qwilleran said, "Your partner seems like an astute individual. Does he have any idea who really killed Hawkinfield? The man's enemies are easy to identify; the ones who arouse my suspicion are his so-called friends."

Sabrina put down her fork and stared at him. "Well," she said hesitantly, "when it first happened . . . Spencer thought it might be the husband of J.J.'s girlfriend. But now I guess there's no doubt it was Beechum."

Qwilleran stroked his moustache. "Hawkinfield had a girlfriend? Was it well-known?"

"This is a very small town, Qwill. It was well-known but not talked about. She worked at the *Gazette*—still does, in fact—and she thought J.J. walked on water. That's the kind of woman he liked. She used to bake cookies for him all the time, and he called her Cookie, even around the office. Everyone knows he paid for her face-lift."

"But she had a husband?"

"Not until a few years ago. She married a run-of-the-mill house builder who immediately landed the contract for all the houses on Big Potato, and he turned out to be a real Hawksman."

"Did he know about his wife's connection with Hawkinfield?"

"Who knows? He was a simple soul—sort of a male Pollyanna. We all liked him when we worked with him on interiors. He had a massive heart attack and died . . . Don't quote me on any of this.''

When dessert was served—almond ravioli with raspberry sauce—Qwilleran returned to the subject of the biography. He said, ''In doing my research I'd like to explore Hawkinfield's relationship with his children—just for background information, so that I feel comfortable with my subject.''

''Yes, I can understand that,'' she said. ''The three boys were the center of his universe, you know, and they were really bright kids, but J.J. neglected his daughter because she had the misfortune to be female. He gave the boys bikes, skis, golf lessons, even private tutoring. Sherry got piano lessons, which she hated.''

''How did she feel about her father?''

''Not enthusiastic! She referred to him flippantly as her male parent and scorned her mother for being weak. When I was doing the interior of Tiptop, Sherry latched onto me as a sort of role model. That's how she acquired an interest in selling decorative accessories.''

''Was she as smart as her brothers?''

''She was shrewd, rather than book smart—even devious,'' Sabrina said. ''I think her second-class standing in the family slanted her that way; she had to look out for Sherry. And now that she's in business for herself, that's not a bad quality to have.''

''I saw a family photograph,'' Qwilleran said, ''and she looked like an unhappy girl—certainly unattractive.''

''Yes, her teeth needed attention, and she desperately wanted a nose job, but J.J. considered that an extravagance. Fortunately, her maternal grandmother left her some money, so she was able to have orthodontal work and esthetic surgery. What a difference! Her personality

blossomed, and she became quite popular. In fact . . .''
Sabrina glanced around the room and dropped her voice,
''her father sent her away to school because she was dating
a Lumpton boy—a really good-looking kid. Two years
later, after graduating from her school in Virginia, she
sneaked off and married him.''

''I'll bet there were fireworks on Big Potato when that
happened,'' Qwilleran said.

''Were there ever! J.J. was sure the boy just wanted to
marry an heiress and get into a 'good' family. You see,
he was the son of the infamous Josh Lumpton! So Sherry
was given a choice: annulment or disinheritance. She was
no fool; she opted to stay in her father's will, thinking
she'd inherit millions. Actually, all she got was Tiptop.
The rest is in trust for her mother.''

''What happened to Josh Lumpton's son?''

''He and Sherry are still close. They'll probably marry
when she sells the inn and gets her million plus. He went
on to law school and passed the bar, although he doesn't
have much of a practice. He'd rather play golf . . . Are
you interested in all this small-town gossip?'' she asked.

''I live in a small town,'' he said, ''where gossip is the
staff of life. I live in a barn.'' He told her about his converted apple barn with its balconies and tapestries and
contemporary furnishings.

''It sounds fabulous! I'd love to see it,'' she said.

There was no lingering over the espresso. Thunder
storms were gathering, according to the local weathercast,
and Sabrina wanted to be home before the deluge. ''Driving in the mountains is spooky during an electrical storm,''
she told Qwilleran as she drove him home. ''By the way,
did you find the letter I lost?''

''Yes, I did,'' he replied without revealing that it was

still languishing in a drawer of the huntboard. "It was in the house. I found it on the floor. If you'd lost it outdoors, it would have been rain-soaked, I'm afraid."

"I'm fed up with these storms," she said. "Basements are flooding on Center Street, and a bridge washed out downriver." She declined his offer of a nightcap. "Some other time. Meanwhile, if you decide to buy Tiptop—"

"You'll be the first to know, Sabrina," he promised. "Perhaps we can have dinner again soon—my treat."

"Perhaps," she said with a glance he was unable to interpret.

Qwilleran walked slowly and carefully up the twenty-five steps to Tiptop, thinking, She's a charming woman, interesting, very friendly . . . probably in her middle thirties . . . seems to live alone . . . an acquaintance worth cultivating. Then he thought, What could she do with Tiptop? It wouldn't hurt to ask for a design proposal and an estimate . . . Her eyes looked green tonight. I thought they were blue . . . What's her relationship with Spencer Poole? She has an enormously warm regard for him. Mentions him often . . . .

He unlocked the door, expecting a greeting from two excited cats with tails held high. It was always dark in the foyer, day or night, and he switched on the lights, but no pale fur bodies emerged from the gloom. Nor were there any welcoming yowls. Instead, he heard human voices upstairs.

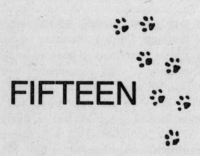

FIFTEEN

WHEN QWILLERAN WALKED into the house and heard muffled voices upstairs, he instinctively looked around for a weapon before realizing he had a formidable one in his left hand. Brandishing the carved walking staff, which had the heft of a cudgel, and forgetting to limp, he started up the stairs two at a time. Halfway up he stopped.

He heard a man's voice saying, "Well, thanks for being with us, Bob; good luck at the tourney . . . and now a look at the weather . . ."

Qwilleran finished the flight of stairs at a slower pace and found the cats on his desk: Koko lounging sphinx-like on the yellow legal pad and Yum Yum lounging sphinx-like on the radio, the controls of which were unwisely located on top. Neither of them stirred; both regarded him with infuriating complacency.

"You rascals!" he said after counting to ten. "Why didn't you tune in some good music?"

Only then did he realize he was walking without pain. Filled with immediate ambition he busied himself with activities neglected in the last few days: putting candles in the eight-branch candelabrum, throwing the baker's white duck uniform into the washer, writing a thank-you note to Mrs. Beechum with a testimonial for her homemade lini-ment. The storm roared in on schedule—with crashing thunder, flashing lightning, and pounding rain, and the Siamese were glad to huddle in Qwilleran's bedroom and listen to a chapter of *The Magic Mountain*. He had to shout to be heard above the tumult outdoors. When he tuned in the eleven o'clock news, flood warnings were in effect.

The next morning he opened his eyes and rotated his left foot painlessly; his elation knew no bounds. He was ready to plunge into the bogus research for the biography he had no intention of writing! He was eager to drive again after being grounded for three days. When he raised the blinds in the bedroom, however, the view from the win-dow suggested that Tiptop was flying through a cloudbank at an altitude of 35,000 feet. Furthermore, the meteorol-ogist on the radio predicted dense fog on the mountains until late afternoon, with heavy humidity. The flood warn-ing had been changed to flood watch after last night's rain.

Qwilleran stepped out onto the veranda and inhaled the moist smells of fog and drenched treebark, noting that only three of the twenty-five steps to the parking lot were visible; the rest were shrouded in mist. Sherry Hawkin-field's plane would never be able to land, he told himself.

Indoors he warmed a sticky bun in the oven, but his fingers faltered over the controls on the coffeemaker: Extra Strong or merely Strong? Three cups or two? Remembering the fate of Wilson Wix, he opted for moderation. Then he fed the cats and watched them gulp and gobble with jerking of heads and swaying of tails. In his earlier days he would have had neither the time nor the inclination to watch animals eat. In many ways Qwilleran had changed since Kao K'o Kung came to live with him.

After he had showered and shaved and dressed, he again checked the veranda; there were now four steps visible. He went upstairs and made a pretense of straightening his bed; housekeeping was not one of his strong points. Koko was back on the desk, sitting on the legal pad.

"Let me see that thing," Qwilleran said.

It was the editorial that Hawkinfield had written before he died, intending to run it the following week, and it brought a tremor to Qwilleran's upper lip. Rushing into the cats' room to use their phone, he called the editor of the *Gazette*.

He said, "Colin, I want to start my research on the Hawkinfield bio by interviewing Josh Lumpton. Can you break the ice for me and give me a good reference? Don't mention my book on crime."

"How soon do you want to see him?"

"This morning. Immediately."

"Sounds as if the ankle is okay and you're rarin' to go. How's the fog on the mountain? It's not too bad down here. The airport's still open. But the river's raging."

"The fog is dense, but I can get through. Where is Lumpton's place of business?"

"South of town on the Yellyhoo, half a mile beyond the city limits—that is, if he isn't flooded out. If I don't call you back in five minutes, it means he's still high and dry and willing to see you. He's an agreeable guy."

There was no return call. When Qwilleran ventured down the steps, the mist swirled about him. When he drove down Hawk's Nest with fog lights on, nothing was visible except a few feet of yellow line on the pavement. Houses had disappeared in the whiteout, but he could tell their location by counting the hairpin turns. At the foot of the drive the visibility improved, however, and he dropped Sabrina's letter to Sherry Hawkinfield in a mailbox.

South of Spudsboro the flooding had almost reached the pavement, and the ramshackle Yellyhoo Market had virtually washed away. Truckloads of sandbags were traveling toward the downtown area where banks, stores, and offices could not afford to wash away. Lumpton Transport was located safely on higher ground—a fenced parking lot for truck cabs, trailers, flatbeds, refrigerated trucks, tankers, and moving vans. There was no name on the headquarters building, but an oversized sign painted on its concrete-block front shouted: YOU GOT IT? WE MOVE IT.

The receptionist conducted Qwilleran into the boss's private office, a plain room with a large girly-type wall calendar as the sole decoration. There, surrounded by a bank of computers, was a jolly mountain of flesh in khaki chinos, seated regally in a huge chair. His pudgy face was wreathed in smiling folds of fat.

"Come on in," he called out affably. "Sit you down. Colin said you were comin' over. What's the name again?"

"Qwilleran. Jim Qwilleran spelled with a QW." He leaned across the desk to shake hands.

"Want some coffee? . . . Susie, bring some coffee!"

the booming voice shouted in the direction of the door. "How d'you like our weather? Colin says you're stayin' at Tiptop."

"It's much wetter than I expected. Did you ever see it as bad as this?"

"Only once. In 1963. The Yellyhoo looked like the Mississippi, and Batata Falls looked like Niagara. I don't worry about the river reachin' us here, but if the county has to close South Highway, we're out of business."

The coffee arrived in heavy china mugs decorated with dubious witticisms, the boss's mug bearing the good-natured message: "I'm Fat But You're Ugly." "How about a jigger of corn to liven it up?" he suggested with his great, hospitable smile.

"No, thanks. I like my coffee straight."

"So you're gonna write a book about my old buddy! Great fella! Smart as the dickens! Never be another like him! But he was jinxed—had one stroke of bad luck after another."

Qwilleran wondered, Was it bad luck or was it calculated retaliation? He asked, "Didn't Hawkinfield make a lot of enemies with his outspoken editorials?"

"Nah. Nobody took that stuff serious. He was okay. Did a whole lot of good for the community. Everybody liked him."

"How long were you sheriff?"

"Twenty-four years!" Lumpton patted his bulging stomach with pride.

"That's an illustrious record! Everyone talks about you."

"My constituents been bendin' your ear? Hope they didn't tattle too much." He wheezed a husky chuckle.

Genially Qwilleran asked, "Should I infer that you're covering up a few secrets?"

The trucker gave him a sharp look before chuckling again with the aplomb of a seasoned politician.

Qwilleran continued: "How did you feel about losing your last campaign for office, Mr. Lumpton?"

"Didn't waste no tears over that. Twenty-four years of bein' a public servant is long enough! It was time I got out—and started makin' some money." He gestured toward his computers.

"But wasn't J.J. responsible for your losing the election?"

"Hell, no! I just didn't feel like campaignin'."

"Do you think Wilbank's a worthy successor?"

"He's okay. He's doin' a good job. Got a lot to learn, but . . . sure, he's okay. Me, I know the county inside out. I know every man, woman, and child in the Potatoes."

"How many of them are Lumptons?"

"Plenty! And I did my part—four sons, three daughters, five grandkids." The trucker was leaning back in his big chair, swiveling, and enjoying the interview.

Qwilleran switched his approach from amiable to serious. "If Hawkinfield was so well liked, why was he murdered?"

"You don't know the story? There was this nutty young fella on Li'l Tater—a real troublemaker. He had some kind of crazy grudge against J.J.—even threatened to kill him. J.J. paid no attention. I guess editors get letters from cranks all the time. But . . . it finally happened. The kid just blew his stack."

"Wasn't it your son who represented him at the trial?"

Lumpton nodded. "Court-appointed. They all take a few cases like that."

"I hear the trial was remarkably brief."

"Sure was! Our judicial system at its best! Everybody doin' his job and doin' it well! That way, it didn't cost the county a whole lot of money. A long jury trial can wreck a county's budget for the year!"

"But wasn't there radically conflicting testimony?" Qwilleran asked.

"Sure, the defendant pleaded not guilty and told some cock-and-bull stories, but you can't believe them Taters."

"What do you know about Hawkinfield's daughter? She seems to be the last of the family."

"Don't know her. Knew the three boys that got killed. Don't know the daughter."

"I believe she's the one who was married to your son briefly."

Lumpton frowned. "Guess so. They weren't married long enough to notice."

"Also, she's the one who gave the incriminating testimony at the trial."

"Oh, her! She doesn't live around here."

Qwilleran gazed at his subject with a cool eye and paused before saying in a deeper voice, "Who really killed Hawkinfield, Mr. Lumpton?"

The big man's eyes popped. "Did I hear you right?"

"You certainly did! There are rumors in the valley that they convicted the wrong man."

"Somebody's crazy! If there's any rumors in this county, I start 'em. Whatcha gettin' at, anyway? You ask a lotta questions. Are you one of them investigative reporters?"

"I'm an author trying to get a handle on my subject matter," Qwilleran said, softening his approach. "No one can write a biography without asking questions. Since you were in law enforcement for twenty-four years—and know everyone in the county—I thought you might have a lurking suspicion as to the real motive for Hawkinfield's murder.''

"Look here," said the trucker, standing up and losing his official smile. He was a mountain of a man, Qwilleran realized. "Look here, I'm busy. I don't have time to listen to this—"

"Sorry, Mr. Lumpton. I won't take any more of your time. Sherry Hawkinfield will be here this weekend, and I'll get her to fill in some of the blanks." He was on his feet and edging out of the office. "One more question: Exactly what is the Hot Potato Fund?"

"Never heard of it!" The trucker was lunging around the end of his desk in a manner that hastened Qwilleran's departure.

"Thank you, Mr. Lumpton," he called out from the hallway.

He drove directly to the office of the *Gazette*. Downtown Spudsboro was misty, but the mountains had disappeared in the fog. When he entered Colin Carmichael's office he was carrying a plastic sack from the Five Points Market.

"Qwill! You're walking like Homo sapiens instead of an arthritic bear," the editor greeted him.

"I see you're sandbagging the building," Qwilleran observed.

"We're also moving our microfilm out of the basement. Did you see Uncle Josh?"

"Yes, he was ready to talk, but he disliked some of my questions . . . May I close the door?" he asked before sitting down. "First, let me confess something, Colin. I have no intention of writing a biography of Hawkinfield—and never did. All I want is to find out who killed him . . . You look surprised!''

''Frankly, I am, Qwill. I thought that matter had been put to bed.''

Qwilleran tamped his moustache. ''I've had doubts about the case for several days, and last night I found something in Hawkinfield's study that leads me to suspect Josh Lumpton.''

Carmichael stared at him incredulously. ''On what grounds? I know Hawkinfield hounded him out of office, charging corruption, but that was a few years ago. Josh runs a clean business. His computerized operation is unique in these parts. We gave it a spread on our business page. He's treasurer of the chamber of commerce.''

''Be that as it may,'' Qwilleran said, drawing the legal pad from the plastic sack. ''I have here in my briefcase one of Hawkinfield's unpublished editorials, datelined for the Wednesday after his death. It's my theory that he was killed to forestall its publication. Someone—and who could it be but his daughter?—knew it was going to be published and tipped off the murderer. Her false testimony at the trial—and I do mean false!—suggested that she was protecting someone. Was it her once-and-future father-in-law? No doubt she also collaborated in trapping Forest Beechum. In court he was defended *incompetently* by Josh's son, who is also her lover, if my information is correct.''

''Let me see that,'' the editor said, reaching for the legal pad.

''I'll read it to you. You have to imagine anywhere from one to four exclamation points after each sentence. J.J. liked to yell in print.'' Qwilleran proceeded to read:

In our hysterical and ineffective war against drugs and drug lords around the world, we are tricked into forgetting those home-grown murderers who not only prey on the poor but rob the government of millions in lost revenue!! Bootleggers, some of you may be surprised to know, are still operating illegally and profitably!!! Perhaps you think the manufacture and sale of illegal whiskey died with the repeal of Prohibition. Not so! Cheap booze is still killing people!! And networks of respected citizens are involved in this heinous racket!!! Are we talking about some far-off sink of iniquity in crime-ridden New York or California? No, we are talking about this blessed valley of ours, this ideal community, this latter-day Eden, which is sinking into an abyss!

First, the local moonshiner produces the whiskey, running it in filthy stills hidden in mountain caves and using additives to fake quality, as well as dangerous short-cuts to make a cheaper product!! Then the hauler has a contract to transport it out of the mountains disguised as honest cargo—in a furniture van or under a load of logs!!! Finally the big-city bootlegger waters it down and sells it to the dregs of society! Everyone makes a profit except the consumer, who dies of lead poisoning!!

Now brace yourself for the most shocking fact!!! The distilling and hauling operations are financed by local investors who innocently or not so innocently buy shares in the illegal and aptly named Hot Potato Fund, which is purported to promote the local economy! Civic leaders, church deacons, and elderly widows are sinking their savings in this profitable, damnable underground venture!! They never question

that their quarterly dividends are unreported and said
to be non-taxable! Or do they?

Who is guilty? Look around you!! Your next-door
neighbor is guilty! Your boss is guilty!! Your golf
partner is guilty!!! Your good old uncle is guilty!!!!

When Qwilleran finished reading, he looked up at his
listener and waited for a reaction. Carmichael was thinking, with lowered eyes and twirling thumbs.

"How about that?" Qwilleran demanded. "Have you
heard of the Hot Potato Fund? Is this why Taters discourage outsiders from prowling around their mountain? Is this
why Lumpton Transport is doing so well?"

"What are you going to do with that information?" the
editor wanted to know.

"If I'm on the right track, it'll be used as evidence in
court. There'll be a new trial."

"Give me that pad," Colin said, "and forget you ever
saw it."

"Why?" Qwilleran asked mockingly. "Is the *Gazette*
involved in this, too?"

"All right, I'll tell you something I'm not supposed to,
but for God's sake, keep it under your hat. Okay?"

Qwilleran held up his right hand. "I swear," he said
lightly.

"We received an anonymous tip about a week ago. I
don't know why informers like to tip off the media, but
they do. I spoke to Del Wilbank about it and learned
that the feds have been investigating the Potatoes for
months. They have undercover agents in the valley and the
mountains. We can expect a major bust any day now. And
believe me, it'll be a big story when it breaks, hitting all

the wire services. So . . . until then, you don't know anything.''

Qwilleran pushed the pad across the desk. "You can
have it, but keep it in your safe. How do you suppose
Hawkinfield knew about the operation?"

"From what I hear, he had everything but wire taps."

"I still want to find his killer, but I need evidence before I take the matter to the police . . . How would you
like to break for lunch, Colin?"

"Not today. How about Monday?" the editor suggested.

Qwilleran went alone to The Great Big Baked Potato,
after he had stopped at Five Points for some delicacies for
the Siamese, including the white grape juice that was
champagne to Koko. Just in case Sherry Hawkinfield's
plane landed, he put in a supply of cashew nuts, crackers,
and a chopped liver canape spread.

His enforced confinement had whetted his appetite for
steak, and he ordered a twelve-ounce cut, medium rare.
"But no potato," he specified to the waitress.

"No potato? Is that what you said?" she repeated in a
whining voice.

"That's right. No potato."

"But that's our specialty."

"Be that as it may, *hold the potato*!"

She returned with the manager. "Sir, is this your first
time here?" he asked. "We're famous for our baked potatoes."

"Where are they grown?" Qwilleran inquired, expecting to hear Idaho or Maine or Michigan.

"Right here in the foothills, sir, where the soil is ideal
for growing potatoes with flavor."

Now Qwilleran knew why these were the Potato Mountains! As he pondered a decision, a young woman at the next table leaned over and said in a pleasant voice, "Take the potato. It's better than the steak." He noticed that she was eating only a potato with a variety of toppings. He noticed also that she had hair like black satin. He took her advice. She had left the restaurant when his meal was served; otherwise he would have thanked her. The steak tasted of tenderizer, but the potato was the best he had ever eaten.

By the time Qwilleran drove home, the fog had burned off in the valley, but halfway up Hawk's Nest Drive it closed in like a white blanket, and he reduced his speed. Although it was difficult to see anything but a small patch of pavement, he was aware of rivulets of water running diagonally across the road. Farther along, the asphalt was covered with mud, and he slowed even more, hugging the cliff on the right and watching for downbound foglights. He had just passed the spot where the Lessmore house should be, when something loomed up in front of him. He eased on the brakes, leaned on the horn, and veered across the yellow line, stopping his car just before crashing into the obstruction. It was another vehicle, skidded diagonally across the road and smashed against the roadside cliff. Backing into his own lane, he turned on the flashers and hurried to the wreck. The cause of the accident was obvious: a mudslide . . . fallen rocks . . . a tree across the road.

As he approached the driver's side of the wrecked car, a woman behind the wheel signaled frantically and shouted, "I can't open the door! I can't open the door!" It was the woman with black satin hair.

SIXTEEN

THE WOMAN TRAPPED in the wrecked car on the mountainside was in a panic. "I can't get out!" she screamed.

"Are you hurt?" Qwilleran shouted through the glass as he tried the door handle. It was jammed.

"No, but *I can't get out!*"

"Turn off the ignition!"

"I did! *What shall I do?*"

"Can you roll down the window?"

"Nothing works!"

It was a two-door model, and Qwilleran tried the opposite door, but the fenders were folded in, and the car was wedged between the wall of rock and the large tree that had tumbled down from the top of the cliff.

"I'll go for help!" he shouted at the driver.

"It might explode!" she cried hysterically.

"No chance! Stay cool! I'll be right back!"

Starting uphill at a jogtrot, he was amazed that his ankle would support the effort. Running downhill to the Lessmore house might have been easier, but he was sure the couple were both at work downtown. He knew how the road curved near the Wilbank residence, and he was sure Ardis would be at home on a day like this. If not, he was prepared to run all the way to Tiptop. Now he wished he had invested in a CB radio or cellular phone.

At the Wilbank driveway he shouted "Hallo! Hallo!" while jogging toward the house. By the time the front door materialized through the mist, Ardis was standing on the deck.

"Trouble?" she called out.

"Accident down the hill! Call the police and a wrecker! A woman's trapped in the car but not hurt!"

"Del's home," she said . . . "Del, there's an accident!"

Qwilleran started back downhill and was picked up by the off-duty sheriff on the way to the scene. Together they set out flares. Already the sirens could be heard in the valley, amplified by the stillness of the atmosphere.

The trapped driver was pounding on the window glass. "Get me out! Get me out!"

"Help's on the way! The sheriff is here!" Qwilleran reassured her, shouting to be heard. He noticed the rental sticker in the rear window. "Are you Sherry? I'm Qwilleran from Tiptop! Didn't expect you in this fog! When did your plane land? I thought all flights would be canceled.''

He was trying to divert her attention, but she was too frightened for small talk. *"Could it catch fire?"*

"No! Don't worry! You'll be out in a jiffy!''

She only glared at him and hammered on the window uselessly. So this was Sherry Hawkinfield! If she were not so terrified she would be quite attractive, he thought.

Police, fire and rescue vehicles arrived, and Qwilleran stepped back out of the way, talking with Ardis, who had walked down to see the wreck. One man with a chainsaw was working on the tree trunk that barricaded the road. The rescue crew was cutting open the car with the Jaws of Life.

When the woman was finally helped out of the wreckage, her first words were, "Hell! I didn't buy insurance! How stupid! Why didn't I take out insurance?''

"Hi, Sherry,'' said Wilbank. "What are you doing up here?''

"Going to Tiptop to discuss business . . . Where is he?''

"Here I am,'' said Qwilleran. "As soon as they clear the road I'll drive you up there . . . Hold on!'' he shouted to the driver of the tow truck. "Let's get her luggage out of the trunk!''

"Howya!'' said the man. It was Vance, the blacksmith. "Glad you're gittin' around ag'in.''

The sheriff said to Qwilleran, "How's everything at Tiptop?''

"Wet outside, comfortable inside. Is this your day off? Why don't you and Ardis come up for drinks at five o'clock?''

On the drive to the mountaintop he said to Sherry, "Would you like something for your nerves when we arrive? A drink, or a nap, or a shower?'' She was looking disheveled in her travel denims and rumpled hair.

"All three," she said peevishly, staring at the dashboard. "What rotten luck!"

He tried to relieve the leaden silence that followed by making such insipid remarks as, "This is the worst fog I've ever seen." . . . And then, "Well, at least we don't worry about flooding up here." . . . And as he carried her luggage up the stone steps, "Fog has an interesting smell, doesn't it?"

When at last they entered the foyer of Tiptop, she was composed enough to say, "I could use that drink. Can you mix a sherry manhattan?"

"Six-to-one? Lemon peel?" asked Qwilleran, who had worked his way through college tending bar.

"I want to freshen up first."

He gestured toward the stairway. "Make yourself at home. You have your choice of the four front rooms, and you know where the towels are kept. I'll take your luggage up."

"I can carry it," she said sharply. "First I need to make a phone call. Now that I have no car, my friend will have to pick me up here after work."

"Go ahead, and ask your friend to stay for a drink."

Soon he heard her on the phone saying, "Honey, you'll never guess what happened to me!"

After she had gone upstairs, Qwilleran quickly retrieved the old-fashioned key from the drawer of the huntboard and hung it on the picture hook behind the Beechum painting—just in case she might be nosy. Her offhand manners led him to expect anything. What had she learned at that school in Virginia?

A moment later he heard a scream on the second floor,

and he dashed up the stairs three at a time. Sherry was standing in the upper hall looking wild-eyed and petrified. "Those cats!" she cried. "I'm deathly afraid of Siamese!"

Koko and Yum Yum, who had emerged languidly from their bedroom after their midday nap, were yawning widely and showing cavernous pink gullets and murderous fangs. Sherry screamed again.

"Take it easy," Qwilleran said. "They won't pay any attention to you. Didn't Dolly tell you I had two cats?"

"I didn't know they were *Siamese*!"

He settled the matter by announcing, "Treat!" and two furry bodies rippled down the stairs to the kitchen. He followed and gave them something crunchy to eat while he mixed a sherry manhattan for his guest. For himself he poured white grape juice and also gave Koko half a jigger in a saucer.

As he was carrying the tray into the living room, Sherry came downstairs slowly, looking at everything. "It's different. You've done something to it," she said.

"Sabrina brought in the plants and accessories to make it look more comfortable," he explained.

Sherry had changed into white pants and a white blouse with a red scarf—a striking complement to her pearly white skin and shiny black hair. It was a severe cut—shoulder-length like Sabrina's, with bangs like Sabrina's, and she tossed it back with a gesture he recognized.

Qwilleran served drinks in the living room, which Sherry studied minutely as if inventorying the accessories and estimating their retail price. After he proposed a toast, she said, "Thanks for getting me out of that scrape."

"One good turn deserves another," he replied. "You recommended the potato in the restaurant, and it was the best potato experience I've ever had. Why haven't I been served one before?''

"This is turnip country. Most of the commercial potato crop is shipped to gourmet centers in New York and California—"

"—where they're called Potato potatoes, no doubt," he said, hoping to get a smile, but she was still stiffly out of sorts.

Losing no time in getting down to business, she said, "So you're interested in the painting." She nodded toward the foyer.

"That's why I phoned you. Is it for sale?"

"Everything's for sale."

"What are you asking for it?" He recalled that Sabrina estimated it would bring $3,000.

"Well, it's been appraised at $5,000, but you can have it for $4,500."

"It's a good painting," Qwilleran said, "but isn't that a trifle steep for the work of an unrecognized artist?"

"Ordinarily it would be," she said, "but this is no ordinary situation. It was painted by a convicted murderer, and the painting has notoriety value. I suppose you know what happened."

Qwilleran nodded sympathetically, but he thought, My God! She not only sent an innocent man to prison, but she's profiteering from her treachery. Wasn't the original price $300, including delivery? To Sherry he said, "I'll give your offer some serious consideration."

"What about the Fitzwallow chest? You said you were interested. I'd let that go for $1,000."

"It's a unique example of folk art. The question is: What would I do with it—unless I bought the inn?"

"The way things are going in the Potatoes," she said, "Tiptop will be a good investment."

"It needs a lot of work, though, chiefly lightening and brightening. The veranda makes the rooms dark even in broad daylight, as you must know. Today's vacationers like sunlight."

"You could take off the veranda and build open decks all around the building," Sherry suggested, showing some animation. "That's what my mother always wanted to do."

"It would be a costly project," Qwilleran objected.

"The building's listed for $1.2 million, but if you want to buy from me direct, I'll let it go for a million. You can use the difference for remodeling."

"Is that ethical? Dolly Lessmore has the listing."

"She's had it for almost a year and hasn't done a damn thing. I'd like to unload it so I can concentrate on my retail business."

"Your shop has a clever name," Qwilleran remarked. "Did you think of it?"

"Yes," she said, looking pleased. "Glad you like it." She held out her glass. "Is there another one where this came from?"

"Forgive me. I'm being an imperfect host," Qwilleran apologized. "But only because I find our conversation so engaging."

When he carried the tray to the kitchen, both cats were in the foyer in their listening position—extremities tucked under compact bodies, ears pointed toward the living room. "You two behave yourselves," he said quietly as he passed.

Sherry was beginning to relax, and she accepted her second manhattan with more grace. "You mix a good cocktail, Mr. Qwilleran," she complimented him.

"Call me Qwill," he reminded her.

"What are you drinking?"

"Just the straight stuff. I never combine the grape and the grain." He clinked the ice cubes in his white grape juice. "Incidentally, white looks very good on you."

"Thank you," she said. "I wear it a lot. Well, tell me about you. What do you do?"

"I'm an author," he said with an appealing display of pride mixed with modesty and a hint of apology.

"What have you written? Your books must be selling pretty well, but I never saw your name."

"I write textbooks," he said, exercising his talent for instant falsehood. "They're rather dull stuff, but they pay well."

"What's your subject?"

"Crime."

"Oh," she said, and her eyes were momentarily downcast. "That must be fascinating. I'm afraid I don't have much time to read. What brought you to the Potatoes?"

"I was looking for a mountain retreat for the summer, where I could work without distractions, and the Potatoes were recommended by a friend who had camped here. I didn't expect to rent anything this large, but I wanted to be on the summit of the mountain." He decided it was unwise to mention the cats again.

"Are you accomplishing anything?"

"As a matter of fact, I've decided on a new project. I'm planning to write a biography of your father."

"No! Do you mean it?" Qwilleran thought her surprise was tempered by qualms rather than enthusiasm.

"Yes, he was a remarkable man. I don't need to tell you that. He made a great contribution to the growth and well-being of the community. He practiced an aggressive, adversarial style of journalism that is rare in these times, and his editorials were blockbusters. Yet, there was a warmly human side to him as well." Qwilleran thought, I can't believe I'm saying this! "I'm referring to his love of family, his deep sorrow at the loss of his sons; the pain he must have suffered over your mother's illness . . . I suppose you were a great source of support and comfort to him." Searching her face for reactions, he found her attempts to assume the right expression almost comical. "The city is planning to name a scenic drive after your father. Do you think he would approve?"

"I think he'd rather have the city named after him," she said in a burst of candor brought on by the second man-hattan.

"Did you have a good father-daughter relationship?" he asked innocently.

"Well, to tell the truth, Qwill, I was one of those early mistakes that happen to young couples. My parents were still in college when I was born, and my father was not too happy about it. Besides, he preferred sons to daugh-ters. But in recent years we developed a real friendship. That happens when you get older, I guess."

Or when the prospect of an inheritance looms on the horizon, Qwilleran thought.

"We'd reached the point," she continued, "where he'd confide in me and I felt free to discuss my problems with him. So his death was a terrible loss to me . . . *What's that?*" She stiffened with fright and looked toward the foyer, where sounds of thumping and muttering and whimpering could be heard.

Qwilleran said, "The cat's talking to himself. He's faced with some kind of problem. Excuse me a moment."

Koko was on the floor, writhing and biting his paw, and

Qwilleran released him from the entanglement of a long hair, thinking as he did so, This is the second time! Most unusual!

"He had something caught in his toes," he explained to his guest when he returned.

She had been sitting on the sofa with her back to one of the folding screens, but now she was walking around to inspect the rented furnishings. It appeared to Qwilleran that she kept glancing at the secretary desk at the far end of the room.

He said, "How do you like Sabrina's idea for foreshortening the room with folding screens?"

"Neat," she said without enthusiasm. She sat down again and helped herself to cashews.

"Gray was apparently your mother's favorite color. Sabrina said she had beautiful gray eyes."

"Yes, she liked gray. She always wore it."

"You have your mother's eyes, Sherry."

"I guess I do," she replied vaguely as if preoccupied.

"Sorry to hear about her illness." Sherry was fidgeting, and Qwilleran was working hard to engage her attention. "I haven't been able to find Lake Batata. Is it a myth?"

"No, it's there. That's where my brothers used to go fishing."

"I assume that you don't care for fishing."

"I was never invited," she said with a half-hearted shrug.

"Do you remember when Lake Batata was a waterfall?"

"Uh . . . yes, I remember. In winter it was one big icicle as high as a ten-story building . . . Excuse me, Qwill, but I think I could use that nap now. The accident, you know . . . and the drinks . . ."

"Yes, of course. I understand."

"Uh . . . are they still out there?" she asked timidly.

"If you're apprehensive, I'll run interference for you," Qwilleran offered, "but the cats won't bother you."

Koko and Yum Yum were still in the foyer, listening, and he shooed them into the kitchen. Locking them up there might be the courteous thing to do, he was aware, but he was disinclined to do so. A hunch was making itself felt on his upper lip.

Sherry went upstairs, holding on to the handrail, and as soon as she was out of sight, he inspected the secretary desk in the living room. The obliging Mr. Beechum had replaced it as requested but without entirely covering the door to Hawkinfield's office. An inch of the door frame was visible on one side. If Sherry had noticed it—and he was sure she had—what thoughts would cross her mind? If he now positioned it properly, would she notice the change? He was sure she would. Her gray eyes always appeared to be observing, intently.

As he wrestled with this decision, an unusual noise in the foyer alarmed him. It was a soft thud accompanied by a gentle clatter and the tinkling of a bell. "Now what the devil is that?" he muttered.

It was the telephone, lying on the carpeted floor alongside the huntboard, and Koko was sitting there looking proud of his accomplishment.

"Bad cat!" Qwilleran scolded as he picked up the instrument and checked the dial tone.

Koko expressed his nonchalance by rolling on his back at the base of the cabinet, squirming and stretching as he had done many times before, but this time, one long elegant foreleg was stretched halfway under the piece of furniture. The pose, combined with the importunate telephone maneuver, was sufficient to arouse Qwilleran's curiosity. The cat was trying to communicate!

There was a flashlight in the drawer, and he beamed it under the chest, but all he could see was a collection of dustballs wafted in by drafts from the French doors. It was clear why Mrs. Hawkinfield disliked it; not only was it an ugly piece of furniture, but it was built too low for a vacuum cleaner, and to use the attachments would mean lying flat on one's face.

"Forget it," Qwilleran said to Koko.

"Yow!" the cat replied in a scolding tone, and he toppled over on his back and extended his forepaw under the huntboard again.

Qwilleran stroked his moustache and obeyed. From the umbrella stand he selected a slender bamboo cane with a crook handle. Then, getting down on his knees and touching his head to the floor, he took a few blind swipes under the chest. Out came several dustballs or "kittens," as his mother used to call them—fluffy balls of lint, dust, and hair that collected under furniture. Fuzz from the gray carpet made the Hawkinfield kittens predominantly gray. The cane also dredged up a short length of ribbon and a fragment of tissue from some long-forgotten gift.

"That's all," he said to Koko, who was prancing back and forth, obviously excited about the show, and he turned off the flashlight that was projecting its narrow beam of light under the huntboard.

"Yow!" Koko protested.

"There's nothing under there, and I don't enjoy standing on my head to entertain man or beast."

"Yow-ow-ow!" the cat insisted in a loud, clear voice, and Yum Yum appeared from nowhere to add her supportive "N-n-NOW!"

Qwilleran felt a creeping sensation on his upper lip, and he went down on his knees again, turned on the flashlight, pressed forehead to floor, and combed the space under the chest with the crook handle. Out came a rubber dogbone.

"Dammit! Is that all you wanted?" Qwilleran said in consternation, his face flushed.

"Ik ik ik," Koko chattered, ignoring the bone.

"I do this under duress, I want you to know." Once more he used the cane to explore the murky back corners. First he snagged another kitten . . . and then a hard rubber ball . . . and then a kitten so unusual, so significant, that Qwilleran dropped it in a drawer of the huntboard. After returning the cane to the umbrella stand and cleaning up the debris, he sat down to plan his course of action.

SEVENTEEN

WHEN SHERRY WANDERED downstairs after her nap, she had added gold jewelry and a whiff of perfume. She looked refreshed. In Qwilleran's opinion she also looked stunning. She had style, but it was style copied from her role model. Tossing her hair back with both hands, she asked, "How much did Sabrina charge you for decorating all this?"

He was glad to be able to say, honestly, that a bill had not yet arrived from Peel & Poole. "If I buy the inn, Sabrina will re-design it inside and out," he said, partly to needle Sherry for her tasteless query. "She has some clever ideas. Also a charming personality,'' he added to carry his taunt further.

"Have you met her husband?'' Sherry asked, not without malice in her attitude. "He's a real charmer!''

"Husband?'' Qwilleran repeated casually, feeling a mild disappointment.

"Spencer Poole. He taught her everything she knows. He's an older man with white hair, but he's a virile type and lots of fun.''

"Would you care for coffee? Or other refreshment?'' he asked absently. He was remembering the souvenir he had found under the huntboard—a dusty ball of hair. White hair.

"Other,'' she replied slyly. "Same thing. But I'll wait until my friend gets here. The wind's coming up. I hate it when it whips around the house and howls.''

She watched Qwilleran light the eight candles in the dusky foyer and ran her hand over the smooth interior of the rough burl bowl, asking how much he had paid for the bowl and the candelabrum.

"What time do you expect your friend?'' he asked.

"Right about now. He's Hugh Lumpton. Do you know him?''

"I've heard the name. Isn't he an attorney and a golfer?''

"Yes, but the other way around,'' she said with an impish grimace.

"How long have you known him?''

"Since high school. I think I hear his car.'' She ran to the front door. "Yes, here he is!''

The man she greeted had a gauntly handsome face with that look of concentration that Carmichael had mentioned, plus a golfer's suntan emphasized by a light blue club shirt and a shock of ash-blond hair. It was easy to understand why he had a female following.

Their meeting was reasonably ardent, with most of the ardor on Sherry's part. "Lucky you weren't hurt," he said to her.

"This is Jim Qwilleran, who came to my rescue . . . Qwill, this is Hugh Lumpton."

They shook hands. "What was the last name again?" the attorney asked.

"Qwilleran, spelled with a QW. But call me Qwill." He waved his guests into the living room. "What may I serve you to drink?"

"Qwill makes a super manhattan," Sherry said as she settled familiarly on the sofa.

"Go easy on those things," Lumpton warned her. "I'll have bourbon, thanks, with a little water."

As Qwilleran prepared the drinks, he was wondering, Has Josh talked to him? How much does Hugh know? Does he know how much I know?

"No!" he said to Koko, who was ready for another swig of grape juice. "You've had your quota."

When he carried the tray into the living room, Sherry and Hugh were sitting on the sofa with their handsome heads close together—a striking couple. They were whispering—not necessarily sweet-nothings, Qwilleran guessed; more likely they were comparing notes, such as: *He says he's a crime writer. He's asking a lot of questions. Someone's been in the office, or tried to get in . . . He's been talking to my dad. He knows I defended Beechum. He's questioning the trial.* They were only conjectures on Qwilleran's part. Nevertheless, the pair on the sofa pulled quickly apart and assumed sociable smiles as soon as he entered the room.

Lumpton proposed a toast. "Tip of the topper to Tiptop!"

Sherry said, "Qwill may buy it, honey."

"What would you do with it?" the attorney asked him.

"Open a country inn if I could find a competent manager. Hotel keeping is not exactly my forte."

"Qwill is an author. He writes textbooks on crime," Sherry said. "He's going to write a biography about my father." She recited it as if reading a script.

"Is that a fact?" Lumpton said without looking surprised.

Qwilleran said, "J.J. would make a challenging subject. You have a famous father yourself, Hugh. I met him this morning."

"Famous or infamous? He's always had a penchant for getting his name in the headlines, sometimes as a hero and sometimes as a villain, but that goes with the territory when you're sheriff. I'm glad to see him established in the private sector now."

Sherry said, "Hugh makes a lot of headlines himself. He's going to Michigan next week to play in an invitational."

"Bob Lessmore and I are competing," the golfer said. "Ironically, the course here is under water, while Michigan is in the throes of a drought."

It was not much after four o'clock, and Qwilleran had a bombshell of a topic that he wanted to drop a little later. Meanwhile, it was important to keep the conversation polite, and he steered it through the details of Sherry's accident . . . Lucy's rescue mission in the woods . . . the preponderance of Lumptons in the Potatoes.

Qwilleran was sitting in Yum Yum's favorite lounge chair facing his guests, who were on the sofa in front of a folding screen. After a while he became aware of movement above their heads, and glancing upward he perceived Koko balancing on the top edge of the screen, having risen to its eight-foot summit without effort and without sound. Qwilleran avoided staring at him, but in the periphery of his vision there was an acrobatic cat teetering precariously with all four feet bunched on a very narrow surface. He was looking down on the visitors with feline speculation like a tiger in a tree, waiting for a gazelle.

Don't do it! Qwilleran was thinking, hoping Koko would read his mind. Koko could read minds, but only when it suited him.

Somewhat worried about the impending catastrophe, Qwilleran asked questions about white-water rafting, the new electronics firm, and the history of Spudsboro. Soon another air-borne bundle of fur appeared on top of the screen; Yum Yum had chosen this vantage point to observe the chopped liver on the cocktail table. Nervously the host talked about book publishing, the weather in Moose County, and the peculiar spelling of his name.

Eventually it was time to serve a second round of drinks, and he rose slowly from his chair and moved quietly from the room, hoping not to provoke the Siamese into any precipitous action.

Despite the menacing sound of the wind, his guests seemed to be enjoying the occasion. Conversation flowed easily, with a modicum of pleasant wit.

Qwilleran decided it was the auspicious time to launch his wild shot. It was his only recourse, considering his lack of credentials as an investigator.

"If either of you can suggest sources of information on J.J.," he began, "I'll appreciate your help. For dramatic effect I propose to start the book with his murder. Sherry,

I hope this subject is not too painful for you . . . Then I'll flash back to his career and family life throughout the years, ending with the trial. And that brings up a sensitive question. In doing my research, I find reason to believe that the wrong man may have been convicted. It seems some new evidence has been brought to light.''

"I was the defense attorney," Lumpton said briskly, "and this is the first intimation I've had of any new evidence—or even a rumor of such. What is your source of information?"

"That's something I don't wish to divulge at this time, but I suspect that the murderer was not a hot-headed environmentalist! Why does this interest me? First of all, I don't like to see an innocent man sent to prison. Secondly, to be perfectly frank, the exposé of a crooked trial would make a damned good finale for my book. How do you react?"

Sherry was looking scared. Lumpton was moistening his lips. Both of them had set down their glasses on the cocktail table.

Lumpton said, "This is preposterous! I defended Beechum at the court's request, but there was no doubt from the very beginning that he was guilty."

Qwilleran said, "I'm reluctant to doubt your statement, but I'm led to suspect that more than one person was involved in the murder, and one or more persons may have committed the big P."

"What?" Sherry asked in a small voice.

"Perjury!"

What happened next may have been caused by the sudden gust of wind that slammed against the building. Whatever the cause, the cats' timing was perfect. Both of them flew down from the screen, narrowly missing the two heads on the sofa, and landed on the cocktail table, scattering drinks, nuts, coasters, and chopped liver.

"I knew it!" Sherry shrieked. "They're dangerous! Where are they? Where did they go?"

Qwilleran rushed to the kitchen for towels, while the guests dropped to their knees, sopping up wet spills with cocktail napkins, collecting cashews and ice cubes, and avoiding broken glass.

"I apologize," Qwilleran said. "They've never done that before. I think they were spooked by the wind. I hope you didn't cut yourselves. Let me get some fresh glasses, and we'll have another round."

"Not for me," said Sherry, noticeably shaken.

"No, thanks," said the attorney, "but I'd like to ask what you intend to do with your information."

"Naturally, I'd prefer to hold it for the publication of my book, but I feel morally obliged to report my findings to the police at once, namely, that J.J. wrote a blistering exposé of certain criminal activities in this area. *Someone* knew the editorial was about to be published. *Someone* found it necessary to stop its publication by eliminating the editor. *Someone* came to the house at a prearranged time and threw him over the cliff. *Someone* forged death threats purportedly from Beechum, which conveniently disappeared before they could be introduced by the prosecution, but *someone* testified to having seen them."

He stopped, and there was silence in the room as his listeners considered his threatening statements. Outdoors the wind was banging a loose shutter or downspout.

"My only contribution to the inevitable investigation," he went on, "is some material evidence found in the foyer here, where the assault is said to have occurred. It's been hidden under a piece of furniture for a year. Would anyone like to see it?''

As he strode to the Fitzwallow huntboard, Lumpton sprang to his feet and followed. With the only light coming from the eight candles in the iron candelabrum, he half-stumbled over two cats streaking toward the staircase.

Qwilleran opened the drawer slowly and produced a handful of ash-blond hair mixed with lint and dust. ''This is it,'' he said calmly, keeping his eyes on the attorney.

It took Lumpton a split second to recognize it and reach for the Queen Anne chair. As he swung it over his head, ready to crash down on his accuser's head, a burst of loud music from the second floor broke the rhythm of his swing just enough to give Qwilleran the edge. Qwilleran seized the iron candelabrum and rammed it into his attacker's midriff like a flaming pitchfork. The chair fell and Lumpton bellowed and sank to his knees. Sherry screamed! Dropping the candelabrum, Qwilleran picked up the heavy burl bowl and overturned it on the attorney's head, rendering him a limp lump on the floor.

Candle flames were licking the carpet, and Sherry screamed again. ''Fire!''

''Shut up and sit down!'' Qwilleran ordered as he stamped his feet on the smoldering carpet. ''Pick up that chair and sit in it!''

''Can I—''

''No! Sit there. Put your feet together. Fold your hands. You won't have long to wait.''

In minutes a car could be heard pulling into the parking lot, and soon the Wilbanks were climbing the steps, struggling against gale-force winds.

''*Treat!*'' Qwilleran yelled, and two cats came running down the stairs fast enough to resemble a continuous streak of pale fur. "Koko, you keep an eye on this woman. Don't let her move or open her mouth."

As if he understood his instructions, the cat assumed a belligerent stance, lashing his tail and staring at his captive in the Queen Anne chair. Yum Yum sniffed Lumpton's loafers but found no shoelaces to untie.

When Qwilleran admitted the Wilbanks, they stepped into the foyer with gasps of relief, Ardis saying, "Isn't this wind awful?"

"We can only stay for one drink," Del said. "We're moving to a motel in the valley."

"We're worried about mudslides," said his wife. "Why is it so dark in here? Did the power go off again?"

Qwilleran flicked a switch, lighting the six wall sconces and three chandeliers. They illuminated a grim tableau. He said, "Allow me to introduce our other guests. On the floor, under the wooden bowl, we have the attorney for the defense, actually J.J.'s murderer. In the chair, scared speechless, is the accomplice before and after the fact, guilty of perjury . . . There they are! Do your duty, Del. The telephone's over there."

As the sheriff was calling for an ambulance and a deputy, Ardis said, "What's wrong with Sherry? She looks as if she's in a trance."

"She's all right. Talk to her," Qwilleran said. Then he yelled, *"Treat!"* Both cats shot out of the foyer, and he followed them to the kitchen, where he gave them a crunchy snack.

Wilbank wandered into the kitchen, too. "I saw Colin this afternoon. He told me everything that you and he talked about. He said you suspected Josh Lumpton of killing J.J."

"I did, until I found some evidence incriminating Hugh.

When I confronted him with it, he picked up the same chair that clobbered J.J. and would have pitched me over the cliff, too, I imagine, if I hadn't been ready for him. If my guesses are right, he killed J.J. to protect himself and his father. I see Hugh as the mastermind of the Hot Potato Fund, while Josh was the organizer of the bootleg operation. J.J.'s editorial would have exposed both of them. Hugh's future wife collaborated because she wanted to inherit her father's estate. They compounded their crime by conspiring to send an innocent man to prison. This time around, justice will be done. If it isn't, my attorneys are going to raise the roof of the courthouse, and I daresay the *Gazette* won't let the prosecutor get away with anything this time."

"The prosecutor was defeated in the last election," said Wilbank. "A woman holds the office now."

"She'll find some former witnesses guilty of perjury, including Sherry," Qwilleran predicted.

"Ardis and I know Sherry pretty well. It's hard to believe she'd be a party to it."

"Sherry was a would-be heiress who wanted to see her male parent underground, although she found it expedient to profess filial friendship. On the weekend of the murder, perhaps J.J. read his inflammatory editorial to her. Writers with any ego like to read their stuff to a friendly ear, you know. Did Colin show it to you?"

Wilbank nodded. "It's in his safe. He said he made the situation clear to you."

"Quite clear! What will happen to Sherry now?"

"We'll take her with us and work something out with the prosecutor . . . I think I hear the sirens."

* * *

As the paramedics maneuvered the stretcher down the twenty-five steps, the Wilbanks told Qwilleran they'd take a raincheck on the drink; they left with a silent young woman in tow, who tossed her hair back nervously.

He had a strong desire to call Polly Duncan and break the news of his successful investigation. Now that it was all over, he could tell her the whole story without alarming her. He felt free to boast to Polly; she listened with understanding. But first he had to wait for the discount phone rates to go into effect.

Tuning in the eleven o'clock news on the local radio station, he heard this brief announcement: "A police prisoner in Spudsboro General Hospital is a new suspect in the Father's Day murder of J.J. Hawkinfield last June, name withheld pending charges. A spokesperson for the sheriff's department refused to predict what effect the suspect's apprehension will have on the previous murder trial. Forest Beechum is currently serving a life term for the crime."

Before the announcer could conclude with dire predictions of damaging rain and severe flooding, Qwilleran's telephone rang, and an excited voice cried, "Did you hear the newscast? They have a new suspect! Forest may be coming home! Wouldn't it be wonderful?"

"I'm very happy for you, Chrysalis. I've recently talked to my attorneys in Pickax, and they expressed an interest in the case, so if you want legal advice, you can call on them."

"Are they high-priced?"

"You don't need to worry about that. The Klingenschoen Foundation makes funds available for worthy causes."

"I'm so happy! I could cry!"

Qwilleran himself was exhilarated by the events of the day, and when he called Polly he said, "G-o-ood e-e-evening!" in a musical and seductive voice. She knew it well.

"Dearest, I'm so glad to hear from you!" she cried. "I've had a most unnerving experience!"

"What happened?" he asked in a normal tone, thinking that Bootsie had swallowed a bottle cap or fallen down a heat register.

"I'm still trembling! I attended that formal dinner I told you about and arrived home after dark. Just as I approached my driveway, I saw a car in front of the main house, parked the wrong way, and someone was behind the wheel. It was standing there with the lights off. I thought it was strange, because no one's living in the main house, and curb parking isn't allowed on Goodwinter Boulevard, you know. When I turned into the side drive, the car started up and followed me—without lights! I was terrified! When I reached the carriage house, I parked near the door, left my headlights on, and had my doorkey ready. Then I jumped out, almost tripping on my long dress, and saw this man getting out of the car! I was able to get inside and slam the door before he reached me, and I sat down on the stairs and bawled like a baby!"

Qwilleran had been speechless as he listened to the chilling account. "This is terrible, Polly! Did you call the police?"

"As soon as I could collect my wits. Gib Campbell was on patrol duty, and he was there in three minutes. The prowler had gone, of course."

"You weren't able to see his face?"

"The outdoor lights weren't on, unfortunately."

"You should always leave them on when you go out in the evening."

"I thought I'd be home before dark; the days are so long in June."

A specific dread swept over Qwilleran. "I don't like the sound of this, Polly. I'd better get back to Pickax. I'll leave tomorrow morning."

"But your vacation has only just begun!"

"I'm canceling it. I can't have anything happening to you."

"It's a sweet thought, dear, but—"

"No buts! Can you stay home until I arrive?"

"I have to be at the library tomorrow and Monday."

"Well, don't go anywhere after work, and if you see anyone who looks the least bit suspect, ask for a police escort. I'll be home Tuesday and I'll call you every night while I'm on the road."

"Qwill, dear, you shouldn't do this."

"I'm doing it *because I love you, Polly*! Now hang up so I can call Brodie!"

Qwilleran called the Pickax police chief at his home. "Andy, I'm sorry to bother you. Do you know about the prowler on Goodwinter Boulevard tonight?"

"Just happened to pick it up on my radio on the way home from the lodge meeting, Campbell responded. No trace."

"The prowler was after Polly. He was waiting for her when she came home."

"Where are you?" Brodie asked.

"I'm still in the Potato Mountains, but I'm leaving for Pickax tomorrow. This worries me, Andy. Polly's connection with me is well known around the county—around

Lockmaster County, too. I'm a prime prospect for a ransom demand.''

"You're talking about . . . kidnapping? We've never had a kidnap case in a hundred years!''

"Things are changing. Outsiders are coming in, and you can expect more incidents. I'll be home Tuesday. What can you do about it in the meantime?''

"We'll step up the patrols on Goodwinter, and I'll talk to Polly tomorrow—see that she gets a ride to work. We don't want to lose a good librarian!''

After the two calls to Pickax, Qwilleran paced the floor anxiously, and the roaring of the wind added to his agitation. Soon the nightly downpour started, hitting the veranda roofs and the upstairs windows like hailstones. Before retiring, he packed for the journey and assembled his luggage in the foyer. The Siamese were nervous, and he allowed them to stay in his room. They promptly fell asleep, but the events of the day churned in his mind.

Sometime in the middle of the night, as he was tossing restlessly and listening to the wind and rain, a sudden, deafening roar drowned out all other sounds. It was like a locomotive crashing into the side of the house, like a jet shearing off the mountaintop, like an earthquake, a tornado, and a tidal wave! He turned the switch on his bedside lamp, but the power was off. Gradually the booming pandemonium receded into the distance, and he ventured downstairs with the bedside flashlight and even stepped out onto the veranda. Nothing seemed to be damaged, but there was an unearthly moaning on the mountain.

Somehow he made it through the night, trying the radio on batteries from time to time, but the local station never transmitted after midnight. When he finally managed to catch a few hours' sleep, he was aroused by the fitful behavior of the Siamese, pouncing on and off the bed. The sheriff's helicopter was circling the mountain.

Once more he tried the radio and found the station on emergency programming. Along with directives, warnings, and pleas for volunteers, there was this repeated announcement:

"Big Potato Mountain and parts of Spudsboro have been declared a disaster area, following the collapse of Lake Batata Dam early this morning. The dam burst at 3:45 A.M., dumping tons of water down the mountainside, washing out sections of Hawk's Nest Drive, and destroying homes on the drive as well as certain commercial buildings on Center Street and at Five Points. The Yellyhoo River, already overflowing its banks, has been swollen by the rush of water from the artificial lake, and it is now feared that debris carried down the mountainside will collect in the Yellyhoo south of town and dam the rampaging flood water from the north. Residents on both sides of the river are being evacuated. The power has failed in most of the county, and most subscribers are without telephone service. The hospital, municipal buildings, and communications centers are operating on emergency generators. At this hour there is no report on casualties. The sheriff's helicopter is searching for survivors. Stand by for further information."

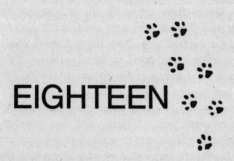

EIGHTEEN

"WE'RE TRAPPED!" QWILLERAN said to the cats after hearing the news of the Batata washout. "It could be days before we get out of here! And we don't have a phone, water, refrigeration, or even a cup of coffee! Don't sit there blinking! What shall we do?"

Then he remembered the old logging trail down the outside of the mountain. It emerged from the forest onto the highway north of town, beyond the golf course and near the airport. "Okay, we're going out the back way. Fasten your seat belts!"

There was no way of knowing what had happened to

the Lessmores, or their house, or their place of business, but after reaching Pickax there would be time enough to return the keys and explain his sudden departure to Dolly, Sabrina, Colin, and Chrysalis. In his hurry he abandoned most of his purchases, having lost interest in the objects bought so impulsively at Potato Cove. Only the five bat-wing capes went into his luggage. Even his box of sec-ondhand books was left behind with the exception of *The Magic Mountain*, and there was no point in taking the expensive turkey roaster that the cats had declined to use.

The Siamese were silent while Qwilleran packed the trunk of the car and placed their carrier on the backseat. Soon he headed for the trail that Chrysalis had shown him. In passing the gazebo he stopped to admire Dewey Bee-chum's handiwork: a handsome hexagonal structure that the cats would never use. It had a cedar shake roof and a cupola and carved wood brackets supporting the roof be-tween the six screened panels. There was one puzzling detail, and Qwilleran left the car to walk over and confirm his suspicions. No door! There was no way to get into the thing! He could imagine Beechum removing his moldy green hat to scratch his head while saying, "Y'didn't let on as how y'wanted a door."

The logging trail was hardly more than a set of tire tracks between the trees, and as long as he stayed in the muddy ruts, Qwilleran thought, it would be navigable. The trail wound in and out, up and down, back and forth—always descending—but the lower the altitude, the muddier the tracks, enough so that he became alarmed. He gripped the steering wheel and hoped for the best. Despite the swerving and jolting, there was not a sound from the back-seat; that in itself was ominous. The small car bounced in and out of ruts and wheeled successfully through large puddles until a misleading depression in the road swallowed the wheels, and the car sank axle-deep in the mire.

Qwilleran gunned the motor and spun the wheels; the second-hand, three-year-old, four-cylinder, two-tone green sedan would move neither forward nor backward. It only sank deeper. Stunned by this new misfortune, Qwilleran sat behind the steering wheel and felt his throat tightening and his face burning. Why? Why? Why, he asked himself, did I ever come to the Potatoes?

He considered leaving the car and slogging the two miles back to Tiptop through slimy clay that would be shin-deep—lugging the cat carrier, slipping and falling and dropping it. And if he stayed in the car, what would happen? No one in Spudsboro would know that he had left Tiptop. No one would miss him. No one would come searching for him. Worse yet, no one ever used this route! Occasionally he heard the chop-chop of the helicopter, but that was scant help; trees arching over the trail provided complete camouflage.

The Siamese had been mercifully silent during this crisis, and once more he considered struggling back to Tiptop, leaving them in the car until he could return with help, but the phones were out of order. How would he make his plight known? He leaned forward with his arms circling the steering wheel and his head on his arms, in an effort to think logically, yet nothing even remotely resembling a solution occurred to him.

"Yow!" said Koko, for the first time that day.

Qwilleran ignored him.

"YOW!" the cat repeated in a louder voice. It was not complaint nor rebuke nor expression of sympathy. It was a cry of excitement.

Qwilleran looked up and caught a glimpse of a moving

vehicle approaching through the trees. It was lurching slowly up the hill—a rusty red pickup with one blue fender, the body of the truck riding high over the wheels. It stopped inches away from his front bumper, and Chrysalis leaned out of the driver's window.

"Where are you going?" she called out.

"Nowhere! I'm stuck!"

She jumped out of the truck cab, wading through the mud in rubber boots that reached above her knees. "I was going up to Tiptop to see if you were all right. I heard about the washout on the radio and thought you'd be marooned."

"I was, and I should have stayed that way," Qwilleran said, "but there's a serious emergency at home. I need to get there in a hurry. If you'll be good enough to drive me to the airport, I'll rent a car."

"Perhaps I could haul you out and tow you down," she suggested.

"Around these sharp turns? No thanks!" From where he sat in his stalled car he could see a thousand-foot drop down the mountain. "Let me put my luggage and the cats in your truck and leave the car here."

"Do you have boots? The mud's over a foot deep here."

"I'll take off my shoes and roll up my pants."

With his shoes hanging around his neck and his socks in his pocket, he transferred the baggage. The cat carrier went on the seat between them.

"Nice cats," Chrysalis said. "Siamese?"

"Yes. They're good companions and very smart."

"Yow!" said Koko.

"He knows we're talking about him," Qwilleran explained. "His vocabulary is limited, but he expresses himself well."

She said, "Don't worry about tracking mud into the cab; we've got enough dirt in this thing to grow strawberries. When we get to Bear Crossing, there's a stream where you can wash your feet and put on your shoes." She backed the truck down the trail and around two hairpin turns before crashing through underbrush to make a U-turn.

"You handle this swamp buggy like a stunt driver," he said with admiration.

"This old crate will go anywhere, and it's a lot more fun than the school bus!" She was a different person since hearing about the arrest of a suspect, and Qwilleran almost regretted that he was leaving. "When are you coming back to the Potatoes?" she asked.

"Probably never. I'm needed at home. I've checked out of Tiptop, and if you can haul my car out of the mud, you're welcome to keep it. I'll give you the keys and send you the title." Before Chrysalis could adequately splutter her surprise and thanks, he changed the subject. "Were you surprised to hear about the washout?"

"Not really. We always knew it would happen someday. Too bad, though. Damage is already estimated at ten million, according to the latest on the radio. I hope no one got hurt, but it'll be a miracle if they didn't. The air is so full of disaster news that they haven't mentioned any more about the suspect. I wonder who it is. I wonder how they found out. I wonder how soon Forest will be coming home."

"George Barter of Hasselrich, Bennett & Barter can probably expedite things for you. He planned to fly down here Monday."

"I hope he's bringing boots," she said.

"The disaster may delay his visit—I'm sure it's being

reported on national news—but when he arrives, he'll have some good news. The Klingenschoen Foundation wants to establish a conservancy to save Little Potato. They'll buy any property that's for sale, to insure that it's never commercially developed. Some Taters may opt to sell and retain lifetime rights to live on the property. And the price paid will be fair. No gouging.''

"I can't believe this!" Chrysalis said. "I've heard about the conservancy idea, but I never dreamed it would happen to Li'l Tater! Was it your suggestion, Qwill? We're so lucky that you came to the Potatoes! How can we thank you?''

"In the mountains we aim to be good neighbors,'' he said.

"Yow!'' was the affirmation from the carrier.

Later, driving away from the airport in a rental car, Qwilleran tried to organize his ambivalent feelings about the Potatoes. So much rain! So much corruption and prejudice! And yet he had never seen so many rainbows . . . witnessed such dramatic skies . . . felt such magic in the mountain air! Too much had happened in one week. One week? To Qwilleran it seemed like a year! Time became distorted in the mountains. Look what happened to Rip Van Winkle!

He and the Siamese again spent a night at the Mountain Charm Motel, famed for its uncomfortable beds and country-style fripperies. Despite its shortcomings, it was the only hostelry in the area that welcomed pets. After dinner he turned on the television, minus the sound, to keep Koko and Yum Yum entertained. It was a nature program, and they huddled together at the foot of one lumpy bed, staring at the screen, while Qwilleran lounged on the other lumpy bed, trying to read the newspaper. His mind could not focus on world news. Unanswered questions plagued him: What really triggered Wilson Wix's heart attack? Did Robert Lessmore's investment firm promote the Hot Potato Fund? Was Yates Penney a baker from Akron or a federal agent?

Then he reflected, If Koko had not found that key behind the painting and that door behind the secretary desk, Forest Beechum would be spending the rest of his life in prison. Did Koko know what he was doing? Or was he simply on the scent of a postage stamp and a dog's mattress? As for finding the key, was Koko pursuing his hobby of tilting pictures? Or did he know that something was not where it should be?

Though Qwilleran found it difficult to rationalize Koko's behavior, he could understand why Sherry had hidden the key as she did. Were not women prone to hide things in the sugar bowl, behind the clock, under the carpet, or in their underclothing? Sherry wanted no unauthorized person in her male parent's office until she could find time to examine, and possibly burn, his personal papers.

Picking up *The Magic Mountain*, Qwilleran thought a good read would relax his mind, but he was unable to find his place. Yum Yum not only untied shoelaces; she stole bookmarks.

Either Koko lost interest in the mating rituals of Brazilian beetles, or he knew he was on Qwilleran's mind. With a stretch and a yawn he deserted the tube and hopped onto the other bed, saying a cheerful "Yow!"

"Yow indeed!" Qwilleran said. "Is that all you have to say? When you sniffed the label on the sherry bottle, were you getting high on the adhesive? Or were you trying to tell me something? And all the time you were wallowing on the floor in front of the Fitzwallow huntboard, you knew there was something of interest underneath it. Was it the dog's toys? Or the ash-blond hairball?''

Koko's large black eyes—black in the dim lamplight of the motel—were brimming with concentration, and Qwilleran told himself, He's trying to transmit a thought; I must relax; I must be receptive.

Koko was concentrating, however, on a spider crawling up the wall, and after springing at it and knocking it down, he ate it.

''Disgusting!'' Qwilleran said and went back to his own thoughts, recalling his incredible week in the Potatoes: getting lost in the woods, the unpleasant episode at the golf club, the horrifying accident at the waterfall, the pain and incapacitation that resulted, the washout and the prospect of being marooned on Tiptop, the ordeal on the muddy trail . . .

''I don't know why I came to the damned Potatoes in the first place! Do you know, Koko?'' Then he answered his own question. He remembered the party celebrating his inheritance . . . all those good friends . . . all that mediocre food . . . someone suggesting the Potato Mountains for a vacation . . . himself jumping at the idea and pursuing it like a fool, persevering against odds, agreeing to pay $1,000 a week for a white elephant. Why? What attracted him? How could he explain his stubborn resolve?

Koko was watching him with twitching whiskers, and Qwilleran put a hand to his own moustache. Slowly the cat rose from his lounging position on the bed. He arched his back and stiffened his tail and pranced, stiff-legged, around the mattress. Qwilleran watched the performance and wondered what it was supposed to convey, if anything.

Round and round Koko paraded until Qwilleran recalled the revolving circle on top of Little Potato—the silent marchers with lanterns, believing in the power of thought and fervently *willing* their kinsman to be returned to them.

No! he thought. How could their influence be felt in Pickax, many hundreds of miles away? ''Impossible!'' he said aloud, and yet he stroked his moustache with a heavy hand, and as he pondered the cosmic conundrum, Koko caught another spider.